Parlor Games

THE LAUGHING GAME

AE LISTER

The Laughing Game
ISBN # 978-1-80250-750-8
©Copyright AE Lister 2024
Cover Art by Kelly Martin ©Copyright September 2024
Interior text design by Claire Siemaszkiewicz
Pride Publishing

Published in 2024 by Pride Publishing, United Kingdom.

Pride Publishing is an imprint of Totally Entwined Group Limited.

Pride Publishing Publishing books by AE Lister

Persuasions
Various Persuasions
Various Distractions
Various Intentions

Northern Horizons
760 Miles
Repentance and Absolution
Return to Telegraph Creek
A Port Essington Christmas

Parlor Games
Are You There, Moriarty?
Forfeits
The Laughing Game

Collections
Dark and Deadly: Skeletal Equation
We Three Kings: A Spoonful of Sugar
His Harem: Alternative Medicine
Hot Bite: Bloodlines

THE LAUGHING GAME

Dedication

To the members of my street team, who help get
the word out!
*(stonedbish, lady_starscream, pitch7742, trioseven7,
zian_nhite, snakeyghost, thera_loves_to_read,
allthedarkvibes, camm13, michelleh.e., kristy_lynn,
kjnrose, loveislovereview, kitvesper, galerr__,
andrea00087, sprgrl_07, heather5952,
heathermmromancereviewed, amos24601, kellyp0129)*

A Note on the Title

The rules of the Laughing Game are straightforward. One player begins by saying the word "ha" with a straight face. The second player continues saying "ha ha," followed by "ha ha ha" and so forth in a circle. The object is to keep going as long as possible without cracking up. If a player breaks so much as a smile, he's out of the game.

—*Mental Floss*, November 15, 2016.

Chapter One

Before I left my home, I texted the redhead that had departed in the quiet hours of the morning.

Me: Thanks. That was fun.

Rebecca: Yes! Hit me up if you ever want a repeat.

Me: Will do.

I smiled and pocketed my phone. That was unlikely. It had been fine, and she was very attractive. But the casual sex with strangers thing was starting to wear thin. My life had been a bit of a shit show the last few years, and I hadn't had time for more.

My dad had passed away and I'd had to arrange for my mother to be cared for, first in her home and then in a retirement facility, where she lived currently. None of my siblings lived in town, and although I could discuss my options with them over the phone, the responsibility fell on my shoulders since they were busy with their children and husbands. Luckily, she liked the place and was settled and mostly content. The stress of the situation had eased and I was starting to feel like I could enjoy life again.

The physical release of my hookup had been sorely needed, and I was feeling good when I climbed the steps to Maverick Molly's for my meeting with Jacob and Sebastian.

"Oh, please, keep the cold out!" someone shouted as I stepped inside. I recognized the voice of Robin Webb, Maverick Molly's most flamboyant server-slash-performer.

"Sorry," I said, shutting the door and stomping my boots.

"Jacob!" Robin yelled down the hall. "Mr. Barnett is here!"

He turned back and looked me up and down. I might have imagined the saucy lilt to his expression, except that Robin flirted with anyone and everyone who stepped through these doors.

"Mr. Barnett," Robin said.

"Mr. Webb," I said, grinning at the curvy man in vintage underclothes that contrasted beautifully with his dark skin. The 'molly boys' at the club wore white cotton bloomers, corsets in a variety of shades over cotton chemises, black stockings and little leather booties from another time.

"Oh, now, you don't have to be so formal. I'm not supposed to use your first name, but you can use mine, you know," he said with a wink.

"How are you, Robin?" I said, moving past him to the full coat rack.

"Oh, I'm just dandy, Mr. Barnett. How are you?"

I shrugged and luckily found an empty hanger. "Pretty good. I like that shade of eyeshadow. Is there glitter in it?"

Robin batted his lashes. "Of course! And thank you so much, Ange—" He put a hand to his lips. "Mr. Barnett."

"Do Sebastian and Jacob *really* make you use men's last names? Is that a hard rule?"

"Oh, Mr. Barnett. It's a very *hard* rule." Robin winked again, then rolled his eyes and touched his velvet choker. "They say it helps with the historical ambience. People were so bleeding polite back then, you know? Except when they were stabbing you in back alleys." He scrunched up his face in thought. "Or maybe even then. Who knows?" He shook his head, the lamplight bouncing off his brown curls. "Anyway, I just like your name so much. And I wonder if..."

"What?"

"Well, I just wonder if—"

Jacob Moriarty strode up the hall toward us. "Robin, would you leave poor Mr. Barnett alone? He doesn't need any of your tomfoolery."

Robin gave Jacob an amused look. "Tomfoolery? *Really?* You know we're not actually living in the Victorian age, right?"

Jacob pointed to the gaming parlor to his right.

"Aren't you supposed to be in there?"

"Yes, but—"

"Uh uh. I'll have none of your nonsense tonight, Robin Webb. Get your cheeky British arse in there and serve customers," Jacob said. His skin was darker than Robin's, and he loomed over the younger man who was even a little shorter than I was, although Robin had the attitude of someone taller.

Robin put a hand to his chest. "Well!" He stepped forward and gave Jacob a quick kiss on the cheek. "I honestly love it when you're strict with me."

Jacob narrowed his eyes but his face softened. "Robin. That's inappropriate. You're my employee."

"Mr. Barnett can vouch that it was my idea. How can I resist? You're so strong and..." He looked Jacob Moriarty up and down. "Fit." He turned back to me while Jacob watched with benign tolerance.

"Lovely to see you, Mr. Barnett. Be sure to pop in for a drink when you're done with these killjoys." He threw me a stunning smile and strolled back into the parlor with a sway of his saucy backside.

I couldn't help uttering a laugh.

Jacob rolled his eyes, but he grinned.

"Angel. Glad you're here." He shook my hand and ushered me down the hall to the office in the back. "Sebastian's manning the bar, but he helped me get everything together for the taxes."

"Super," I said, following Jacob's imposing form as he led me to the office.

"Brandy?"

"Hell, yeah."

Jacob and Sebastian had commissioned a spacious room beside the kitchen as an office. They'd decorated it with dark paint and antique pieces of furniture, including three wood armchairs with padded leather seats. There was even a Victrola in the corner, but I'd never asked if it worked.

"Have a seat," Jacob said.

I did, placing my briefcase on the floor, while Jacob went to the rolling bar cart and poured brandy from a decanter into two cut tumblers. He placed one before me then went to sit in the rolling leather chair opposite, on the other side of the desk.

He held up his glass. "These are real crystal. The ones we use in the gaming parlor are glass."

"Very fancy," I said, lifting mine and examining the way the colors of the liquid danced in the light.

"Long time no see! What have you been up to?"

I took a sip of the brandy and swallowed. "Oh, that's nice." I shrugged. "Nothing that exciting. Work. The gym sometimes. Same old, same old."

"Any, uh, hope on the romantic side?" he asked, gazing at me in a peculiarly intense way.

"Uh…no. Not really. Why?"

Jacob shrugged. "I hate to see you alone. Surely there's someone out there who can intrigue the great, straight, Angel Barnett."

"I haven't met any 'intriguing' women lately. But I did hook up with someone nice last night, as a matter of fact. I met her at the bar near my place."

"Hmm. And she was…nice?"

"Yeah. She was," I said. "It was okay. The sex, I mean. And why am I telling you this? Jesus. I sound like a dick."

"Because I'm your friend. You don't sound like a dick, Angel," he said. "But you do sound a bit confused. And definitely lackluster." He rubbed the side of his glass. "You know there have been rumors…"

I sat forward and put down my glass. "What rumors?"

He held up his hand. "Sorry, not rumors, exactly. Speculation."

"About…about me?"

"Maybe."

I blinked. "Why would there be rumors about me?"

Jacob looked at me like I was the only one not in on an obvious joke.

"Angel. Darling. You're talking about a club filled with kinky gay men."

"Okay…"

"You also profess to be straight."

"So?" I said. "Wait a second, *profess* to be…"

Sure, maybe I was questioning my sexual orientation in private, but I hadn't realized it was up for public debate.

"Sorry, sorry. I shouldn't undermine your sexual orientation. If you say you're straight, you're straight."

I looked at him. He looked at me.

"I don't think I ever *said* I was straight."

"Uh…I'm pretty sure you did. But what does *that* mean? You might *not* be straight?" He grinned and leaned forward. "Angel Barnett, are you exploring your options?"

I hesitated. "I don't know. Maybe?"

"This is turning into a very interesting conversation."

"Well, I know I'm not gay. I had sex with a woman last night. I've never had sex with a guy."

"Mmm. The question is, have you thought about it? Which of course, doesn't mean you're bisexual. But it might."

I narrowed my eyes. "Is this a come-on? Because unless Sebastian knows about it—"

The man in question appeared, carrying a sheaf of papers.

"I heard my name. What do I not know?"

"It's not a come-on," Jacob groaned, leaning back in his chair. "I'm only curious if you've ever thought about other men in that way."

"That's kind of personal, Jacob," I said.

"Yeah, that is really personal, Jacob." Sebastian agreed, putting the pile of papers down on the desk and sitting on the corner. "So, Angel, we all want to know."

He grabbed a handful of peanuts from a nearby bowl and popped one in his mouth.

I rolled my eyes.

Jacob laughed. "Yes, well, telling a bunch of kinky gay men that the hot accountant who comes to the club every month or so is straight is like putting a honey-covered beehive in front of a bear's den. I've had questions."

"From who?" I asked. I wondered which of the Maverick Molly's regulars were speculating about my sexuality, and why.

"Well...let's see, now. I think the molly boys have a bet going."

I opened my mouth, then closed it again. Of all the—

Sebastian pointed at me. "They do. They totally do. Most of them think you're at least a *bit* bi." He chewed and swallowed. "Come on. You're not *completely* straight, Angel. The universe isn't that cruel."

Jacob stared at his husband. "What do you care? You can't have him anyway."

"Oh, wow, hold on now." I held up my hand.

"How do I know *you're* not trying to land him?" Sebastian shrugged. "Anyway, I'm the hot one in the relationship."

"Wait. No-one's going to land me. I had sex with a woman *last night!*"

"Doesn't mean you're not bisexual. Honestly, doesn't even mean you're not gay."

"I'm not gay! I'll admit that I might be a *little bit* bi. I'll put that on the census form next time it comes around. Happy?"

"Yes, actually. And I know someone else who will be," Sebastian said.

Both Jacob and I said, "Who?"

Sebastian only smiled.

"Who?" I repeated.

He regarded me more seriously. "Do you really want to know?"

I thought about that for a split second.

"Yes. Yes, I do."

"Gideon Foster."

A strange white-hot flash went through me from head to toes. I pretended that that name had had no effect.

"Gideon Foster," I said. His name felt good in my mouth. Holy shit. I was probably at least a bit bi.

"Yes," Sebastian said. "I believe he and Vihaal have a bet also."

My breathing picked up. I uncrossed my leg, then crossed the other one. *Be cool, be cool.*

"Look at him," Jacob said to Sebastian. "It's as if you just handed him a surprise Christmas gift."

"Or a grenade."

Gideon Foster and Vihaal Petrovsky were friends of theirs, and I'd been getting to know them slowly over the past few months. Casually. As friends. They were prospective business clients, and I liked to get to know people before I committed to working with them. At least, that was what I told myself.

I laughed but it sounded totally fake, even to my ears. "Don't be ridiculous. I don't even care. Why would I care?"

"Oh fuck, you're *totally into them*!" Sebastian said. He turned to Jacob. "You owe me fifty bucks."

"Seriously?" I said, standing up. I couldn't keep still. It was like a bomb had been dropped, but I couldn't tell if I wanted to run or if I wanted to let it shatter me into a million horny pieces. "*You two* have a bet?"

"So, Gideon thinks you're bi, and he thinks you're *into* him and Vihaal. At least a little teensy bit," Sebastian said with glee, holding his thumb and forefinger a few millimeters apart. "I think you're into them about this much," he said, moving them apart. Quite far apart.

"Come on," I said, my voice barely there.

Jacob leaned forward. "Angel. Are you into Vihaal and Gideon? We'd understand if you were. They're really quite something."

"Um," I murmured, squirming and trying to hide the fact that my cock was swelling at the mere thought of them, even though I hadn't been a horny mess when I'd walked into the club. At least not tonight. "Ah...maybe a little bit?"

"I knew it!" Sebastian shouted, standing up. He turned to Jacob. "I told you."

Jacob slowly smiled as he stared at me with a strange kind of satisfaction. "Won't Gideon and Vihaal be delighted."

"You can't tell them. Please, don't tell them," I muttered. "God. This is so embarrassing."

"Why is it embarrassing? It would be embarrassing if we'd found out you had a crush on Justin Trudeau or something like that." He narrowed his eyes. "*Do* you have a crush on Justin Trudeau?"

"No, I don't have a fucking crush on Justin Trudeau! I don't have a crush on anyone!"

"Well, maybe Vihaal and Gideon. A little one," Sebastian said.

I seemed to be panting. Why was I panting?

"Is it hot in here? Did you turn the heat up? I can't breathe."

"Oh my God, I think he might be having a panic attack," Jacob said. "Have some more brandy."

Brandy? Oh yes, brandy. There was brandy in a glass on the table. For me.

I grabbed the glass and lifted it to my lips. My fingers were shaking. I took a sip. Then another. I put the glass down and leaned back in the chair, counting to ten and back until I'd calmed down.

Jacob and Sebastian had gone quiet. I opened my eyes and stared at the ceiling.

"What am I going to do?"

"Here, let's talk about the financials," Jacob said. "I'm so sorry we upset you."

"Yes, that's a good idea," I admitted. "Can we keep the...other stuff...under wraps for now?"

"Angel, we'd never out you without your permission."

"Oh, thank God."

"But aren't you curious as to *why* Gideon and Vihaal have a bet going?"

I lifted my head and stared at Sebastian. "Should I be?"

Sebastian looked at Jacob. Jacob looked at Sebastian.

"We probably shouldn't be telling you this, but Vihaal and Gideon have a bit of a crush on you."

"*Both* of them?" No, that couldn't be true. How could that be true? They thought I was straight...oh... Oh! "Do gay men really find straight guys *that* alluring?"

"Frankly, yes. Especially intelligent straight guys who look like they should be on the cover of *Men's Health*."

I snorted. "Oh, please."

"Angel. You're a hot guy."

"I'm *maybe* average. I've got a belly, you know."

Jacob laughed. "Do you think that matters to them?"

"Doesn't it?"

Sebastian rolled his eyes. "You're still thinking like a straight guy."

"Up until a few months ago, I thought I was one."

"Wait. You've been questioning your sexual orientation for *months?*" Sebastian said.

"Ever since..." I put my head in my hands. "Since I started hanging out with them."

Sebastian and Jacob gaped at each other.

"Since when have you been hanging out with them?"

"Oh, it was nothing, really. Coffee here and there. We went to lunch once. Maybe we had dinner?"

We had definitely had dinner. It had been the best time. I thought, now that I was looking back on things, that dinner had been what turned the tables. Had they been...dating me? Had that been a date?

"Hold on. They invited you to *dinner?*"

I nodded. "I. Yeah. I thought it was a business-owner-slash-client thing."

"Did it feel like a business-owner-slash-client thing?"

"Oh fuck," I whispered. "Have they been seducing me?"

"I'm sure they've been trying," Sebastian said, barely keeping a straight face. He seemed delighted.

"Sounds like they succeeded," Jacob muttered.

"But...but they're *married*. Why would they be trying to... I don't get it."

"Angel, Angel. Sweet summer child. Vihaal and Gideon are married, yes. But their marriage is far from traditional, in any sense of the word."

"Oh my God."

My brain was exploding, my belly was swirling at the thought of getting together with them for more than a coffee or a meal, and my palms were definitely sweating. I gazed at Sebastian with desperation.

"So…what do I do now? Now that I know?"

"That you've been denying a part of yourself your whole life? That you have a crush on them? That they've been *trying to get you into bed*?"

I whimpered. "Help."

Chapter Two

Talking to Jacob and Sebastian about taxes calmed me down. I was in a bit of a spin, but the brandy helped.

"You can have more, you know," Sebastian said, gesturing to my glass.

"I'm driving," I said.

"You know, Angel," Jacob murmured from his place behind the desk. "It's not always as easy as saying 'I like girls' or 'I like boys'. Sometimes you have to leave room for the possibility that your heart—and other organs—don't fit into a tidy little box. Plus, there are so many gender variations out there. Why limit yourself?"

"Yeah. I've been...*curious*...before. But I never expected to find another man—*or men*—to be more alluring than any of the women I've ever encountered." I shrugged.

Sebastian smiled and gave Jacob a knowing look.

"Anyway, I'd better get out of here. You'll email me the files and information?"

"Already done," Jacob said, closing his laptop. "How long do you think for you to prepare and submit?"

"Not long. A couple of weeks, maybe? I haven't got a ton of other business clients, and my personal clients have fairly straightforward paperwork."

I rejected their kind offer of a round of cards in the gaming parlor. I needed to get home, if only to wrap my head around everything I'd learned — about myself, and Vihaal and Gideon — and decide what the hell was happening and what I was going to do about it.

It was hard to believe there were so many bets on my sexual orientation. I'd mostly assumed I was straight and that I looked straight. Although if anyone had asked what looking straight meant, I couldn't have defined it.

Then again, the fact that I was comfortable hanging out with so many gay guys and coming into Maverick Molly's on a frequent basis was perhaps courting speculation. Maybe I was drawn to Jacob, Sebastian, Gideon, Vihaal and Maverick Molly's because it addressed something I'd been denying about myself for a long, long time.

Gideon and Vihaal seemed very happy together. Were they looking for something outside of their relationship? A fling? A fun afternoon? Initiate the supposedly straight, but probably bisexual, man into the world of gay sex?

What *exactly* did they want from me? The question left me with a strange, excited feeling in my gut. Maybe I should start listening to that normally quiet place inside me that seemed to be sending out flares to get my attention.

We shook hands and they followed me into the hall. I glanced toward the door to the Bordello—the kink room that Jacob and Sebastian rented out by the hour.

"You, uh, got anyone in there right now?" I asked, pretending a casual curiosity.

Jacob shook his head. He glanced at Sebastian, who seemed to be trying to keep from smiling.

"First booking is for eight," he said.

"Ah," I said. When we got to the rack of coats by the front entrance I gave them a wave goodbye. "I'll let you know when I've got everything ready for your signatures."

"Great meeting with you, Angel," Sebastian said.

They headed into the gaming parlor, from which the screech of microphone interference could be heard right before an amplified voice said, "Fuck this thing. Testing, testing."

I put on my coat as I headed for the door, but my finger caught in the sleeve and I tripped on a roll in the burgundy rug. I fell forward onto my knees, bracing myself with my hands so I didn't end up on my face.

"Fuck," I cursed, as the front door opened and a blast of cold air came in with two pairs of legs.

"Well, well, well. If it isn't Angel Barnett."

I froze for a moment, my body reacting to that voice and tone before my brain did. My gaze tracked up the closest pair of legs, over an expensive-looking leather coat, up, up, and up, to a face the color of copper and a striking pair of blue eyes.

"Vihaal," I murmured, from my position near the floor as he gazed down at me with amusement and…something else.

I glanced to the man beside him.

Gideon, dirty blond hair artfully coifed and hazel doe-eyes dancing, crouched down to meet me at eye level, his blue cashmere coat draping softly over his thighs.

"Oh my God, Angel. Are you okay?" he asked.

"Hi," I said, finding myself transfixed by Gideon's pretty face, as if I'd jumped into another dimension.

I cleared my throat, blushing as I scrambled to right myself.

"Sorry. I was just with…" I gestured at the gaming parlor. "Jacob and Sebastian. Taxes. You know."

Gideon helped me up, while Vihaal gazed at me sedately.

"I've often wondered how you'd look on your knees before me, Angel," he said, with a benign smile.

Gideon threw him a look, then turned back to me.

"Are you sure you're all right?" he asked, gazing at me with concern. "Don't listen to him, he's extra horny tonight. We have an appointment in the Bordello, doncha know."

Gideon glanced at Vihaal, and the conflagration of desire between them was almost a visible phenomenon. Vihaal looked at Gideon like he was picturing him splayed out naked on a table. Maybe that's what they were planning. I found myself wondering how that would look.

Another check mark in the bisexuality file.

"I'm fine. Thank you." I dusted my pants and straightened, gazing at Vihaal and pretending he hadn't made a reference to my knees. "Sorry."

He was watching me as if I were a strange species of bird or mammal.

"Why are you apologizing?" he asked, in that deep, dark voice that made me question everything about myself.

"You know what, Angel? In the Bordello," Gideon murmured, leaning forward. "V does nasty things to me and I fucking love every minute of it."

Air seeped out of my lungs in an audible sigh as my cock jerked and my brain went fuzzy.

Another check.

"Gideon. Don't be naughty," Vihaal said.

Gideon shrugged, blinking soft eyes at me.

"I might as well let him know what kind of man you are," Gideon purred.

Vihaal regarded me with those stunning green-blue eyes. "I'm very glad you didn't hurt yourself."

"Takes more than that to make a mark on me," I said, but only Gideon laughed.

I almost choked on my tongue while Vihaal looked me over.

I had to get out of here.

"Well then, have a good time," I said. "I've got to get home."

I made a hasty exit, making sure to be careful as I went outside and down the steps in the snowy darkness. The door shut behind me and I stopped, gulping deep breaths of frigid air.

I looked at the closed doors of Maverick Molly's. Part of me wanted to turn around and go back in, to join Vihaal and Gideon in the gaming parlor before they went to the Bordello. But they were on a date, or so it seemed, and maybe they would head directly to the back to do…whatever they did there.

I started walking again, imagining what *nasty things* Gideon *fucking loved* having done to him, and unable to stop the thought that came unbidden to my mind. Namely, that the view of Vihaal from my knees had not been so bad.

My car coughed and spluttered when I turned the key and I realized I'd need to take it in for a check-up soon. It was on its last legs but I was procrastinating shopping for a new one. I didn't want to research the options and go back to having a monthly car payment, although at this point that might be less expensive than maintaining this car.

As I drove I contemplated everything I'd learned from Jacob and Sebastian, while becoming progressively more distracted and horny. Now that I'd admitted that *maybe* I was physically attracted to two men whom I'd gotten to know over the past few months, my body had taken over like a dog let off leash for the first time.

It might have been the lingering effect of realizing I was attracted to them, and coming face-to-face — or face-to-leg — with them afterward. It also didn't make a whit of a difference that I'd had my dick sucked and more the night before. That all paled in comparison to the way I felt now, and I wondered what *that* meant.

My modest townhome was about a fifteen-minute drive from the club. It didn't look like much from the outside — or from the inside either, if I was being honest. But it was mine and it kept me and my two cats comfy and warm.

I felt relief at being home and somewhere familiar, and my cats greeted me at the door as if they'd never been fed in their lives. I felt like I was already a different person, because I'd finally realized something important about myself. Even though I didn't know if I was going to act on these unusual but undeniable feelings.

You're going to act on these feelings, a voice inside my head said in a smug tone, and I knew it was true.

A sudden realization hit me.

That when I'd been on my knees in the hallway at Maverick Molly's, staring up at Vihaal and Gideon, I'd been much more turned on than I'd been with the redhead from last night, even when she'd been naked in my bed and I'd known we were about to fuck.

What did *that* say about me?

I fed the cats, then took the half-drunk bottle of Chardonnay out of the fridge, pouring what was left into a tumbler-sized glass. This was no time for half measures. I put the now empty bottle on the counter and took the glass into the living room, sitting on the couch and absently picking up the remote control. For the next fifteen minutes I flipped through channels and drank the wine, until a sense of ease came over me. Maybe it was time that I faced the truth — that I wasn't only attracted to women, and that I had a thing for Gideon and Vihaal.

It seemed like I was the last to know. I didn't carry any internalized homophobia — my parents had been very openminded. In fact, my mother was bisexual — although now past the point of acting on it — and both of my parents had been open about sexuality and gender non-conforming people. My mom would speak fondly of her university days and the girlfriends she'd had during that time of her life. It occurred to me that refusing to entertain any departure from the straight narrative might have been my own small way of rebelling against my, admittedly unusual, upbringing. But I was thirty-six, and apparently my horizons were begging to be expanded. It was time I gave those feelings room to grow.

A sense of anticipation and excitement began to replace the feeling of being thrown off course, and upside down. Life was full of promise.

* * * *

I sat with this new awareness for two days, wondering what the hell to do or how to go about approaching the men with whom I was obsessing.

On the third day, as I was tidying the kitchen after lunch, my phone vibrated with Vihaal's number. The amount of joy that hit me when his name showed on the screen of my phone informed me that, for whatever reason, I had become very, very fond of him and Gideon. Then again, there was also nervousness, because Vihaal was an imposing and commanding presence. And I wanted to impress him.

"Hey," I said, trying to act casual. "Vihaal."

"Angel."

The sound of our breaths filled the silence. I tried to think of something to say.

"I heard you and Gideon had a bet going."

What the fuck am I doing?

There was silence, then Vihaal started to laugh.

"He knows about our bet," Vihaal said, and it took me a second to realize he wasn't speaking to me.

"Oh fuck," Gideon said. "Is he mad?"

"I've got you on speaker, Angel. That was Gideon. Are you mad?" he asked, with something that seemed like delight.

"Uh...not mad exactly. Surprised by all the... speculation."

"So, tell me then. Who won this bet? I'm very curious to find out."

My breathing got louder.

I swallowed. "Well…what was the exact wager?"

Vihaal gave a slow soft chuckle.

"Tell you what. Why don't you come over for a visit and we'll discuss it. Gideon has a recipe for tiny sandwiches he wants to try."

"Tiny sandwiches?" I asked.

"Also, I'm wondering if you'd look over some financials from Tarnish, the antique store I own. Sebastian suggested it might be a good idea."

"Sure. Yeah, I can do that."

"Angel!" Gideon spoke again. "I have a silver tiered platter and a recipe for triangle sandwiches that I don't get to use very often. We'd love to have you for afternoon tea!"

"Extravagance," Vihaal said in the background. Then he huffed a laugh. "Did you just make a rude gesture to me, Gideon?"

"Will you come? We haven't seen you properly in ages!" Gideon pleaded.

"How can I possibly refuse a silver tiered platter and triangle sandwiches," I said, only after the words had left my mouth realizing just how strange that sounded.

"Exactly. Is tomorrow okay? About three o'clock?" Gideon asked.

"Yes, that's fine," I said.

I was free. I wanted to see them. And this was absolutely happening.

"Wear something nice," Gideon whispered.

"What?" I said, my cock reacting to the timbre of his voice.

"Gideon, I am not amused. Give me the phone."

"Ta, ta," Gideon said.

"I'm so sorry, Angel. He's impossible."

I laughed.

"It's fine. He's..." I tried to think of a word to describe Gideon. "...something."

"Yes. Yes, he is. See you tomorrow."

After we'd ended the call, I thought about what Gideon had said. Did he want me to dress fancy? It was afternoon tea, after all. Or did he want me to dress... sexy?

I didn't have a clue how to dress sexy for two men who had finally made me realize I'd been living a lie.

* * * *

I wasn't used to losing sleep over anyone, but I tossed and turned with anticipation over the prospect of seeing the two of them again. I finally gave in and jerked off, mostly as a form of stress relief and a sleep aid, and if I'd had any doubt as to the sexual nature of my obsession with Gideon and Vihaal, their sexy performance in my fantasies laid that to rest. I'd never felt this way about any of the women I'd dated. I felt so out of my depth and like a total newb.

I'd already known about Tarnish, Vihaal's antique store. But I'd never seen the place and now I wanted to. I grabbed my phone and Googled it.

It looked like a cute spot. It was in Hintonburg — not exactly close to where they lived in Old Ottawa South. The word Tarnish was painted in fancy lettering over the front door.

I put my phone down and closed my eyes, finally drifting off to thoughts of Gideon making his triangle sandwiches.

* * * *

A soft 'pat, pat, pat' on my cheek woke me out of a sound sleep.

"Fuck off," I mumbled, turning over.

Blessed silence for a few moments, then the sheet ever so subtly shifted and a 'brrrrr' noise sounded in my face as a rough tongue swiped across my nose.

"Toff. Fuck off!" Seriously, this goddamn cat.

I opened my eyes. A fluffy white face, with a black patch over half of it, and two soft green eyes stared back at me.

"Brrrr?" Toff said. Which I translated to *When the fuck are you gonna get up and feed me?*

"Hi."

He lay down, but continued to stare at me with expectation. I glanced over to the chair by the window to see Rummy in her usual spot, letting Toff do all her dirty work.

Thoughts of two attractive, kinky gay men came back to mind, and I remembered the epiphany I'd had the day before.

"Oh, fuck," I said, groaning and reaching out a hand to ruffle Toff's fur. "I am so fucking fucked, it's not even funny." I couldn't help smiling. "And that might not be a euphemism."

When I sat up, Toff launched himself in the direction of the door, then stopped and looked back, his gaze saying *Hurry the fuck up, you loser*. Rummy gazed at me placidly from her perch. She was smart enough to know it would take me a minute to get going.

Their names were from the musical *Cats*. The really annoying one was Toff, short for Mr. Mistoffelees and the calmer one was Rummy, short for Rum Tum

Tugger. I loved them, but man, it would have been nice to sleep in on occasion.

I reached over to unplug my phone and checked the notification screen. There was a message that was an obvious scam, and another from a Discord group I was a member of. But nothing as interesting as the text from Vihaal.

See you later today. We're really looking forward to it. Winky face.

I grinned, but nerves hit me at the thought of what might await me. Did he know I was questioning my sexuality? Did they already know how caught up in them I was?

I texted back.

Did you talk to Sebastian? He wasn't supposed to say anything…

There was a terrible crash from downstairs. I threw my phone onto the bed and ran behind Rummy down the stairs, skidding to a stop at the bottom.

Toff sat on the breakfast bar, licking his paw. What had been a semi-expensive vase was now in pieces on the kitchen floor, the bouquet of sunflowers I'd bought to cheer myself up scattered amongst the broken glass.

Wait a whole hot minute.

I remembered my phone, and the text from Vihaal. Then I recalled what I'd typed in response, and realized that if they hadn't known I'd discussed something relating to them with Sebastian and Jacob, they sure did now.

I ignored the mess on the floor, knowing the cats would be persnickety enough to avoid the area, and ran back upstairs. I launched onto the mattress and grabbed the phone. Was it possible to unsend a text?

But it was too late. Vihaal's reply had already come in.

Say anything about what? What does Sebastian know that I don't???

Oh, fuck my life. Maybe I could pass it off as a joke.

Laughing face emoji. I'm looking forward to afternoon tea.

Distraction was also effective. I kept typing.

I hope Gideon's making lots of little sandwiches. I can't wait to try some.

I hit send and waited with breathless anticipation.

The typing bubble popped up and the three dots danced for a few seconds.

Hmm. Is there something you'd like to tell me, Angel?

Fuck. No, no, no. I wasn't ready for this. I hadn't even had coffee.

He knew. He had to know. Everyone suspected. But I wasn't in the least bit prepared for this conversation.

See you at two. Waving hand.

Oh my God, I was such a coward. And my life had been a lie.

See you later. Face with a monocle.

Then a face with sunglasses. Then a...face with a birthday hat blowing a party favor?

Ha ha. It's not my birthday?

I know.

Wait. He knew. I knew he knew. Without even talking to Sebastian.

But...he didn't *know* I knew he knew. So, I would simply remain oblivious until he said something. And I'd face *that* when it happened.

Chapter Three

I had no idea what to wear.

Sure, it was afternoon tea, but I wasn't a fifty-year-old woman. I decided on a pair of dark-wash jeans, and a navy-blue button-down shirt, tucked in—more formal—with the top two buttons undone. I grabbed the leather choker that I wore to the clubs off my dresser, and fastened it around my neck.

I might as well look pretty.

I moisturized my face and put some gel in my hair, feeling like someone waking up to a new world. Getting ready to visit Vihaal and Gideon was a completely different experience from heading out to try to meet women. I felt so much more vulnerable, and at a loss as to what might impress them. And I wanted to make an impression.

I knew what women liked, but I had no idea how to make myself attractive for two men. As I gazed at my face in the mirror, seeing the faint freckles that spanned my pale nose and cheeks, and the reddish hair that curled in a neglected shag around my ears, I wondered what they saw in me to draw them in. I was nowhere near as hot as they were. My eyes were a boring brown color and I'd never been able to grow a respectable beard.

And I had so many questions. Did they romance other men frequently? Did they have an open relationship? Did they have other men over all the time to share their bedroom or their playroom? Wait, Vihaal had said they didn't have a 'dungeon' in their home, and that was why they used the Bordello frequently. Did they take other men there, or just each other?

Fuck, I was getting ahead of myself. It was entirely possible that I would only be offered a cup of tea and some teeny tiny sandwiches.

My car made troublesome sounds the entire way to their place. I had an irrational attachment to my silver Honda Civic. It had been with me a long time, but maybe it was a good idea to move on.

I turned left onto Cameron Avenue from Riverdale, then took an immediate right onto Bellwood. The picturesque street spanned out under what would be lots of tree cover in the summer but at present were bare branches and snowy bushes. Number fifty-seven was a charming three-story Victorian-style home about three quarters of the way down, with red brick walls and a porch with white railings and a balcony directly above it. There was space on the street to park nearby. I noticed a small red Mazda in the drive.

My car made a rattle and a sigh as I turned it off with the manual ignition and I prayed it might still have a few weeks left. Like I'd said, it had been a stressful and busy few years, and I hadn't maintained it properly.

I sat there for a moment, taking in the view out the windshield. Old Ottawa South was a beautiful but pricey area to live and I wondered how rich Vihaal actually was. Sebastian had implied that he had family money, and I knew he owned the antique store, which he had other people managing. They could obviously afford to live here.

I took a deep breath and got out of my car. Maybe I could pretend that nothing had changed, and we were only good friends who enjoyed hanging out together in a socially approved way. But what the hell was the fun of that? If my parents had taught me anything, it was to take some risks and find out what you really wanted. Now that I had some breathing room, maybe it was time I took that advice.

Gideon answered the door wearing tiny cut-off jean shorts and a mesh crop top, and holding a black feather duster. If there had still been any question that I might be a little bit gay, it left me in a spike of desire as I gazed at him, noticing the curves of muscle in his thighs and calves and the slight pooch of his belly under the see-through shirt. I couldn't help staring at him, in blatant desire and with some confusion, since it was quite chilly out here.

"Angel!"

Gideon's expression went from delighted to concerned and he looked down at himself, as if only now remembering his outfit.

"Oh, shit, sorry." He rolled his eyes. "V's punishing me and he made me wear this and I'm supposed to dust the tchotchkes. Actually, I'm just wandering around bending over and reaching up and driving him mad with desire."

He crossed his arms over his chest and gave me a proud look, as if challenging me to criticize.

"Punishing you?"

"Yeah." He grinned. He waved the feather duster and rolled his eyes. "We have this thing… Never mind. Come in, come in!"

He backed up and beckoned me in.

As I stepped inside the small entryway, Vihaal's voice echoed from another room.

"Gideon, when you're done welcoming our guest you can stop pretending to dust."

"Cool! Thanks, man. It's exhausting pleasing you," Gideon shouted in a bright, happy tone. "Here, just put your coat on one of these hooks and your boots in the tray. Ooh, you look hot! Did you do something to your hair?"

I shrugged, then cleared my throat. "What? No, this is the way I always look."

"Oh, it's the choker. That's super sexy. Did you make yourself extra pretty for us?"

I laughed but it sounded totally fake. "What? No!"

He narrowed his eyes at me. "It was a joke, but okay." He gazed at me with contemplation. "Huh."

"What?" I asked, knowing I should just keep my mouth shut.

"You seem different. Nervous, for some reason. Why are you nervous, Angel? We're just having tea."

I did the fake laugh again. It sounded only slightly more authentic. "Don't be ridiculous. It's only that my car sounds like it's dying."

"Oh, damn."

I went through as Gideon led me past a stairway directly ahead and into a cozy living room, where Vihaal stood by the picturesque bay window. As if a fog had lifted, I saw him with the new awareness of my feelings and could not deny that I was very much drawn to this imposing, compelling man who had more charisma in his little finger than most of the women I'd dated.

I also couldn't deny that my dick had moved and swelled in response to the alluring presence of not one, but two, captivating men.

Settle down, I told it silently. I needed time to get used to the idea of the three of us possibly being more than *just friends*.

"Angel," Vihaal said, smiling. His hands were in his pockets, his gaze quickly running over me. "My, don't you look nice."

Those words hit me in a place I'd not expected.

"Thanks. I...made an effort," I admitted, blushing. Why did this man make me feel so off center, but in an entirely agreeable and welcome way?

At that information, Vihaal's eyebrows shot up and his smile broadened.

"I'm going to change," Gideon said. "Don't worry. Vihaal won't bite. At least, not unless you give him permission." He threw Vihaal a look. "*Be. Nice.*"

Then he was gone.

I looked about the room, trying not to be obvious about stealing glances at Vihaal, even though my gaze was drawn to him. Each time I did look at him, he was watching me with the same kind of predatory calm that a lion would use to assess an antelope. It was unnerving, but also arousing, since I was pretty sure he wouldn't pounce and kill. But he might be contemplating a different kind of attack and that thought was, honestly, thrilling.

The living room was a lovely space, with what looked like an original oak floor, painted brown trim, and white plastered walls. I'd been here before, but it all seemed more relevant now. There was a whole wall of bookcases, filled with books that overflowed the shelves, and with small artistic items scattered in front and in between — probably what Gideon was supposed to have dusted.

For the first time I noticed a dark wood secretaire against the wall with an open notebook upon it, and some other antique pieces like the coffee table and a side table that looked very expensive. They had probably come from Vihaal's antique store.

I looked closer at the rug on the floor.

"It's Turkish," Vihaal said, in a neutral tone that didn't indicate any kind of show-offy vibes. "You seem more...present today."

"I noticed it before. It's very soft. Is it from the store?"

"Well, it never made it to the store. I saw it before it was tagged and immediately had it delivered."

"It's beautiful."

"Yes, well, I like beautiful things," he said, staring at me in a way that made my balls pull up tight and my cock thicken.

"Oh?" I said, flushing. "You said you had some work for me?"

"Oh no. Don't try to distract me. I want to know what you told Sebastian."

Fuck. Fuck, fuck, fuck.

"Ha ha ha, what do you mean?"

Vihaal leveled a gaze at me and my bravado shriveled. He reached for his phone and showed me the screen. The text I'd sent was on there.

Did you talk to Sebastian? He wasn't supposed to say anything...

"Explain this."

It sounded like an order, because he didn't say 'please'.

"Oh, I, uh, nothing…" I said, feeling very brave for defying him.

I laughed again, but it sounded like a choke. Then I *did* choke on a bit of spit I'd inhaled. I held up my hand and leaned forward, coughing uncontrollably.

"Sorry…" I rasped. "Spit…down my wind…pipe."

I gasped, sucking in air when I could.

Vihaal stepped forward and took my elbow, then helped me to the antique settee.

"Goodness," Vihaal murmured. "Are you all right?"

Fuck no. I wasn't. I had to come clean. I hated being deceptive to people I cared about. And it was becoming obvious to me that I did care about Gideon and Vihaal.

"Sebastian—" I began, then had another coughing fit just as Gideon returned, wearing more appropriate clothing.

"God, what is happening? Is he dying?"

"Please get Angel a glass of water, Gideon. He's simply choking on secrets. Secrets that he's about to tell us. Isn't that right, Angel?"

God, he was good.

I nodded. "Water. Please."

Gideon dashed away to the kitchen and returned with a tumbler of water as Vihaal and I had a stare down. It wasn't aggressive per se, but there was a challenge in his blue-eyed gaze.

I took the glass from Gideon and tipped it to my lips, sipping a bit of water.

"If it helps," Vihaal said, "I'm pretty sure I know what you're hiding."

His gaze landed on my groin, where, despite the coughing fit, my dick was still filling out my pants.

"Or…not hiding very well," he continued.

"What?" Gideon said. His gaze followed Vihaal's, then he was blushing.

"Oh!" He glanced at Vihaal, then back at me. "Huh."

"Fine. Okay." I took a deep breath. "I told Sebastian and Jacob that I...that I didn't know...if I was... y'know..."

"I'm afraid you'll have to spell it out."

"Straight. I don't know if I'm straight. I'm probably a little bit..." My gaze tracked down Vihaal's body, then returned to his. "...gay. Well, bi. Or pan. Fuck, I don't know. Just not as straight as I thought I was."

I glanced at Gideon in his tempting outfit.

Vihaal crossed his arms and gazed at me. "And what prompted you to do that? I'm very curious to know."

I'll bet you are. Speaking of bets...

"Hold on. When I told him, he said that the molly boys and you and Gideon had bets going about it."

"Well. You can't blame us for speculating."

"Can't I?" I said, raising my chin. I wasn't mad about it, but I did take offense to people using something so personal for entertainment.

He grinned. "Well, I suppose you can. But now I want to know who won."

Oh damn. "Who won...the bet? What were the exact terms?"

"Gideon bet that you were bi or pan," Vihaal said.

"And Vihaal said you were as straight as they come," Gideon stated.

"Although I might have only said that to be contrary," Vihaal said, stepping closer. "And because I never thought we could be so lucky."

"Fine. Well, I guess you win," I said to Gideon.

"Yes! I knew it!" He threw Vihaal a victorious look, then turned a contrite one on me. "Oh, shit, sorry." He laughed, and how could I be mad?

"It's fine," I said, shrugging, but my heartbeat was out of control. "I seem to be the last to find out."

"That's the way it works sometimes. Congratulations," he said, regarding me with a look that made my cock harder.

"There's more."

"There usually is."

"I told Sebastian that it almost seemed like the two of you were trying to…seduce me."

"Well, well, well," Vihaal murmured, looking me up and down. "You did pick up on that."

"Are you fucking kidding me right now?" I asked.

Vihaal laughed from deep in his chest. "No, not at all. We've been desperate to get your attention. And it's worked."

"Finally," Gideon grouched, rolling his eyes and coming closer. "We've been trying so hard!"

"For fuck's sake! Why didn't you say something?"

"Like what?" Vihaal asked. "Should we have propositioned you at dinner?"

"Well, I don't know. You could have said that you were…hoping for more than a friendship."

"But if you were straight, that might have sent you running for the hills. And we didn't want to risk it," Gideon explained. "We wanted to make friends with you because you're a cool person."

"But you're a very attractive man, Angel. You must know that. You can't have had too much trouble pulling at the local bars," Vihaal said. "Women, I mean."

"Well, no. But that whole scene is getting a bit…old," I said, gazing at Vihaal, then glancing at Gideon. My gaze tracked down the younger man's body then over to Vihaal's. "And boring. You know."

Vihaal smiled in such a smug way I was surprised he didn't reach out and undo the fly of my jeans. "Well, I *don't* know, to be honest, but I'm very glad to hear it."

Vihaal wrapped his hand around my bicep, then tugged me forward.

It felt awkward for a split second, but he smelled amazing and his stature and solidity made me feel strangely subdued. We were almost the same height, but that was where the similarity ended. I didn't struggle, even when I realized that I could feel exactly how much he was enjoying our proximity.

"Angel. We would be happy to help you figure out exactly what you want."

"More than happy," Gideon murmured, watching us like it was the most thrilling episode of a new reality show.

Vihaal held me for a moment, gazing at me with an incendiary look. Then he let go and stepped back.

I reached out and grabbed his wrist, pulling him back to me, and our mouths came together as my world exploded.

He responded to my amateurish attempts at kissing him. I knew I was overthinking it, and probably making a mess of it, but I didn't care.

"Fuck," Gideon whispered. "Jesus."

My body was combusting, and I would have given him whatever he'd wanted.

I was breathless and aching with need when Vihaal finally ended it, carefully drawing back as I tried to stay with him. But he gave me a stern look and shook his head once, which was enough.

"Sorry," I murmured, dazed. I touched my lips with my fingers, still feeling the electricity of our connection. "I'm sorry."

"For fuck's sake, don't apologize."

I laughed. "Too desperate?"

Vihaal continued to regard me with an intense expression. "Oh no. I enjoy desperation, as a matter of fact. Very much."

Gideon rolled his eyes. "Well, there you go. You've had a taste of the Dommiest Dom this side of the US border," he said. "There's no point resisting."

"Yeah. I think you're right," I said, feeling dazed.

"I don't mean to break up this little"—Gideon waved his hand—"exploration. But. I made sandwiches. And I really want to use my tiered stand."

"Of course, Deo," Vihaal said, still gazing at me. "And anyway, I'm famished."

He licked his lips and a thrill of desire coursed through me at the memory of that kiss and at the way he looked like he could eat *me* for afternoon tea.

The silver tiered platter was a thing of beauty and Gideon wielded it like it was The One Ring. He placed it gingerly on the coffee table and stepped back, smiling with pride. Sweet triangle sandwiches with the crusts cut off were piled high on every tier. He'd arranged them to make an attractive design and I was loath to ruin it.

"Help yourselves. There's egg salad, tuna salad, cucumber and cream cheese, and ham."

"Gideon, I'm impressed," I said. "You must have spent the whole morning making them."

"Oh, no, it's nothing. They're fun to make. And I wanted to try a new tuna salad recipe. The egg salad is my own that I've been perfecting. And I think I might have nailed it this time."

I sat down on the settee and took a plate, then took one of each and arranged them in a circle.

"He did a wonderful job, didn't he? My little Deo likes to play housewife on occasion, and I certainly don't mind," Vihaal said, taking a plate of his own. He put three of the tiny sandwiches on his plate, then resumed his seat.

"Well, it's nice to be fancy once in a while," Gideon said. "Oh, shit! The tea!"

He hurried back to the kitchen.

I tried a bite of the egg salad. Flavor burst in my mouth. I tasted something spicy and something sweet, and the texture of the egg was just right. It was delicious.

"Wow," I commented.

"Good, aren't they?" Vihaal said with a smile. He was looking at me in a way that made me feel self-conscious. "You've really surprised me today, Angel."

I swallowed the bite of sandwich I'd taken. "You think *you're* surprised," I said, smiling at the unexpected turn my life had taken.

Chapter Four

Gideon came in with a tray on which was a large tea kettle in a flowered knit cozy, surrounded by an arrangement of three china teacups and saucers with various designs on them.

"Can you tell, I like flowers?" He placed the tray on the coffee table and looked at Vihaal. "How are the sandwiches?"

"Wonderful. You spoil me."

Gideon looked at me. "Do you like my sandwiches, Angel?"

"This egg salad is really good. It's…" I shrugged, taking another bite and chewing slowly. "Zingy."

"There's some sweet onion and minced gherkin, and chili powder in there. But don't tell anyone." He leaned forward and spoke in a whisper. "It's my secret recipe."

"Hmm," Vihaal said, "Angel, you'll soon find that Gideon has quite a few secrets."

"Not as many as you," Gideon said, making a face at Vihaal.

Vihaal smiled. "And not as many as Angel's been keeping."

"Touché," I said, picking up my tuna sandwich. "I've kind of been on autopilot, not really spending time on self-examination."

There were things they weren't telling me. Important things about them, their relationship. But I didn't give a fuck at the moment. And a part of me couldn't wait to find out.

"Shall I play Mother?" Gideon asked, lifting the teapot and a saucer and cup, and pouring the dark amber liquid into it.

"Can I possibly stop you?" Vihaal asked, grinning, and taking two more sandwiches from the platter. Ham this time. "Angel? Still hungry?"

"Oh yeah." I was famished, and the sandwiches didn't seem to be filling me the way they should.

"Here you go," Gideon said, passing me the filled teacup on its pretty saucer.

I took it carefully. Vihaal waited until I'd put it down.

"Plate?" he said.

I held it out, and Vihaal placed two small sandwiches on it. Gideon filled a cup for Vihaal and passed it to him, and one for himself.

"Do you need sugar, Angel?" Gideon asked, lifting a silver holder from the tray.

"But he's so sweet already," Vihaal murmured, sipping his tea and staring over the edge of his cup at me.

I rolled my eyes. "Look, I don't know what Sebastian and Jacob told you, but I'm far from sweet."

"Now that you mention it, Jacob said—and I quote—Angel never sleeps with the same woman twice."

"Oh, come on. How on Earth would he know that? Honestly."

"Is it true?" Gideon asked, regarding me with interest.

"Ha! No," I said, trying to remember. "Wait. Yes. It might be. I don't know."

Vihaal's eyes went wide. "You don't know if you've ever slept with a woman more than once?"

"Oh my God," Gideon said, gazing at me in awe.

"Now hold on a minute. Maybe I've never had a relationship with a woman, but it's because I enjoy being single." I gazed at Vihaal. "Unfettered."

At that word, his eyes widened and he couldn't stop his smile. "Sleeping with a woman more than once is not a relationship, Angel. It's a nightcap."

"Oh, fuck, well of course I've gone a few rounds with the same woman in one night."

"Glad to hear it," Vihaal said, grinning around his teacup. "Stamina is going to be an important asset if we..."

"If we..." I swallowed my tea and put my cup down. "If we...what exactly?"

"If we are going to explore this strong attraction between the three of us," Vihaal said. "I'm glad to hear you've been a bit of a slut."

I frowned. "Well...that might be the wrong word for it."

"Oh no," Vihaal said. "I think it's a perfect word for it."

I gazed at him. "You think I'm going to be slutty with you and Gideon?"

"Well, I certainly hope so. Gideon?"

"Oh, fuck yeah." He smiled, gazing at me over his teacup.

"Holy shit. I feel like I'm being hunted."

"Yes, but do you mind?" Vihaal asked.

"Maybe not," I admitted. "But I am curious about a few things."

"Only a few?" Vihaal said with an arched eyebrow.

"Okay, fine. About a lot of things."

"What do you want to know, Angel?" Gideon asked.

I gestured back and forth between them. "How long have you been married?"

"Three and a half years," Gideon said, leaning in to give Vihaal's cheek a kiss.

"But...I take it it's not a traditional marriage."

They both smiled.

"Nothing about us is traditional," Vihaal said.

I shrugged. "Fair. Do you...make it a habit of inviting other men in for physical...dalliances?"

Vihaal glanced at Gideon.

"I wouldn't call it a habit," Vihaal said. "But we have had the occasional third as a bit of a laugh."

I frowned. "A bit of a laugh?"

"What Vihaal means is that we've occasionally brought someone cute home that we met by chance at an event or something. But we've never tried to seduce someone in particular before."

"Oh," I said.

"We've put quite a bit of effort into you, Angel," Vihaal explained. "I'm glad you've decided to give us a chance. Sebastian seems to think you'd complement our dynamic."

"Whoa," I said, swallowing. "Um..."

"No pressure. I simply wanted to let you know that we don't usually make these sorts of invitations. And we don't do the casual thing anymore."

"Not since we got married," Gideon added. "It's just...it's not us."

"That's why we wanted to be friends with you, first."

I nodded, trying to wrap my head around all of this. "You've given me a lot to think about."

"Understood. I'd also like to ask you to look over the financials at my antique store."

"Sure. I can do that."

"Oh, thank God," Gideon muttered. "It's honestly such a mess and I think there's something underhanded going on—"

"And I think Gideon is paranoid. But. That's why we'd like you to go over Tarnish's financials. To see if anything jumps out at you."

"Oh. I see," I said, becoming serious as I added milk to my tea and stirred it with the little spoon Gideon passed me. "Tarnish is your store?"

"Yes," Vihaal said, sitting back and crossing one long leg over the other. "It does pretty well. But over the past few years there's been a decline in profit, which concerns me."

"I don't trust Dominic," Gideon stated.

"Gideon," Vihaal sighed.

"Look, I'm sorry, but I never have trusted him. He doesn't like me."

"That's not true. And he's a friend of the family..."

"A buddy of your asshole father's, you mean."

My gaze flashed to Vihaal as he closed his eyes, then opened them again, seeming to be mustering patience.

"V, I'm sorry. But it's true. Your dad is an asshole. You've said it, yourself, many times."

"Yes, I have. And yes, he is. But there's a difference between me saying it and you saying it, especially in front of someone I'm trying to impress."

"Vihaal, I've been impressed since I met you."

Vihaal regarded me with curiosity. "Really."

I cleared my throat. "Yeah."

"What's your going rate for business accounting? I don't know how long it will take."

"Do you want me to look at this year's financials? Or the past three years? That will give me an idea."

Vihaal nodded. "Start with this year. If everything looks fine, then I doubt there will be a need to dig further. But, if anything gives you pause, then you can look at the previous year. And so on."

"I'll give you the rate I give Sebastian and Jacob, which is two hundred dollars per hour," I said.

Gideon, who was pouring another cup for himself, spilled tea over the edge of the cup as he stared at me.

"Whoa. If only I was better with numbers," he said, adjusting his aim.

"You're wonderful at what you do," Vihaal said.

Gideon was a registered nurse and worked part-time in the home of an elderly man whose middle-aged children had hired him so that their father could stay in the family home.

"I can't complain," Gideon said. "But can we circle back to where you said you were a bit of a slut? I'd really like to know more about that."

The way Gideon looked at me, with eagerness and bashful excitement, was absolutely adorable, and I laughed.

"I guess I was kind of…"

"Slutty?" Gideon asked.

"Sure. Okay."

"That word has fairly positive connotations in the gay world, Angel. It's not the insult you think it is," Vihaal clarified. "I've known quite a few sluts and they were all absolutely charming."

I sat there, with my teacup and saucer in my lap, the taste of Gideon's fantastic egg salad in my mouth, and the two of them looking at me like they wanted me to be the main course.

"Which is a great segue into what I wanted to ask you next."

I paused, another tiny sandwich halfway to my mouth, and raised my eyebrows.

"We were wondering if showing you some of our favorite porn videos would satisfy your curiosity about what Gideon and I do together. In an intimate way."

His words echoed in my brain as my cock pulsed. I put the sandwich down.

"What?"

Vihaal smiled. "Surely you watch porn, Angel."

I did watch porn. I used to watch straight porn, exclusively. Up until about two years ago. When I'd started satisfying my own curiosity.

"I...uh. Yes. I watch porn." *Should I tell them?*

I laughed, to stall. "This is the last thing I expected during afternoon tea." Then I sobered. "Actually, maybe not the last thing. But it's up there."

"Up there?" Gideon said, giving me a look. "Is it?"

I glanced at my crotch. "Yes."

Vihaal chuckled and stood. "Let me get my laptop. I'll stream it to the TV."

Okay. Well. So we were going to sit here eating tiny sandwiches and drinking tea while Vihaal streamed gay porn to the TV to see what my reaction would be. This was turning into the strangest afternoon.

Vihaal opened his laptop and fiddled about, while Gideon turned on the TV.

"Ready?" he asked, with a mischievous look on his face.

"I sure hope so," I said, pretending to be nervous.

"Here we go," Vihaal said.

But I couldn't do it. I couldn't lie to them. "Wait."

"Hmm?" Vihaal gazed at me, a question in his eyes.

"I..." I put my head in my hands. "I've watched it before."

Gideon looked at me, then at Vihaal. "What? This video?"

Vihaal's eyes narrowed.

"No, I mean, I don't know. It hasn't started yet."

"What are you telling me?" Vihaal asked, in measured tones.

I stood up. "I've watched gay porn, okay? Fuck, I've watched a fuck ton of it."

Gideon stood up. "What?"

"That doesn't mean I'm gay!"

"It probably means you're not straight," he said in measured tones.

"Yes, well. We already established that."

Vihaal was smiling. He sat back against the sofa cushions, the remote in his hand.

"Yes, but...we thought you were still in the early stages of accepting it."

"Okay, fine. I've been questioning things a lot longer than I mentioned to Sebastian or to you."

"Uh huh," Vihaal said. "Well. I'm fucking delighted."

I looked at him, then I looked at Gideon. Then I looked at the TV and sat back.

"Well? You gonna start it, or what?"

Vihaal hit play, and the three of us watched some cute twink get stripped and fucked over the back of a ratty sofa by two muscly bears. It was incredibly hot, and I definitely enjoyed it. For some reason it seemed like Vihaal and Gideon were watching me the whole time.

After it was finished, I said, "Okay. I have one question." I glanced at Vihaal. "Does...getting fucked like that hurt?"

"Not if it's done properly," Gideon said, a saucy glint in his eye. "And Vihaal, well...he does it more than properly."

"I didn't ask because I necessarily want...that. I'm just curious."

Vihaal leaned forward. "You don't have to do anything you're uncomfortable with, Angel. Not all gay men like to bottom. I'm not a fan. But Gideon..."

"Oh, I fucking love it."

I barked a laugh at how sincere he was.

Vihaal sighed. "All right, enough of this. Anyone for more tea?"

Despite the fact that I was having a good time, it all started to overwhelm me. "Actually, do you mind if I get going?"

"No, of course not," Vihaal said, while Gideon gazed at me with affection.

"This has all been a lot," I said. "Good. But a lot."

"I'm sure."

"Can you email me the Tarnish files?"

"Yes. We won't keep you," Vihaal said.

Gideon leaned forward, becoming serious. "Now, about the accounts. I don't trust Dominic. I wouldn't put it past that son of a bitch to sabotage V's store."

"Don't worry. I know exactly what to look for."

Chapter Five

Just as I was getting into bed my phone notified me of an incoming email. I checked to see if it was the one I was expecting.

Here you are. Accounting info from the past twelve months.
And the link to the video we watched earlier. Just in case you want to watch it again.

I had actually tried to find the video, but without success. So I'd pulled up one of my favorites, in which the bottom was cuffed and blindfolded and the top kept him in a state of arousal for a long time before letting him climax, and jerked off to it, coming right when the bottom was allowed to.

Now I clicked on the link Vihaal had sent, and felt my desire return in no time.

I'd known at least a year ago that I was into men, as well as women. But I hadn't had the time to explore that discovery. And maybe I'd been in denial, thinking that all I liked was a different kind of porn. That maybe it was the novelty of it, and the theater of seeing two burly men going at it.

It had taken another month or two to realize I hadn't watched a straight porn video in a long, long time.

* * * *

Over the next few days, my thoughts kept returning to the two men who had put my body and mind into a whirlwind of desire and curiosity. They reminded me of Jacob and Sebastian, who were also married but seemed to have a more traditional idea of what that meant, even though they ran a kink club together.

Vihaal and Gideon were different, although they had the same sense of respect and care for each other. But there was something else. I was eager to find out more about the power dynamic between them — the way that Gideon seemed to defer to Vihaal much of the time, and that Vihaal had a natural sense of authority that I could sense when we were together.

It was obvious from things that Gideon had said — *V does nasty things to me and I fucking love every minute of it* — that the two men were kinky, with Vihaal being the Dominant. I wondered how it would feel to give over to someone in that way, to let them control and subdue me. I got hard just thinking about it.

Vihaal was a flesh-and-blood man who liked to control and dominate his partner. It was obvious now that he might want to do the same to me. The very thought of it caused my body to ignite like nothing I'd ever experienced before, and I had to do something else to take my mind off imagining the three of us together in a room and what that might involve.

So I'd started going over the financials that Vihaal had sent. Nothing seemed out of the ordinary at first, everything looked fairly standard and well-documented. But I began to notice repeating vendor invoices for a company called Divine Treasures. Generally for small amounts — under five hundred dollars — except for a few that were bigger.

One invoice was for close to four thousand dollars.

The smaller invoices listed items such as fine linens, bedding, pillow cases. The big invoice was for 'Various furnitures' which seemed a little vague for such a large purchase. All the other invoices for amounts over one thousand dollars contained very specific descriptions like 'Vintage Victorian escritoire, circa 1854', or 'Genuine marble bathroom fixtures, seventeenth century Italy'. It seemed odd to me that 'various furnitures' would describe such a large purchase.

I found another invoice for Divine Treasures, for the exact same amount, again for 'Various furnitures'. It seemed strange that Tarnish would purchase a different collection of furniture from Divine Treasures for the same price, but it was possible they had a contract to buy a certain amount of small antiques in bulk from the company.

I flagged these items, just in case. It was most likely legitimate, but Gideon particularly had asked me to check for strange invoicing errors or suspicious activities, and I wasn't going to let it go without an inquiry.

Everything else seemed straightforward, with detailed descriptions. The accounts lined up fine. It took me about five days to go through everything then another half day to write a detailed report outlining what I'd looked at and what the results had been.

I sent it in an email to Vihaal and received a prompt reply thanking me and saying that he'd have a look at my results in more detail on the weekend. It was very professional and he made no mention of our get together, or asked if I'd gone to the link he'd sent. Maybe he was busy, but it felt a bit cold after everything, and since it had been so long since we'd seen each other.

"Maybe I should call," I said to Toff. "Do you think I should call?"

He batted his spring toy and yawned, then flopped on the floor.

"Thanks. You're a big help."

It was very possible that they were waiting for me to make the next move.

I opened Vihaal's contact info on my phone. Then I stared at it for a few minutes, wondering what to say. How did you tell two super-hot men that, yes, you were interested in having sex—quite possibly, very kinky sex—with both of them? That you had decided to make the leap out of default heterosexuality into a bisexual wonderland through which you were expecting them to guide you?

I took a deep breath and hit Call.

Anxiety combined with horniness to make me restless as I waited for Vihaal to answer. Or for the call to go to voicemail, and what would I do then?

"Hi, Vihaal, just calling to let you know if you want to take me to the Bordello the next time you go, I'm down. Okay? Call me back."

Huh. I really hoped he answered.

"Hello, Angel."

I was not prepared for the way my body reacted to those deep, confident tones.

"Vihaal," I said, lost for words. "Hi."

"Hi," he repeated and I could tell he was smiling. "I'm so glad you called."

"Oh. Well, good. I'm glad I called, too."

Silence.

Say something, say something.

"Uh, so...I was wondering if..." I laughed nervously, standing up to go look out of the window. "I mean, I just wanted to say...oh my God. Fuck, this is so awkward."

"Shall I make it easy for you?"

"I'd love for you to try."

"Gideon and I want to fuck you."

I inhaled a sharp breath. "Jesus Christ."

"No, just us. He's not invited."

"Hardy har. You're hilarious," I said, my head spinning.

"And you're a beautiful, wonderful man. And we want more of you. If," he said, "that aligns with your wants." He waited a few beats. "Does it, Angel?"

"Yes. Fuck yes," I said, then realized what I'd agreed to. "I don't know about the... I'm not quite ready for... you know, this is all very..."

"When I say we want to fuck you, that doesn't necessarily mean intercourse."

"Oh. It doesn't?" I asked, an inflection of disappointment in my voice.

There was a chuckle. "Well, it can. But it can mean so much more."

"More?" I whispered, feeling shivers and shudders all over.

"Mmm. I'm thinking about more right now."

"Yeah, me too." I swallowed. "Do you mean the kinky stuff?"

Another beat.

"Do you *want* me to mean the kinky stuff?"

"Yes."

"Then, yes, I mean the kinky stuff."

"Holy fuck," I said.

He laughed. "I'm thrilled by how you're reacting to this conversation."

"Vihaal…"

"Yes, Angel?"

"I've never…this is all going to be completely new to me. I'm going to need you to…" I swallowed again. "Start slowly."

He chuckled. "Oh, my darling. I'm very good at drawing things out, don't worry."

I thought about the video I'd watched with the Dom who had teased his submissive for so long and my mouth went dry.

"Fuck."

"Look, Gideon and I have a session booked in the Bordello on Friday…"

"Yes," I said.

"Pardon?"

"I want to go with you."

"Why don't you join us in the gaming parlor. We can have a drink and discuss…everything."

"You don't want me to come to the Bordello?"

"Angel. Of course I do. But I'm not sure you're quite ready for all of that. You just asked me to go slow."

I had asked him to go slow. What the fuck was wrong with me?

"Yes. You're right. Drinks in the gaming parlor sounds great. I'd love to."

"Excellent."

"Except. Fuck," I said, remembering that my car was out of commission.

"Hmm?"

"My car's in the shop and it might not be ready this week."

"That's fine. We'll come and get you. Text me your address. And, Angel?"

"Yes?"

"*I. Can't. Wait.*"

* * * *

I couldn't stop thinking about Friday, but I didn't know what to wear.

I didn't own anything particularly fancy, besides a few business suits. My fashion tended to be on the conservative side, although now that I was stretching the definition of my sexuality, it might be time to expand my wardrobe. Except I didn't know where to begin and it was too late to find anything for tonight.

The men who went to Maverick Molly's tended to dress well. Probably because it was supposed to be a Victorian gaming parlor, and harkened back to a time when people of a certain social class dressed up to go anywhere.

Surely I could dress myself. But I'd been standing and staring at my closet for much too long, thinking everything I had was too plain for a night out at Maverick Molly's. Why hadn't I realized this sooner than the day of? Although, without my car, I wouldn't have been able to go shopping anyway.

I started pulling things out of my closet and trying to figure out what might go with what. I didn't realize the time until I got a notification and a text.

It's Gideon. We're outside. Are you ready?

I was standing in front of my closet in my boxer briefs and a button-up shirt that I hadn't fully committed to. I texted back.

Sorry, I'm not ready. I don't have anything to wear. Can you help?

A reply came soon after.

Of course!

When I opened the door, a cold blast of air came in with Gideon, who looked me up and down and grinned.

"Hello!" he said, gaze zeroing in on my lower half, where the cool air from outside raised goosebumps. "I see you've got a start."

I gazed down at my state of undress.

"Oh, fuck. Sorry," I muttered, closing the door behind him.

"No, no, don't apologize. I'd suggest you wear that to Molly's but I wouldn't be able to keep the other men off of you," he said, taking off his blue cashmere coat and hanging it on one of the hooks by the door. "Or Vihaal, for that matter."

The cats had come to see what all the hullabaloo was about.

"Oh my gosh! Your kitties! That must be Mr. Mistoffelees," Gideon said, nodding at the correct cat, who took up a spot on the half wall to observe him with disdain.

"Yes. And this is Rummy," I said, leaning down and picking up my sweet girl, who purred and regarded Gideon with curiosity.

"She's soooo pretty! And Mr. Toff is such a gentleman!" He glanced at his surroundings. "This is such a cute place!"

"Thanks."

He kicked off his boots and stepped inside, reaching out to let Rummy sniff his fingers, then giving her a gentle tickle on her head. She made a little mewl, which was a sign of her approval.

"Vihaal doesn't have to sit in the car. He can come inside…"

"Oh, he's fine. He's listening to the radio," Gideon said, fluttering his fingers in the air. "Some classical concert, I don't know. Anyway, he knows that when it comes to fashion choices, it's best to let me work alone."

I put Rummy down.

Gideon clapped his hands together. "Where's your closet?"

I took him upstairs.

After perusing the minimal amount of clothing in my closet, he turned to me. "Oh, sweetheart. You need to buy more clothes."

His use of the endearment gave me a soft, safe feeling.

"Clearly."

"Okay. Let's see what we can figure out." He pulled a pair of dark gray suit pants out of my closet. "We'll start with these. Do you have T-shirts?"

"Yes. Here," I said. Rummy jumped up on the dresser and meowed.

"Oh, look, she likes me!" Gideon exclaimed, obviously thrilled. He leaned down to her level. "Don't you, sweet thing? You think I'm all right."

"Of course she does. You're wonderful."

He blinked at me. "Flattery will get you everywhere."

I smiled, and at the look in his eyes, I simply wanted to get going.

"Should I wear a suit?"

He frowned. "Oh no. No. A suit would be all wrong. At least, a business suit would. Do you have any, like, fancy suits?"

"Uh. Nope," I said.

"Hmm." He rifled through one of my drawers and pulled out a black turtleneck. "This is perfect."

"Really? For a club?" I'd always thought of turtlenecks as things to wear at home, when you were cold.

"Are you going to argue with me, Angel?" he asked, raising his eyebrows.

"Fuck no. You know more about fashion than I do."

He grinned. "Oh, we are going to get along just fine!"

He looked me over like I was a tasty snack.

"Right then. I'm going to go downstairs." He stepped closer and gave me a look like he wanted to eat me. "Get dressed, and come along."

After he'd left me alone, it was as if a summer storm had suddenly died. The air still crackled with his presence. I changed my shirt and put on the dark gray pants, using a black belt Gideon had selected, and looked in the mirror.

Holy shit. I looked like someone else. But I also felt more myself than ever.

Chapter Six

"Hey, do you think I should gel my hair?" I asked Gideon.

Gideon's mouth dropped open. "Uh, yeah. Do you have some good putty or something?"

"Yeah. Do guys like that, too?"

"Honey, we like it when you make yourself pretty. Of course!"

I laughed. "I'm not pretty."

"Angel, you're a shiny penny in a dull world. You're lovely."

My heart just about fainted away.

"Thank you. I don't see it. But, thank you."

I walked to the half bath—I kept some gel down here, so I could do last minute touch ups when I went out. I was still reeling from Gideon's sweet words. My hair had grown since I'd had it trimmed in the fall and I liked the way it looked. The wax made the reddish locks fall haphazardly around my freckled face, so that they softened the sharp lines of my features. I thought the black turtleneck made my skin look too pale. Gingers were having a bit of a moment, and Sebastian had assured me that gay and bisexual men loved guys with pale skin and red hair, so maybe I was okay with it.

When I went downstairs, Gideon's eyes just about popped out of his head.

"Oh, holy shit! You look *so hot*. Wait until V sees you!" he clapped his hands like a kid.

He'd put on his boots and coat, and was standing in the front hall. He peered out of the window and gave Vihaal a thumbs-up.

He turned back to me and his eyes widened. "No, wait!"

"What?" I asked, checking to make sure my fly was done up.

Gideon fumbled around in the pocket of his coat. He pulled out what looked like a pencil.

He gazed at me with a sort of yearning. "Would you let me do your eyes? Pretty please?"

"My eyes? Wait. Whoa."

He lifted the pencil. "Just a bit of eyeliner. You'll barely notice it."

I hesitated. Was I ready for eye-liner?

"Look," he said, drawing the tip across the back of his hand. "It's a soft brown. It'll make your eyes pop but nobody will know it's there."

"But I'll know," I said, not sure about it.

Gideon gazed at me with delightful candor. "You're thinking about getting kinky with two perverts but you're scared of brown eyeliner?"

At the word 'perverts', my dick sprang to attention. And I realized he'd made a good point. And also, it was Maverick Molly's. If there was anywhere to try out a little makeup, it was that place.

"Okay. Sure."

Gideon smiled so wide, I was glad I'd said yes.

He stepped close and put a finger on my chin to tilt my head back, then lifted the pencil. Instinctively, I closed my eyes.

"No. Open them," he said, his voice breathy. I smelled peppermint.

I fluttered my lids and stared forward as Gideon traced the outline of one eyelid and then the other. It tickled and I had to blink, but he simply continued once my eyes were open again. It was a strange, but not unpleasant experience.

"There," he said, putting the cap on the eyebrow pencil and pocketing it. "Look."

He gestured at the mirror over the console. I gazed at myself, not quite prepared for how androgynous and freaking hot I looked.

"Oh, holy fuck," I whispered, turning my face to see every angle. It made a big difference, but instead of feeling self-conscious, I felt a hundred times more confident.

"Yeah, you are. So hot. I told you."

If the men at Maverick Molly's hadn't noticed me before tonight, they definitely would now. The thought gave me a weird feeling of satisfaction.

"Come on. We'd better get going or V is gonna lose his shit."

"Well, I don't want that to happen," I said, getting my jacket and boots on.

"No, you don't. Trust me."

Vihaal sat in the driver's seat of a black Audi sedan, tapping his fingers on the steering wheel as Gideon opened the back door for me to slip in.

"Hello, Angel," Vihaal said in that deep bass voice. It affected me the same every time. I melted and got hard all at once.

"Hi."

Vihaal regarded me in the rearview mirror.

"Did Deo sort you out?"

"I think so. Yes."

"I like the eye-liner," Vihaal said. "Makes you look like such a pretty thing."

My heart beat faster and I felt my dick twitch. I would be a pretty thing for Vihaal any day.

"It was Gideon's idea," I said. "He told me no-one would notice."

"That was a tiny lie," Gideon admitted. "But you look so good!"

Vihaal backed the car down the drive. "I called Sebastian and delayed our reservation by an hour. Luckily nobody had booked the other slot, and we've been members of the club for so long that we do get some perks."

"How long *have* you been members?" I asked.

"Oh, it's been, what..." Vihaal glanced at Gideon. "Has it been a year? Seems like we've been going for a while."

Gideon turned to me. "We used to beg and borrow playrooms from amongst our kinky friends, but it got kind of awkward. So we were happy when Maverick Molly's opened up. There are probably lots of places to rent in Toronto, and a few places where straight kinksters can rent in Ottawa, but as far as we know, Molly's is the only one fully reservable and customized for queer kinksters." He looked at Vihaal. "It can't have been only a year. We pretty much got in when they opened, right? Because you already knew Sebastian."

"It seems like it's been longer," Vihaal said.

"It all starts to blur together after a while," Gideon said, grinning. "At least for me. I'm usually in a different headspace when I'm in that room, aren't I, V?"

Vihaal chuckled softly. "If everything is going to plan, then yes."

"When have things not gone to plan? Except for that one time that I had food poisoning?"

"Oh, God, don't remind me," Vihaal muttered. "A tragedy in three parts."

"And then it hit *you* on the ride home."

"Yes. That was awful. I haven't had octopus since."

"Same. Have you ever eaten octopus, Angel?"

"No. Never tried it."

"Vihaal makes the most delicious fish curry. V, you should make it for Angel."

"Certainly."

"I'd love that."

I sat back and watched the city go by as Vihaal drove us to Maverick Molly's. His driving style was steady and controlled, and he handled the car with practiced ease. When we arrived, he found a spot a block away, deftly parallel parked, and shut off the engine.

We emerged into the frosty evening.

Vihaal wore a long black coat, with a black and gray striped scarf wrapped casually around his neck. Gideon's royal blue thigh-length wrap coat, with his bright orange beret tipped at a jaunty angle, stood out against the darkness and he reminded me of a tropical bird or a sunrise. I would never have thought to put those two colors together but it worked. Then again, he could have worn anything and it would look good.

Gideon reached out and took my hand, his gloved fingers tugging me along. "Come on! Bet you've never been here to have fun, right? Only for business!"

"Only for business," I echoed, gazing up at the familiar club, and wondering why it seemed a magical place today, when I'd been through those doors many times before.

But Gideon was right. I'd only been here to discuss the accounting with Jacob and Sebastian. I may have caught a glimpse of activities in the gaming parlor on my way to the back office, but that was as far as I'd gone.

"Full house tonight," Vihaal murmured as we went through the doors and started hanging our coats. A loud hum of voices from the gaming parlor flooded the space, with laughter and the sounds of jazz mixed in.

"Here, let me take that," Vihaal said, reaching out for my jacket.

At least I had a decent leather coat to wear, so I wasn't embarrassed to hand it to him.

Vihaal was dressed in tapered, wine-colored pants, paired with a gray button-up shirt with a banded collar that was tucked in at his trim waist. He looked effortlessly sexy in a distinguished way.

I had expected to feel out of place, but I didn't, even as a dozen eyes turned to look at us as we walked in.

"There's a new bartender," Gideon whispered to Vihaal as we stepped into the gaming parlor.

A stunning person with long curly black hair, olive skin and strong features in a movie-star-attractive face, worked behind the bar. They were wearing a pin-striped white blouse with a high collar and a chain watch attached at the neck. They saw us and smiled, gesturing to a table by the window that was free.

Vihaal raised a hand in thanks and we went over to it.

"Ah, perfect," Vihaal said, sitting where he could see the whole room. Gideon took a seat beside Vihaal and I grabbed the one that was left.

One of the molly boy servers, in corset and bloomers, with a velvet band circling his throat, came over.

"Good evening, gentlemen," he said. "Do we need a drinks menu? Or do you know what you'd like?"

Vihaal smiled, looking the attractive server over. "Gideon and I are due in the Bordello in an hour or so, and we'd like to keep things non-alcoholic. So, two ginger ales, please. And what would you like, Angel?"

"Oh…a Coke will be fine."

"Perfect. Back in a moment," the young man said, and twirled away.

"No drinks before kinks? What would you have if you weren't going to the Bordello?" I asked, my cheeks heating with the thought of what Gideon and Vihaal might be doing in that back room a bit later.

Gideon laughed. "Oh, I like to try all sorts of different cocktails. As long as it's sweet and has an interesting name, I'm in."

"I'm a martini man, myself," Vihaal confessed. "I often make one myself in the evenings at home. I'm picky about the gin."

Gideon rolled his eyes. "Very picky. What's the brand of gin you like, V? Remind me, please."

Vihaal frowned. "You know exactly what kind of gin I like, Deo."

"Why, yes, I do," Gideon said, giving me a cheeky smile. "It's Hendricks. Do you know why I remember it, Angel?"

I shook my head, looking back and forth between them. Vihaal seemed annoyed, Gideon smug and entertained. I got the impression that he got a kick out of annoying his older husband.

"Well, you see, I bought the wrong kind once."

"Oh, dear," I said. "Did he make you go back to the store?"

Vihaal's face went from annoyance to amusement in a second and he snorted a very inelegant laugh, while Gideon gaped at me like I'd just said the most ridiculous thing in the whole world. But then he gave me a slow smile and a wink.

"If only!"

Gideon shrugged and crossed his arms over his chest, sitting back in the chair and regarding me thoughtfully. He'd worn a soft-looking orange sweater with pale blue jeans and black leather boots with a bit of a heel. He looked fierce and sexy and I felt like I was being watched by a jungle cat.

Vihaal also had a predatory look on his face as he gazed at me. "I have a very interesting idea."

"Oh no," Gideon muttered, pink hitting the tops of his cheeks.

"You'll like this one," Vihaal murmured.

"Will I?"

"I think so. But the real question is, will Angel?"

I gazed back and forth between them, waiting for Vihaal to continue.

"Well, you're going to have to tell me what it is," I said.

The molly boy chose that moment to return with our drinks. When he'd left us, Vihaal leaned forward. "I just thought, that the next step after watching two men fucking in a video might be watching two men fucking in real life."

Gideon gave a little shriek. "*Yes.* Yes, yes, yes."

"What do you mean, exactly?"

"I mean," Vihaal said, "that if you'd like to see what two very kinky, and very gay, men do when they go in the Bordello, you can have that opportunity. Tonight."

Wait, what?

"Hold on a second," I said, lifting my hand to give myself a moment to understand what Vihaal was proposing.

"I simply mean," Vihaal said, speaking in a deep voice that warmed me as much as the fire burning in the hearth. "That if you'd like to join us, you can."

"To watch," I stated.

"Yes," Vihaal said, inclining his head. "To watch."

"Oh, but Angel will have to sign up, won't he?" Gideon said.

"I'll cover it," Vihaal smiled, as if he were offering me a prime seat at a prestigious banquet. Actually...

Gideon's eyes were wide and his cheeks flushed. "Oh, I like this idea."

"Gideon is a bit of an exhibitionist," Vihaal explained.

"Actually, I'm a lot of an exhibitionist. Basically, I like to show off," Gideon said, laughing. "And Angel. I would love to show off for *you*."

Gideon held my gaze and I knew I was fucking done for.

"And Vihaal likes to show off, too. Obviously," Gideon said, with a wave of his hand and an eye roll.

"Why obviously?" Vihaal asked, cocking an eyebrow.

Gideon rolled his eyes. "Because you think you're the best at everything."

"Well, I am most definitely the best at dealing with you," Vihaal said, turning and winking at me. "What do you say? Shall we sign you up?"

A flash of memory—of an itemized list I'd had to go over for the accounts—

Silicon lube - jug
Leather paddle
Wood paddle X 3 (different sizes)
Flogger - Leather, red
Nitrile gloves - black
Nitrile gloves - blue

"All right," I said.

Vihaal nodded, not looking surprised at all.

But Gideon looked like he'd just won the biggest stuffed animal at the fair.

"This is going to be *so, fucking, hot*," he said, the words feeling like firm strokes to my cock.

"Yeah," I breathed, and Gideon's eyes danced.

Vihaal stood. "Come with me, Angel. Gideon, stay here and save our seats."

"Yes, V. Whatever you say," Gideon said, sitting up straighter, his eyes bright with excitement.

And that made two of us. I glanced at Vihaal who beckoned me to follow.

Actually, *three*.

Chapter Seven

As Vihaal and I walked up to the bar, the person behind it tucked the towel they were using to tidy up into their waistband and smiled.

"Good evening. What can I get you?"

Vihaal had opened his wallet and now placed a glossy plastic card on the bar.

Maverick Molly's, Kink Club and Gaming Parlor was embossed in gold on the top.

"I'd like to add another person to my membership profile."

"Of course. I'll just text Sebastian. He's in the office."

"I've not met you before," Vihaal said. "I'm Vihaal Petrovsky and this is Angel Barnett. The young man at our table is Gideon Foster. Vihaal and I are already members, and Angel would like to sign up."

They extended a hand to us. "I'm Darya. My pronouns are she/her."

"Excellent. He/him," Vihaal said. "Angel?"

"He/him," I said. "Thanks."

"Wonderful. Give me one moment and I'll have Sebastian come and get you sorted," Darya said, picking up her phone from under the bar and tapping its surface.

It wasn't long before Sebastian came into the gaming parlor and walked over to us. His eyes went wide when he saw me standing with Vihaal.

"Well, well, well. You look great, Angel. Wait, is that…eyeliner?" he asked, squinting.

"Maybe," I said, grinning.

He laughed. "Super-hot! I love it."

"Gideon convinced me to give it a try."

"Well, it works." He turned to Vihaal. "I see you finally convinced Angel to check out the parlor. Where's Gideon?"

"Over there," Vihaal replied. "Seems to be entranced by whichever molly boy is speaking to him at the moment."

Sebastian looked over at our table.

"Oh, that's Toby. He has a way of entrancing pretty much everyone," he said, returning his gaze to Vihaal. "What can I do for you?"

"Gideon and I decided we wanted some voyeuristic company in the Bordello this evening. And Angel here seems willing to indulge our taste for exhibitionism."

I looked at the floor, but I couldn't help smiling. Talk about going from zero to one hundred. I glanced at Sebastian.

"You fucking liar," he said, glaring at me with mock irritation. Then he raised the timbre of his voice in a way that sounded nothing like me—*I hope*. "Oh, I'm straight, Sebastian. We're just friends. They took me out to dinner. Wait, have they been trying to *seduce me*?" He put his hand to his chest in mock surprise, then laughed gleefully.

I narrowed my eyes as Vihaal gazed on with much amusement.

"Very funny," I said. "I don't sound like that. And that isn't what I said."

"That's pretty much *exactly* what you said." Sebastian held up his hands. "Never mind. I'm glad things have moved forward. It's about fucking time."

"Yes," Vihaal agreed. "Gideon and I are thrilled."

"All right, all right. So, I'm curious," I said, shrugging.

Sebastian lifted his hands. "Hey, you don't have to explain it to me."

I filled out and signed some electronic documents, then a card was printed for me.

"Thank you," I said. "I can cover the cost of my membership."

"Nonsense," Vihaal dismissed me with a wave. "I'm happy to do it. It's on my account, yes, but you can come here on your own or with someone else."

"Whoa, whoa," I said, staring at him in shock. "I'm not gonna come with anyone else."

"What I mean is, there are no restrictions. And if we were to, God forbid, come to a disagreement, it's very easy for Sebastian to take it off my account and create a separate account for you. Isn't that right, Sebastian?"

"Yep. Simple as anything."

I looked at Vihaal. "I'm not worried."

"Well, now that you're all signed up, let's get back to Gideon before he does something silly, and forgets all about us," Vihaal muttered.

Sebastian bid us a good evening and left.

Vihaal smiled and, with a jerk of his head, beckoned me back to the table.

Gideon was still chatting with Toby, who turned to acknowledge us.

"Good evening, Mr. Petrovsky. Mr. Foster and I were just discussing paddles, and which ones were best for an entertaining discipline session." He turned to me. "Oooh, I haven't seen you, before."

"Toby, this is Angel Barnett. Angel, Toby."

"Fuck, what an awesome name. Is your mom religious?" Toby asked, batting his eyelashes at me in a flirtatious manner.

I laughed. "No, no. Maybe it was wishful thinking."

"Toby was telling me about some new items they've added to the kink room," Gideon said, with a mischievous smile.

"Isn't that interesting," Vihaal murmured as he took his seat. "Shouldn't he be giving that information to me? I'm the one in charge."

"It's okay, babe. I'll fill you in," Gideon said as he turned to me. "So, all signed up?"

"Oooh, a new member? Welcome to Maverick Molly's!" Toby said, eyeing me up and down. "Is this your very first time?"

"Not in the building. I'm Sebastian and Jacob's accountant. But it's my first time enjoying the gaming parlor."

"Oh! Maybe I have seen you before. But you didn't look like this," he said, making a sweeping gesture with his hand.

"Thanks... I think."

"Yes, that was a compliment. You look hot."

I felt my cheeks heat.

"Toby, would you get me a refill on my ginger ale please?" Vihaal asked. "We still have some time before we can get the key."

"Of course. Back in a jiff."

Toby left in a swirl of white cotton.

"A lot of men are checking you out, Angel."

"Gideon," Vihaal said in a stern tone.

"What? He might as well know he's a hotty."

"Well, somehow I must be. Or neither of you would have paid any attention to me."

"Regardless of the fact that anyone can be sexy if they're confident enough, I must say that your looks…did come into it," Vihaal admitted.

I stared at him and lifted my chin. "Oh?"

He smiled. "Of course. All those freckles and that mouth…" he said, making a swoony face. "And don't even get me started on the red hair."

"Oh, come on. Really?" I said.

"Yes. You look younger than you are."

I pretended to be shocked. "Vihaal. You reprobate."

"I'm a reprobate?"

I smiled and put my chin in my hand, gazing at him dreamily. "Yes. I think that's what I like about you."

* * * *

By the time Vihaal had retrieved the key from Darya and we were standing in front of the door to the Bordello, I was raring to go and already halfway hard.

Vihaal turned to me. "You'll have a safeword, Angel."

I frowned. "Will I need one?"

He shrugged. "We all have the option to stop the scene if needs be. You might change your mind."

"I won't."

"It might be too much."

"I doubt it."

"You might need to go to the bathroom."

"Vihaal. I just went."

He chuckled. "Darling, anything can happen in there. Safewords are a handy tool." Vihaal smiled. "Ready?"

"Hell, yes," I said.

He keyed open the door while Gideon laced our fingers together.

"This is going to be so much fun!"

I'd never actually been in this room before. I'd itemized every piece of furniture and implement from the receipts, but I'd never been in the Bordello at Maverick Molly's.

Now that I was here, I didn't know where to look first.

"Here, let me show you around. I know this place like it's written on the backs of my eyeballs."

"You should," Vihaal said. "We've been in here often enough."

"True. As soon as I step into this room, I'm ready to go," Gideon said. "Now, look. Here we have a very Victorian set up, with a settee and a rug and a vanity and mirror. There's also a rack of antique or made-to-look-antique clothing here on this rack. Did you ever play dress-up as a kid, Angel?"

"My sisters might have put me in a dress once or twice. When I was little."

Vihaal looked over at me. "Hmm. What interesting information. Would you like to watch me dress Gideon up in something?" He ran his fingers over the edge of the wood frame of the settee in a singularly seductive fashion. "That might be a nice way to start."

"Yes!" Gideon agreed. "Let's ease into it for once." He rolled his eyes. "Honestly, lately it's all been a bit *wham, bam, thank you ma'am.*"

"Has it?" Vihaal asked, a stern tone underpinning his words.

"Well, you know what I mean. We get right to business."

"Well, I usually don't have time to waste."

"*Waste!*" Gideon said, and Vihaal grinned.

Vihaal continued. "Don't forget what you are in this room, my little Deo. You need to start addressing me in the proper way."

"Oh, damn. I did forget," Gideon said, releasing my hand and immediately sinking to his knees on the rug in front of Vihaal. "I'm so sorry, Vihaal," he said.

A blaze of heat went through me at the sight. He looked so demure and sweet, kneeling there.

"Angel, come here," Vihaal said.

I did.

"In this room, Gideon is my submissive. There are certain rules and procedures that we follow."

"Right," I said. "Okay."

"While we are in this room, even though you won't be participating in the scene, you are also my submissive."

I'm what? "Pardon?"

He grinned. "Don't look so scared. I'm not a monster. And we've already agreed that you're only going to watch."

"Yes. Right," I said, my body aflame and we hadn't even started.

"I simply mean that I'm in charge. You'll need to follow my instructions if you want the scene to proceed with any validity."

"Of course," I said, happy to go along if it would get me a front row seat at the Vihaal and Gideon kink show.

"Excellent. Stay here."

I watched Vihaal grab a straight chair and bring it over, my heart pounding. He placed it on the floor just inside the door, where I'd have a good view of the Victorian parlor space.

"Sit."

I grabbed the back of the chair and spun it around so I could straddle it, and sat. Gideon was still staring at the floor, but Vihaal gazed at me with a surprised expression that soon morphed into one of displeasure.

And that look of disappointment made my cock go fully hard even as it sent a thrill of real fear down my spine.

Had I done something wrong? I looked down at the way I was sitting.

My cheeks flushed and I stood, heart pounding, and turned the chair back around, placing it the way Vihaal had put it. I sat on it properly.

"Much better," Vihaal stated.

I swallowed, feeling hot and cold and all kinds of delicious things.

"Yes, Sir," I said, testing the word in my mouth. "Sorry, Sir."

"You don't have to call me Sir, but I appreciate the effort. Vihaal is fine."

"Yes, Vihaal."

He kept his eyes on mine as he spoke.

"Safeword, Gideon?"

"Tambourine."

"And what's *mine*?"

"Tarnish."

"And what safeword shall we give to Angel?"

My body was a combustion of desire and we hadn't even started. How was I going to observe this without embarrassing myself by begging to join in, or worse, coming in my pants?

Vihaal pinioned me with his intense gaze, full of his intrinsic power and a hunger so raw, yet so controlled that it was like a lion pacing its cage.

Gideon looked at the floor as the corner of his mouth curved.

"Devil," he murmured.

"Oh, that's good," Vihaal said. "Repeat it, please," he said to me.

"Devil," I said.

"Pardon? Speak more clearly."

Wow. This was next level stern schoolteacher shit.

I cleared my throat.

"Devil," I said repeated, watching Vihaal and wondering how he made me feel like a little kid and a very grown-up man in way over his head at the same time.

Chapter Eight

"Hands on your thighs. Feet flat on the floor."

He was talking to me. Telling me what to do. And I loved it.

"Yes, Vihaal."

The words echoed in my head as if they were the most natural thing in the world for me to say. Comfort, security, safety. Listen to me. Do as I say. Trust me.

I sat in the position he'd demanded and watched.

"Come, my pretty little Deo. Let's get you undressed," Vihaal said, beckoning to Gideon, who stood, gaze lowered like a humble servant.

"Arms up."

Gideon obeyed in silence. He was normally such a talkative and laid-back presence, that watching him go silent and subdued for Vihaal was something.

The ticking of the analog clock on the wall and the hum of the furnace was the only thing to be heard as Vihaal revealed Gideon's smooth pale skin one piece of clothing at a time. The orange sweater came off. Vihaal tossed it to the vanity stool. Next, he knelt and unzipped Gideon's black boots, and removed them, kissing the top of each of Gideon's feet before he placed it on the floor. It seemed strange for Vihaal, as the Dominant, to do this to his submissive. But it absolutely reflected what I knew to be the reality of their relationship.

Gideon was smooth and slim as a seal. And he must have put on some kind of glittery body lotion because he sparkled under the lights of the Bordello as Vihaal stripped him.

As Vihaal unzipped the fly of Gideon's pale jeans, silver flashed in the lamplight. When the jeans were pulled down to his thighs, they revealed Gideon's cock trapped in a metal cage that curved in a gentle arc, keeping him in a state of semi-hardness.

"Fuck…" I whispered, as my cock throbbed.

Vihaal turned to me and frowned.

"Sorry, Vihaal," I breathed.

"Never seen a cock cage before?"

A cock cage? "Not to my knowledge, Vihaal. I think I'd remember."

I liked the look of the shiny metal and I liked the way it kept Gideon from getting hard. It seemed cruel but I knew instinctively that there could be pleasure in denial.

"Mmm. It keeps him from satisfying himself, because his orgasms belong to me."

His orgasms belong to me. Holy shit.

Beyond that, it seemed a piece of kinky jewelry that enhanced Gideon's beauty and mystery, and the bold nature of his sexuality.

Vihaal cupped Gideon's cock in its metal trap.

"What a pretty little cock, my Deo. My captive pet." Vihaal glanced at me before leaning forward and kissing Gideon sweetly on the lips.

Gideon whimpered and opened his mouth to receive Vihaal's tongue.

My cock throbbed at the sight.

I shifted in the chair. Sitting straight and still was an exercise in obedience and I wouldn't pretend otherwise. I wanted to change position. I *really* wanted to flip the chair around again and straddle it, because that would be the most comfortable way to watch. But that might mean the end of all of this, and I didn't want to risk it. Plus, I had no idea what Vihaal might do if I so blatantly disobeyed him. A tiny part of me wanted to find out, but a larger, more sensible part of me, told me not to push his boundaries just yet.

As Vihaal worshipped Gideon's mouth and kissed his cheek and the shell of his ear, Gideon glanced over.

I inhaled sharply as a wave of arousal hit me so hard I thought I might come. Already. After being in this room for ten minutes.

Gideon's lips moved. Vihaal nodded and gave a soft laugh.

"Turn around," he said, and it wasn't to me.

Gideon spun around.

"Bend over."

As Gideon folded himself smoothly at the waist, his hands braced against his knees, a flat black piece of rubber became visible between his ass cheeks.

"My good boy," Vihaal crooned, flicking a finger against it.

Gideon moaned, and I felt an answering surge of desire.

I knew what a butt plug was.

Had Gideon been wearing it when he was in my bedroom, and in the car, and all the time we were in the gaming parlor? The thought gave me an illicit thrill.

As I looked on, fingers digging into my thighs, Vihaal grasped the flange of the plug and tugged. Gideon uttered a delicious whimper, his thigh muscles trembling as more and more of the black rubber object appeared, shiny with lubrication. He gasped as the plug slipped out completely.

I barely kept myself from making a noise and had to concentrate to regulate my breathing.

Vihaal teased the pointy tip against Gideon's hole — also shiny and wet — and pushed the plug back in. Vihaal lifted his hand and slapped Gideon's ass on one side, then the other. Then he spanked him hard, side-to-side, with a quicker rhythm, until Gideon groaned from the pain of it and Vihaal stopped.

"Vihaal?" I asked, my voice husky.

"Yes, Angel? Make it quick, please, I'm a little busy."

"Please let me take my cock out," I blurted.

Vihaal stared at me as if I'd committed a terrible faux pas. But then his expression softened.

"If you must."

"Thank you, Vihaal," I said as my fingers went to the button at the top of my fly.

"You don't get to come until I say so."

I knew there'd be a catch.

"Yes, Vihaal," I said, unbuttoning and unzipping.

"I'll join you." He held my gaze as his fingers went to his fly. He reached into his pants and pulled out his cock and I got a first look at Vihaal's equipment.

It wasn't extraordinary in any way, but seeing it there, swollen with his lust and dark at the circumcised tip, made me groan with excitement. I had mine out now and I thought it looked awfully pale and silly next to Vihaal's.

I lifted my chin and gave my cock two long strokes.

Vihaal's eyes widened and he grinned, then turned back to Gideon.

"Turn around and suck me."

I felt hot and cold, and a bit lightheaded. I made sure to breathe as Gideon turned and sank to his knees, placing his hands on Vihaal's thighs and taking Vihaal's cock in his mouth.

His gaze slipped to mine as he devoured it with so much slurping and abundant drool that I could almost feel it.

Gideon sucked and swallowed, then backed off to catch a breath and swallowed Vihaal down again. He seemed to treat it like an Olympic sport, or maybe he was trying to impress me.

It worked, but now I was on the verge of embarrassing myself, so I placed both hands on my thighs. I sat there stiffly, with wide eyes and sweat beading on my forehead, as a dirty fantasy played out before me in real time. Sitting in that chair, with my cock out and a good view of the tableau before me, I realized how comfortable I was in this intimate sphere with them. I felt like the luckiest person in the world.

Vihaal appeared as if he wasn't affected in the least by having his cock so expertly sucked. And Gideon seemed to be doing everything he could to get a reaction. It was a study in submission, with Vihaal tolerating Gideon's enthusiasm with bland acceptance, as if this was simply a routine occurrence and barely meant a thing. And perhaps that was true for them.

But I could see how Vihaal's blasé demeanor affected Gideon, who became more and more excited as Vihaal simply stood and watched him. Gideon grunted and moaned, and flashed his gaze upward again and again, in blissful supplication.

"All right, enough," Vihaal said finally.

Gideon either didn't hear him, or didn't care to stop at that exact moment. He kept going and Vihaal had to flick a finger against his chin to get his attention.

"Enough," he repeated and Gideon pulled off of him with wide eyes and a subdued expression.

Vihaal, who hadn't climaxed, tucked himself away and somehow was able to do up his pants. "Time to get you dressed, my pretty thing."

"Yes, Vihaal," Gideon murmured, voice rough and lips swollen. He waited on his knees for further instruction as I tried to calm my racing heart.

This was, literally, the hottest experience I'd ever had and I hadn't even done anything. I took deep breaths and sat obediently still as I watched Vihaal select a few items from the clothing rack and dress Gideon in the Victorian finery.

First, a corset made of thick black cotton that buckled with leather clasps and laced behind. It had silver filigree accents and fastened at the front with bolt snaps—like the clasps at the end of a dog's leash—to keep it snug.

Then a frilly black bolero jacket with long sleeves, that he helped Gideon into and tied closed with a cord. The frilled edges of the piece flared out at Gideon's hips, keeping his caged cock visible. It gaped at the chest to expose Gideon's pert nipples and the pale skin over his delicate collarbone.

A wine-colored Victorian collar of some stiff fabric circled his neck, tied with ribbon at the back. It came to a point at his nape and went high under his chin, giving him a statuesque and elegant appearance.

Vihaal had Gideon step into a pair of sturdy boots with a fabric accenting the ankle. Vihaal laced them up then stood, gazing at the vision before him. Gideon looked beautiful and obscene, all at the same time.

"Hmm. What do you think of him?" Vihaal asked, taking Gideon's hand and bringing him to stand directly before me.

"He's fucking gorgeous," I said. "I've never seen anything so lovely, Vihaal."

Vihaal frowned.

"There's something missing," he said, looking Gideon over. "But I'm not sure what."

I thought about it for a second. "A mask, perhaps," I said.

"Brilliant. I'm sure there are a few to choose from."

Vihaal returned to the clothing rack. I returned my hand to my cock with lazy strokes as Gideon, dressed in his pretty finery, watched. Now that things had calmed down, I didn't seem at risk of having an accident and I wanted Gideon to see what this was doing to me.

"Ah, here we are," Vihaal said, sifting through some items hung along the top of the rack. "There are no eyeholes, so it's a blind as well as a mask. Turn around."

Gideon did as directed. Vihaal placed the blind over Gideon's eyes and tied it with the ribbon.

"Spin back around, Deo. I want to see how you look."

Gideon turned.

The eyeless mask went from the top of Gideon's forehead, swooped over his diminutive and perked nose, and descended to the tops of his cheeks. Two silver wings arched outward over his cheekbones, and delicate chains hung, curtainlike, beside Gideon's perfect mouth and dangled past his chin.

"Now he's ready."

"Yes, Vihaal," I agreed, my words breathy and light.

Vihaal placed his index finger beneath Gideon's jaw and tipped his face up, so that the fine chains draped to the sides and he could give his supplicant a gentle kiss on his upturned lips.

Gideon sighed.

"Now, my beautiful slut, a spanking over my knee seems like a good idea, don't you think?"

"Yes, Vihaal," Gideon whispered, as he was led over to the settee.

I watched, entranced, as they got into position.

Vihaal sat and patted his lap. In one smooth movement, Gideon kneeled on the settee and bent himself over Vihaal's lap, supporting himself on his elbows on the cushion. The frilly edge of the bolero jacket rode up to his waist, revealing his plump and perfect ass.

"What a pretty bottom you have, Deo. So smooth and soft. Isn't it a pretty ass, Angel?"

"Yes, Vihaal. So pretty," I breathed. It was like watching a performance, a very sexy one, that was just for me, and for them. I gave my cock a couple of pulls then put my hands on my thighs again.

"Perfect for spanking," Vihaal said, although he continued to caress Gideon's bottom, while Gideon squirmed and sighed, trying to find a comfortable position.

Vihaal raised his gaze to mine and the intensity in his eyes made my balls ache.

"Do you think this naughty boy deserves a spanking, Angel?" Vihaal asked, his voice low and husky.

"Of course he does," I responded, forgetting the formal response in the moment.

Vihaal's eyebrows shot up and he quirked the corner of his mouth.

"And why do you say that?" Vihaal asked, stroking the smooth globes of Gideon's behind.

I shuddered a breath. "Because he knew I wouldn't be able to resist this. And now I'm caught up in something that's going to…leave a mark on me."

Vihaal smiled fully now. "Oh, I certainly hope so. But you're right. He's put you in a very awkward situation, to be sure."

I sat there, watching Vihaal play with his sexy pet, the beating of my heart a frenetic soundtrack.

"Nonetheless, spanking Gideon when he's wearing the cage and plugged up good and tight is one of my favorite things. Because Deo loves a good spanking. In fact, when he isn't caged, he'll often come from it. Isn't that right, Deo?" Vihaal asked, sweeping a hand up Gideon's over the blind to move his hair out of the way.

"Yes, Vihaal."

"And that's one of your favorite things, isn't it, my darling? Coming from a good, over-the-knee spanking?"

"Yes, Vihaal," Gideon said. He moved his head as if trying to see out of the solid mask, sounding resigned and sad instead of excited.

"But, you see, Angel, when he has the cock cage on his pretty little penis, he's prevented from it. And for someone like me, with a sadistic, cruel, and vengeful side, that fact makes this all the more enjoyable."

I moaned, because the very idea was so filthy and depraved and cruel. Vihaal continued playing with the flange of the plug and stroking Gideon's pale backside.

"Although I know that my little, masochistic Deo gets a great deal of pleasure out of being denied and controlled. So it all works out in the end. Doesn't it, my little slut?"

"Yes, Vihaal," Gideon sighed, rocking over Vihaal's lap and making soft little grunts.

"He hasn't had a proper orgasm in days. Gideon tells me it's like riding waves of pleasure that never end. Whereas if he were allowed to orgasm, it would all be over in an instant."

Gideon groaned then whimpered, licking his lips and grunting as he futilely humped his caged cock against Vihaal's thigh.

"Well. Let's get this going. We have thirty minutes to fill."

Vihaal rolled up the sleeves of his shirt and sat there with one hand on Gideon's rump and the other in Gideon's hair. They reminded me of a Renaissance painting. With Gideon in his frilly and depraved finery, bare from the waist but for the cage and plug, and shoed in the pretty boots, they did make quite the picture. I took a photo of it in my mind to remember.

"Do you want it hard or soft, my precious, sweet boy?"

"Hard, Vihaal. So hard."

Vihaal glanced at me.

"Don't forget about Angel. He can't take his eyes off of you," Vihaal murmured. "And he's so fucking hard, and leaking for you, sweet Deo."

I was. I was so fucking hard. And my cock was crying for the two of them.

"Put your cock away, now."

It took a second for me to realize who Vihaal was speaking to, but it could only be me, since Gideon's cock was locked up tight. I hadn't even realized I was touching myself again.

"If you keep that up you're going to get off before I do. And that is not allowed, my boy. Not in here."

I held his gaze as I gave myself one last stroke, then tucked my cock back into my boxer briefs.

"I don't think I can get it back in my jeans," I said.

"Fine. But put your hands on your thighs and leave them there."

"Yes, Vihaal."

I'll do whatever you say because I do not want any of this to stop.

Chapter Nine

Vihaal knew how to give a good spanking.

It was something I wouldn't forget. The sharp slaps of flesh-on-flesh rang off the soundproofed walls of the Bordello along with Gideon's gasps, cries and groans. The smell of sweat and arousal wafted up my nostrils.

If Vihaal were to get out from under Gideon, come over and order me to my knees to resume what Gideon had started earlier, I would have done it. In fact, I was pretty sure I wanted to.

I met Vihaal's gaze and I think he knew it too. I think he'd always known it. The electricity that passed between us, charged by the triangle of our presence in this room and by the sounds of Gideon's debasement, buzzed like a swarm of bees on the hunt for pollen. I heard it as something real and solid, and not just the spinning of my heady brain realizing something about myself and the two of them, and the way we were meant to be together.

Finally, Vihaal stopped, and rubbed his palm over Gideon's reddened backside, crooning soft words.

"How was that, my precious thing?" Vihaal asked.

"So good. *Fuck*. So good, Vihaal. Thank you," Gideon whispered, his tone sincere and grateful. He turned his face as if to look at me, but the ornate mask blocked our connection. He whimpered and let his head hang down again.

"Off my lap now. You've made a mess of me," Vihaal said, giving Gideon one final slap on the ass.

Gideon scrambled up, swaying and breathing hard, his hair askew. His cock bulged against the bars of the cage, which were shiny with moisture from his leaking arousal.

As I watched, Vihaal reached out and swiped the wetness away with a finger, then sucked it, making audible sounds. Gideon's lips parted and he made a soft noise.

Vihaal stood and stepped forward, unfastening the ties of the mask and removing it. Gideon blinked in the sudden light and they gazed at one another. Then Gideon turned to me.

"Fuck," I whispered. He looked even more beautiful now, his skin glowing with a sheen of sweat, his eyes dazed, and his cheeks — *both sets* — rosy and bright.

"Hmm. Look at you. A decadent treat," Vihaal said as Gideon tore his gaze from mine. "Now…"

He held out his hand for Gideon.

"Let's take this over to the bondage bench, shall we?"

"Yes, Vihaal," Gideon said.

"Angel. Bring your chair. I'll tell you where to place it so that you have a full view of the proceedings."

"Yes, Vihaal," I said.

My mouth and throat were dry. I stuffed myself back into my jeans now that I was in a position to do so. My cock was still hard but at least I was vertical. I picked up the chair, wincing as the denim chafed me.

I followed them to the piece of furniture on the other side of the platform bed, in the seriously kinky end of the room. My gaze fixed on the St. Andrew's cross on the wall, wondering if Vihaal had ever put Gideon on it. I had a funny feeling they'd tried out just about everything in this space, but never with a third person involved.

It felt like a precious gift to be here.

"Put it right there," he said, pointing to a spot behind the bench. "I want you to see everything from my angle," Vihaal said.

I put the chair down and sat, waiting with bated breath for what might happen next. I slipped a finger under the collar of my turtleneck for some relief. Clammy sweat stuck to my skin.

"Why don't you take off your shirt, Angel," Vihaal suggested. "They keep the heat on high in here, as normally at least one person is naked."

I nodded, lifting the suffocating item over my head and dropping it under the chair. I didn't feel self-conscious at all and now I was much more comfortable, if you didn't count the raging erection in my tight jeans.

Vihaal untied the strings of Gideon's bolero jacket and removed it, tossing it to the floor.

"We'll leave the corset. I like the way it restrains you. And I'm putting this back."

Vihaal tied the silver mask back onto Gideon's pretty face, so he was prevented from seeing again.

Gideon followed Vihaal's instructions to sit on the padded bench and lie back, so that Vihaal could attach his ankles and wrists to points below. He'd kept Gideon in the boots, so it looked even more depraved to have him bound and spread, with the corset and the filigree blind on, and only his nether regions bare to be played with. He'd removed the stiff collar so that Gideon had more range of movement in the neck.

His gaze fixed on his vulnerable supplicant, Vihaal took hold of the small pegs on the foot supports and whipped them apart in one movement, spreading Gideon's thighs wide and making both of us gasp.

"Holy shit," I said.

Vihaal glanced at me, and grinned.

Gideon's chest rose and fell as he lay there, fastened to the bench in such a vulnerable way. The black flange of the plug was clearly visible and his cock in its pretty cage, still wept.

I imagined what it might be like to be at Vihaal's whim in this way, and all I could think was *yes, yes, yes*. I wanted to be in Gideon's place, even as Vihaal played with his trapped cock and flicked the end of the plug to tease him.

Vihaal stepped forward and to the side, so that I had a clear view as he took the flange of the butt plug between his thumb and finger and eased it out.

"Oh, fuck yes. So beautiful the way your body opens for me," Vihaal murmured, as Gideon's breaths stuttered. He moaned as the object slid free.

Vihaal wiped the plug and placed it on a towel on the floor under the bondage bench. He moved back to his position behind Gideon. I watched, transfixed, as Vihaal lifted a bottle of lube and dripped a copious amount between Gideon's spread cheeks.

Gideon moaned, and shifted his knees back and forth, as much as he could with his ankles strapped down. His head rocked from side to side, and his lips parted as he panted with eagerness.

"You look like a full fucking meal, lying there," Vihaal growled.

He moved between Gideon's spread knees and cupped his hands under his legs, leaning forward between them. He bent to Gideon's pale inner thigh, nuzzling in beside the cage and licking and kissing him all around it, tonguing his balls.

Gideon inhaled and arched his back, groaning and giving himself up to it. His cock was still pushing at its confines, trying to get hard, but unable to, dripping with pre-ejaculate as Vihaal teased and tasted him.

It took so much willpower not to touch myself. For one small second I pressed my palm to the front of my jeans and made a sound of relief.

But Vihaal had seen. Or he'd heard me.

"Hands. Off," he said, in a stern voice that only made it harder to refrain.

"Yes, Vihaal," I gasped, curling my fingers around the edge of the seat to stop myself.

Vihaal turned back to Gideon. He gave Gideon's caged cock a kiss, then straightened. The rattle of a belt buckle and the purr of a zipper rang out.

"You want me to fuck you, Deo?"

"Yes, yes, yes. Oh God. *Please fuck me, Vihaal.*" Gideon pleaded. "Please, please, *please.*"

Vihaal gave a soft laugh, squirting lube into his palm and stroking himself. "Oh, you are such a saucy little slut, aren't you? So desperate."

"Yes, yes, yes." Gideon panted.

"See how he wants me?" Vihaal said. "Even though his cock is trapped?"

I couldn't speak. I could only watch as Vihaal used his fingers to prepare Gideon, then sank his cock inside Gideon's supple and welcoming body in one smooth movement.

Gideon cried out, his mouth wide, his head thrown back, as Vihaal crouched over him. Vihaal started slowly, but soon was fucking hard and fast as Gideon came apart in front of me.

Gideon babbled, whimpered and groaned as Vihaal fucked him with a punishing rhythm and murmured words of encouragement.

"Oh, yes, my pretty boy. So sweet and talkative when you're not at my mercy like this. The only thing I like better than listening to your words is hearing you beg and plead and moan for me."

Gideon abandoned all sense of propriety. He was a writhing animal on that bench as Vihaal took him. I watched Gideon's caged cock bouncing at the rhythm of Vihaal's quick and powerful thrusts.

Now Gideon mumbled nonsense, his exclamations increasing in volume, until he cried out in seeming agony as his caged cock overflowed with white fluid. He'd come, even with the cage on. Vihaal cursed and groaned as he jerked against Gideon's ass, achieving his own release.

Vihal shoved the mask off Gideon's face and it clattered to the floor. Gideon blinked, still uttering soft moans as Vihaal continued to pump him. His eyes were glazed and his face glowed with perspiration.

They were beautiful and so fucking sexy. I'd never witnessed anything so arousing or so incredible in my life. If I hadn't been enamored of these two men before, I definitely was now.

Gideon turned his sweat-streaked face to me.

"Angel. Hi."

"Oh my God. Hi," I said, breathless and so turned on I thought I might die if I didn't get to come soon.

Gideon laughed as Vihal kissed his neck and chin then his mouth, the passion of it searing my vision. He still had his cock buried in Gideon and seemed in no rush to decamp.

"Come over here," Vihaal said to me. "You can jerk yourself off on his face if you like."

It felt like I was having a stroke, the way everything kind of went into slow motion as I walked over to them. I unzipped, pulled out my cock, and held out my hand for lube.

"This isn't a fancy hotel. Do it dry," Vihaal muttered, moving his hips with a lazy satisfaction. "I could probably touch you with a feather and you'd come."

Gideon gazed at me with a dreamy expression. When he closed his eyes and opened his mouth, snaking his tongue along his bottom lip, I almost came without trying.

Three quick pulls were all it took. I made a strangled sound as I shot creamy white jizz all over him. It landed on his forehead and lips and chin and cheek, dripping down to the bench in lazy blobs. There was so much, but he made sounds of approval and moaned his satisfaction.

"Fuck yes. Good job," Vihaal muttered, as I squeezed the last bit out and took my hand off myself, standing there in the middle of the Bordello with two men who had become my living fantasy.

* * * *

We were quiet on the ride to my place.

Finally, I couldn't handle the silence.

"So…that was…*something*," I said, rubbing my palms on the tops of my thighs where they were covered by my winter coat.

Vihaal only smiled and looked smug as he drove the car. But Gideon turned a shocked look on me.

"Is that all you've got to say?" he demanded, looking so fucking cute and offended and tired after his experience in the Bordello.

I laughed. "What do you want me to say?"

Now he looked even more offended.

I sighed. "Okay, look. I've never witnessed anything so fucking hot in my life before."

Gideon's expression softened.

"Happy now?" I asked.

He gave me a short nod and smug smile.

"As a matter of fact," he said, "I'm feeling very relaxed and content right now. And satisfied that we gave you a good show, and maybe some insight into how *not straight* you might be."

"Fuck, Gideon. That ship sailed way back at your sexy tea party." I shrugged. "Maybe before that."

Gideon huffed a laugh. "Good."

"I really don't think you're vanilla, either," Vihaal murmured, eyes fixed on the road ahead.

"Vanilla?"

Gideon laughed. "Vihaal thinks you're kinky. Like us."

"I think Vihaal is a very smart and perceptive man."

We were silent the rest of the way to my place.

"I'll walk you to the door, Angel," Gideon said as Vihaal pulled into my driveway.

"Sure," I said, not wanting to argue with the man whose face I'd painted with my jizz about forty minutes ago, even though I was capable of getting to the front door myself.

"I want to give you something," Gideon explained, and as soon as Vihaal had put the car in park, he was opening the passenger door and getting out.

"Angel," Vihaal murmured, as I prepared to exit.

"Yes?"

"Gideon really likes you."

"Well...I'm glad." Warmth filled my chest. "And, uh, what about...what about you?"

Vihaal smiled. "I like you too."

Gideon knocked on the window and beckoned me, but Vihaal wasn't finished.

"I love Gideon. And he loves me. And we are committed to each other," he stated. "But if you are so inclined, we would have you as another person in our...intimate circle. It may not work out. But if it does, won't it be marvelous?"

"I'm...inclined. I am so, so inclined, as a matter of fact."

Gideon opened the car door.

"V! Let Angel out of the fucking car."

"Wait, can I call you V?" I asked, giving Vihaal a cheeky smile.

"I would love it."

I got out of the car. Gideon slammed the door shut.

"Seriously, that man. And he says I talk a lot." He held out his hand. "Come on."

I let Gideon pull me toward my house. On the porch, he tugged me off balance and I fell against him.

"Mmm, hello there," Gideon said as he wrapped me in his arms and gave me a warm hug.

"Hi," I murmured as we gazed at each other. He was so fucking pretty.

"When you came on my face, that was the hottest thing, seriously," Gideon said, as if he was proposing.

I burst out laughing and he frowned.

"What? Didn't you think so?" he asked.

"Sorry, I'm just...I feel a bit giddy. That was the best."

He seemed satisfied. "Maybe you can come down my throat next time."

"Oh, holy fuck," I said.

"Uh huh. And I don't care how much of a dirty slut you've been with other people, you ain't prepared for that," Gideon said, his minty breath puffing against my face.

"I've been such a dirty slut, Gideon," I confessed, my voice a whisper in the darkness.

His smile widened. "Oh, you naughty, naughty boy. Now we can be sluts together. For Vihaal."

"That sounds like a dream," I said.

Then Gideon's mittened hand was on my cheek and he was leaning closer. I moved forward to capture his mouth with mine and lost myself in the warm, soft wetness of Gideon's exploring tongue and soft lips. Our breaths mingled as we tasted and savored each other.

Finally, he pulled back, wiping at his mouth.

"Fuck."

"I know," I said, my gaze greedily feasting on his eyes, his nose, his cheekbones and those luscious red lips.

"Vihaal was watching. He always watches."

I glanced at the car and smiled at Vihaal who was indeed watching us.

"Do you mind it?" I asked.

"Exhibitionist, remember?" He pulled the collar of my jacket up against the chill. "And you, my sweet little voyeur, are going to find yourself with a front row seat to all kinds of hijinks. I just hope you can keep up."

"I'm prepared to die trying," I said.

"I'm going to text you first thing tomorrow, okay? We need to set up our next date."

I swallowed. "Are we going back to the Bordello?"

"Oh, we will, but not for a couple of weeks. We're not animals."

I laughed. "Okay."

"In the meantime, might be nice to do some ordinary things. Do you like to go to the movies?"

"Sure."

"Okay, then. You know we aren't crazy sex freaks. At least not all the time."

"Well, damn."

Chapter Ten

Everything I'd seen in the Bordello replayed like a movie reel in my head over the next couple of days. I tried to get some work done. But every time I closed my eyes I saw my jizz landing on Gideon's cheek and nose and lips.

I wanted to do it again. And I wanted to do more.

I was also fielding texts from Rebecca.

Hey, Angel. I had so much fun with you! I'd love to get together again.

Hi. Feeling horny. Would love to get together again!

Hey, call me. Ready to bone if you're 'up' for it. Happy face emoji.

I had to give her props. She was really trying. But I had no compulsion to reply or to get together with her.

I'd briefly considered hooking up with her again, to see how I felt now that I'd begun exploring a different side of my sexuality, but I'd thought better of it. I didn't want to use her, and I had no real interest in doing so.

To be honest, I was beginning to care less about how to define my sexuality, and more about enjoying the exciting journey of exploring it.

Oh, hey, sorry about that. Normally I would but I'm super busy with work right now. Tax season, you know. Hope you're doing well.

It was lame, and I knew it. Still, we'd only had a casual hookup. Neither of us had made plans to see each other again. And now that this *thing* — whatever it was — with Vihaal and Gideon was progressing, I had absolutely no interest in her.

I was conflicted about who would make the next move in our little three-way neo-relationship. I wanted to text them but I didn't want to seem desperate or clingy. Maybe I was still thinking like a straight guy.

Anyway, the next day Gideon texted me good morning and asked about my plans. I admitted that I had a ton of work to do and he said they were slammed as well, but asked if I wanted to go see the latest *Guardians of the Galaxy* movie on Saturday.

If he'd asked me to go see Paw Patrol I'd have still said yes.

My car had come back from the shop after over five hundred dollars in repairs, so I offered to meet them at the cinema.

The nervous excitement I felt at the prospect of seeing Vihaal and Gideon again made it plain that I was totally falling for them. I'd never felt this way about anyone before, and now I was feeling it for two men? Life was fucking weird. But life was also doing me a solid right now, so I couldn't complain.

I'd had a brief moment of panic and doubt after the Bordello, once they'd gone home and I was alone with my thoughts. What if this crashed and burned? What if we had a lot of super sexy fun but it turned out we weren't good together? Or worse, what if they decided that I wasn't a good fit for them? I'd be devastated.

Then I remembered that we'd already established a friendship, and if it did turn out that we weren't suited as a romantic throuple, they would still be important people in my life. And, what if it did work out? Was I going to miss out on this wonderful possibility by living a boring fucking life?

I got there early and found a seat at one of the tables in the refreshment area. I'd worn a different turtleneck with a pair of gray pants, but I really needed to ask Gideon when we could go shopping. If I was going to keep up with these men, I needed to dress better.

I was playing a puzzle game on my phone, letting the hum of conversation float over me, when the chair beside me was pulled out and Gideon plunked himself down with a sigh.

"Sorry we're late."

"Yes," A deep voice agreed. I turned to see Vihaal standing on my other side. He continued, "I didn't realize that Gideon was dragging me to another Marvel movie until we were halfway here."

"Oh, don't be such a snob," Gideon muttered. "You admitted that you liked the first *Guardians of the Galaxy* movie."

"Which ones are they? The guy with the metal space suit?"

"No, that's Iron Man and The Avengers. You don't like those movies and I would never take you to see one, ever, again," Gideon said with a shudder. "This is the group with the alien tree and the raccoon. Star-Lord? Mantis?"

"Oh, yes," Vihaal murmured. "It's hard to keep them all straight."

"Hardy har. *You* like *Guardians of the Galaxy*, right, Angel?" Gideon asked me.

"I think so. I can't remember, honestly. I get them mixed up, too."

"Oh my God. Seriously, you people." He rolled his eyes in the most adorable way and I smiled.

"Well, hopefully I'll like this one," I said, wanting to be agreeable, and not caring at all what movie we were here for.

Vihaal laughed softly.

"If you don't," Vihaal murmured, "I'll simply have to distract you."

"If you talk during this movie, V, I will murder you," Gideon replied.

"I didn't mean by *talking*."

Gideon unwound his scarf and dropped it on the table, then undid the buttons on his coat.

"Do you want to get some snacks? I'm gonna get popcorn." Gideon stood.

"Nah, I'm good," I said.

"Suit yourself. Back in a flash."

Vihaal sat down in the chair beside mine, his coat falling open to reveal a pair of light wash jeans and a black Henley. I'd never seen him looking so casual and I liked it.

"I don't go to the movies with Gideon very often," he admitted. "Our tastes lie in different directions in this particular area."

I laughed. "Not surprising. You're so different."

"Yes, well, opposites attract I suppose. Anyway, Gideon has been dying to see the newest Guards of the Universe movie for some time."

I couldn't help smiling at that. "It's Guardians of the Galaxy."

"Oh. Yes." He laughed. "See? You're going to come in handy, Angel." His gaze tracked over me. "In a multitude of ways."

A shiver of lust traveled down my spine.

"Did you read my report about the financials?" I asked. "What do you think about the things I flagged? They might be nothing."

"But they might be something. Yes. I'm...concerned."

"Did you tell Gideon?"

"Yes. He is *very* concerned. Thank you for looking them over. I'm going to follow up on this, Angel, I can assure you. Even if it's all perfectly legitimate, I expect Dominic to keep better records of our purchases."

Vihaal and I watched the people gathering in the lobby.

"I was impressed with how our experience in the Bordello went," he said, not looking at me.

I couldn't help admiring his profile for a moment before returning my gaze to our general surroundings.

"Good. Because I liked it very much," I said.

He turned and smiled at me, with eyes that conveyed his pleasure. "You must have grown up in a liberal household, if you don't have any qualms about pushing your sexual boundaries that way."

"My parents were kind of hippies. My mom was older when she had me — I was kind of a surprise, but a happy one. As long as you weren't hurting anyone, they were behind you, no matter what. My parents didn't believe there was only one way of living."

Vihaal sighed. "I wish my parents had been as accommodating."

I frowned. "Did you have a bad home life as a kid?"

"I didn't have a home life."

"What do you mean?"

"My father sent me away. Never mind, it's an old wound," he said, looking at the floor, then back at me with a universe of pain in his eyes. "Maybe I'll tell you about it sometime."

I gazed at Vihaal, my heart expanding for this self-contained and confident man who'd apparently grown up in less-than-ideal circumstances, and realized there was a lot more to him than I'd imagined.

"Well, that was a crap and a half," Gideon said as he dropped a bag of M&Ms on the table in front of me. "You can have my free candy," he said. "I got the value deal."

"Pssht. It's hardly free and it's hardly a value," Vihaal said, reaching out and taking the candy and putting it into his coat pocket. "I'll hold on to this."

"Whatever. Come on, we need to get to our seats."

I stood and grabbed my jacket, following Gideon as he showed the tickets to the hostess.

"Theater ten," she said. "At the end of the hall."

"Thanks," Gideon said. "Bye the way, I love your helix piercings."

The young woman smiled. "Thanks. Your coat is amazing!"

"Thanks, it's very warm."

He turned to me as we moved forward, Vihaal trailing. "I got seats near the back. V tends to get bored and I didn't want him disrupting the whole theater."

"Oh," I said, not sure what he meant, but glad to sit beside him in the back row, where we weren't in the middle of a crowd of strangers. Vihaal sat down on my other side.

"Oh, sorry," I said, "Don't you want to sit together?"

"No," Gideon said, shoving popcorn into his mouth. "Not here."

Vihaal grunted. "I'd rather sit with you, Angel."

"Well, then, this is perfect," Gideon said. He reached for my hand and squeezed it, then placed a buttery kiss on my cheek, checking for other people first.

He went back to eating popcorn and sipping his drink.

"It's like bringing a ten year old to the movies," Vihaal muttered. He stretched his legs out and leaned back, closing his eyes.

"I heard that," Gideon said. "Better than feeling like I'm with my grandpa."

Once the movie started playing, after the teasers, Gideon was entranced. I was less so, but eventually started to get into it, until Vihaal got into distracting mode.

He must have been waiting for just the right moment. There was crinkling as he pulled the bag of candy from the pocket of his coat and ripped it deftly open. After a moment, Vihaal showed me his open hand with a tiny brown M&M in the center.

I took it, popping it into my mouth, giving him a glance and mouthing *thank you*.

He smiled and reached into the bag for another. This time he offered it between two fingers. I glanced over at him and he smiled. I took the candy.

M&Ms were great, but even more delicious was the fact that Vihaal was doling it out to me in measured bits.

The next one he held right in front of my lips. I side-eyed him, and he smiled and raised his eyebrows, as if he was daring me. After a moment of hesitation, I opened my mouth, and Vihaal placed the candy on my tongue. There weren't many things I wouldn't do for chocolate.

I gave Vihaal what I hoped was an incendiary look and licked my lips. He leaned in and whispered in my ear.

"One day, I'd like to have you on your knees, naked, beside the kitchen table—your place or mine, I don't care—with your ankles bound and your wrists tied behind your back."

I tried not to make a sound but my cock bounced in my pants and my heart started beating a frantic rhythm.

"And I'll feed you pieces of food from my hand if you're very good and quiet and patient."

Holy. Fuck. I nodded my head.

"*Yes.*"

"Yes?"

"Please," I whispered.

Gideon glanced over.

"Oh no," he said. "It's started."

Vihaal lifted another M&M to my lips. I had my mouth open when he got it there, and this time, instead of simply placing the candy on my tongue, he used two fingers to apply pressure and cause me to open wide. My gaze flashed sideways and he regarded me with much satisfaction. He held my gaze as he dropped another M&M in my mouth, then withdrew his fingers, rubbing the tips over my teeth and lips as he did.

"You're going to make a lovely, lovely submissive."

At that moment, it was all I wanted to be. I didn't give a fuck about the movie. I wanted Vihaal to take me into the bathroom and put me on my knees and fuck my face.

What is happening to me?

I didn't recognize myself but I really liked the bold, shameless person I'd become.

I turned to gaze at Vihaal as I swallowed the candy down, hoping to convey some of what I was feeling. I saw his eyes widen and lips part in the semi-darkness. After a glance at our surroundings, he leaned close, took my chin between his finger and thumb and kissed me with more passion than I was expecting.

I opened to him without question and lost myself in the surprise and honesty of it. It didn't last long — we were in public — but when he released me, he mouthed *thank you* and smiled with obvious affection.

My cheeks — and other things lower down — heated as he held me with a look. I waited, outwardly patient but inwardly aflame, for another candy.

Vihaal fed me M&Ms, one at a time, playing with my willingness to submit, teasing my tongue and the insides of my cheeks, to see what he could get away with. When he stopped, I looked over and he showed me the empty bag, frowned and shrugged his shoulders.

The disappointment hit me hard. The sweet chocolate, the teasing, and this mild act of submission had been surprisingly lovely. And now there was no more candy, no more Vihaal touching me in such an intimate way, and soon the movie would end and we'd have to go our separate ways.

"You didn't watch any of it, did you?" Gideon asked when the credits started rolling.

"Don't be mad at Angel, it was entirely my fault. I couldn't keep my hands off him."

"I'm sure that's true," Gideon muttered. "And I can't really blame you. Next time, I'm just bringing Angel."

"Oh, thank God," Vihaal muttered.

Gideon narrowed his eyes.

"It's a good thing there was a buffer between the two of you," I said, clicking my tongue. "And it's a good thing it was me."

Gideon snorted. "Oh, honey, you can get between us anytime you like."

"Yes," Vihaal agreed. "Anytime."

We parted with smiles and plans for Gideon and me to go to the mall the following week, even though that seemed like too long a wait.

When I got back to my car, I put the key in the starter lock and turned it.

Nothing.

I tried again, but the engine didn't turn over. It didn't even try to.

Fuck, fuck, fuck. Had I renewed my CAA membership?

I slammed my palms against the steering wheel.

"For fuck's sake!" I cursed. "I was having such a good day."

A familiar car appeared in my rearview mirror. I turned to see Vihaal's Audi and felt some relief. I wasn't stranded.

Gideon opened the Audi's passenger door and slipped out, walking over. I rolled my window down. Yes—actually rolled it. That's how old this car was.

"Hi. My fucking pissant of a car won't start," I grouched.

"Oh fuck," Gideon said. "That's no good. Do you have CAA?"

I shook my head. "I forgot to renew it. So, no."

"Shit," Gideon said.

"Yeah."

I heard the low rumble of Vihaal's voice but couldn't make out what he said.

"Car's dead!" Gideon said. "No, he doesn't have CAA."

Vihaal said something else and Gideon turned back to me.

"Vihaal says to come home with us. I agree. We can figure out what to do in the morning."

"Oh, fuck. Really?"

"Yeah, of course. Or we can drive you home. We're not leaving you *here*."

"I mean, I'd love to go home with you. If it won't be too much trouble."

"What? Of course not. Now come on, it's freezing out here. I'll even let you sit up front, with *the chauffeur*."

Vihaal muttered something and Gideon laughed.

"Oh, now I'm in for it. Better come home and save my skin, Angel."

I got in the car. Gideon got in the back. Vihaal looked at me.

"I would call this a fortuitous circumstance."

"My car dying is fortuitous?" I asked wryly.

"Well, now we get the chance to swoop in and save you. And bring you home," Vihaal said. "Don't you want to come home with us?"

I gazed at Vihaal, then at Gideon.

"Of course I fucking do."

Chapter Eleven

To say that my car refusing to start that night was a strange but welcome development would be an understatement. Vihaal and Gideon seemed delighted to swoop in and save me and take me home, because now they could entertain me.

"Anyone for a drink?" Vihaal asked as we took off our coats.

"Hell yes," I said. "What have you got?"

"Oh, all kinds of things. Wine, spirits, mixers. There might even be a couple of IPAs in the mini fridge."

"A glass of wine would be great," I said, marveling at how my day had turned out.

"Red or white?" Gideon asked.

"Doesn't matter. I guess, white?"

"Gideon, open the bottle of Riesling in the fridge. I've been saving it for a special occasion."

I scoffed. "Oh, you don't have to open a special bottle—"

"Nonsense," Vihaal said with a smile. "We'll do what we like."

He gave me a lingering once-over and I almost combusted.

"Please make yourself at home, Angel," Vihaal said. "Take a seat. Anywhere."

"Sure. Thanks," I said. I chose the corner spot on the sofa from which I could see glimpses of Gideon puttering about, uncorking the wine and pouring three glasses.

Vihaal excused himself, so I took my time looking around their comfortably appointed living room. A built-in bookcase spanned one wall, filled with books of all kinds.

Gideon came back with two glasses of wine, handing one to me and putting one on the coffee table.

"For Vihaal."

He went back to the kitchen and returned with his own glass and the rest of the bottle, which he set on the table.

"I saw you two playing pass the M&M. I don't think you paid much attention to the movie, did you?"

I gave him a look and he laughed.

"Okay, fine. I can't blame you. Vihaal's unbelievably distracting. Particularly when he's deliberately *trying* to be."

"There was a movie?" I joked, giving Gideon a smile.

Gideon took a deep breath. "V can be a lot. Make sure to speak up if he's moving too fast, all right? The last thing we want to do is scare you off."

"Are you kidding?" I said. "I'm having so much fun."

Gideon surged forward and stopped within an inch of me, his gaze moving to my lips as I tried not to spill my wine. His breaths puffed against me and I couldn't resist him. I sat forward and took his sweet mouth with mine and literally devoured him as he struggled to keep up.

"Oh fuck yes," he gasped, opening wide as I kissed him deep and hard, dragging my tongue over his and clashing our teeth together. I moaned as Gideon straddled my lap and cupped my chin in his hands, attacking me with equal fervor.

"Angel. God. You're so hot," Gideon murmured, as we kissed and fumbled together. My arms wrapped around him and I splayed one hand against his back.

I was beyond words but Gideon kept talking in between panted breaths and soft gasps.

"You're like, literally a gay...virgin, but you're not...like...fourteen, which would just be gross." He pulled back and gazed at me quizzically. "How the fuck old are you, anyway?"

I looked at him, dazed and so fucking turned on I couldn't keep still.

"I'm thirty-six. I thought you knew that."

"I thought you were younger. You look younger."

"Good," I said, my gaze fixed on those wet lips that demanded my attention. "How old are you?"

"Twenty-six. Jesus, we're ten years apart," he said, giving me an incendiary look.

"Does that matter?" I gasped.

He grinned. "Only in the best of ways."

I kissed him again, harder, and he met my passion with his own.

He smelled like cinnamon and sugar, and tasted like mint. His solid erection pressed against me.

"No cage?" I gasped, unable to stop eating at his sweet mouth.

"Not today," Gideon replied, moaning as I bit his top lip and stroked the roof of his mouth with my tongue.

"My, my, what have we here?"

Gideon and I pulled apart and gazed dazedly at Vihaal.

"Sorry, V..." Gideon panted. "I couldn't help myself."

"Well, don't stop on my account," Vihaal said, picking up his glass of wine and sitting in the armchair across from us.

Gideon turned back to me and looked like he was about to get back into it.

I held up my hand. "Wait," I said. "I think I need more wine."

Vihaal chuckled and Gideon smiled slyly, slipping off my lap and passing me my glass.

"Not too much, though," Vihaal suggested. "I think this afternoon is beginning to go in another direction."

"V, we were only kissing," Gideon said, picking up his wine.

Vihaal laughed. "That was practically 'just fucking', except you both have your clothes on."

Gideon pouted in the cutest way. "You got to play with Angel at the movies. Now it's my turn. And, by the way, it was super-hot, the way you fed him the candy."

Vihaal raised his eyebrows. "I thought you were watching the movie."

"You underestimate my ability to multitask."

"Hmm. Funny you should mention that," Vihaal said with a grin that made me even more aroused than I already was.

"Why?" Gideon asked, tilting his head and giving Vihaal a look of suspicion.

"Because I'd like to see you suck Angel off while I finger you."

My cock pulsed at Vihaal's words and I had to adjust my position. "What?"

"You heard me," Vihaal said. "And so did you." He turned to Gideon and smiled.

Gideon hummed.

"Or maybe, Angel should spank me. Because I've been very, very naughty."

I gazed back and forth between them, my horny brain unable to process what was happening.

"I suppose that could be fun," Vihaal conceded with grace. "If Angel even wants —"

"I'll do it," I said, not giving it a second thought.

Vihaal laughed. "Wonderful."

Gideon grinned and almost vibrated with excitement.

"Would you like him naked?" Vihaal asked.

"Oh yeah." And now I was smiling. "I'd love to…" I inhaled a deep breath, suddenly lightheaded. "…watch you take Gideon's clothes off."

Vihaal's eyes widened and the corner of his lips quirked. "Fast or slow?"

"Oh. Fast," I said, adjusting my erection again.

"All right."

Gideon held my gaze as Vihaal moved forward and efficiently stripped him, making sure to do it in a way that didn't block my view of the proceedings. I watched, transfixed, as Gideon's clothes came off, until he stood there in nothing but his smooth, pale, unmarked skin.

He was stunning — an ethereal sprite with a rampant erection and a lust-filled, hazel-eyed gaze.

"Well, what are you waiting for? Over Angel's lap. Now."

I took a sudden inhale that made a sharp sound in the quiet room.

"Mind you don't break his cock, though," Vihaal said, nodding to where my jeans were bulging obviously.

I blushed, moving a hand to cover the tent in my pants.

"Don't cover yourself, Angel. I like to see my playthings enjoying themselves."

Playthings.

As Gideon crawled over my lap, his sinuous form undulating in ways that made my dick ache, it didn't seem all that complex. We liked each other. We were attracted to each other. Gideon and Vihaal loved each other and they both wanted *me*, for some strange reason. And something about this whole thing was the answer to a prayer I'd never spoken aloud to *anyone*.

I didn't know what to do with my hands. They itched to touch Gideon, and to see what it felt like to spank a gorgeous naked man over my lap. But I waited for Vihaal to give me leave.

"Oh, don't you two look lovely," he said. "Now look, you can spank him if you want. I'm sure he'll enjoy it. But have fun with him. That's what I like to do."

Gideon whimpered and rocked on my lap, nudging his cock against my thigh.

I licked my lips. I'd expected explicit instructions. I was suddenly paralyzed by the range of options. Gideon was right here and just…giving himself to me.

My left hand moved of its own volition, to rest on Gideon's smooth, plump buttock. And squeeze. And stroke. He was so warm and his skin was like silk. Knowing Gideon, he probably had a whole daily moisturizing routine to keep it that way. It was as soft as any woman's.

My other hand got in on the action. I stared at my fingers as I soothed and stroked Gideon's rump like he was a cherished pet. But he wasn't. Gideon Foster was a flesh-and-blood human man. Over my lap. *Naked.*

I met Vihaal's gaze. His pupils were dilated and full of desire. He was enjoying this.

He always watches.

I returned my gaze to my hands on Gideon's ass.

"Angel," Vihal murmured.

I lifted my hand and brought it down on that beautiful soft flesh — *smack!*

Gideon jerked, then moaned, then cursed.

I repeated the action with the same result. My palm tingled and throbbed.

Vihaal chuckled. "Here we go."

I gave Vihaal a lust-filled glance, then got to work. My rhythm was jerky and uneven at first, but soon leveled out. I'm sure I didn't use as much strength as Vihaal would, but Gideon responded well. He moaned, rubbing himself against my leg.

"Are you going to let him do that?" Vihaal asked.

"I — What?" I said, my hand in mid-air.

"He's rutting on you. He's going to come if you let him."

"Really?" I asked, staring down at him. Gideon was breathing hard and clutching the couch cushion.

"Yes," Vihaal said.

"No, I promise, I won't," Gideon whined. "Keep going…"

I lowered my hand to rest it on the small of Gideon's back. "Shhh, now. Be a good boy for me."

Gideon groaned and then whimpered. "Holy fuck."

"That's the stuff," Vihaal said, and my heart flipped at his approval.

But I needed some direction. I didn't want to waste this opportunity, but I didn't know what to do next. It was so overwhelming, having this beautiful man squirming on my lap, my brain was a thick fog of lust that I could barely see through.

Gideon's head swiveled and he stared at Vihaal. Then he buried his face in the cushions. "Oh, fuck, fuck, *fuck.*"

I massaged his lower back as Vihaal brought a chair from the kitchen and sat down right in front of us. He handed me a small plastic bottle that didn't have a label.

"What's this?"

"Coconut oil," Vihaal replied.

Gideon groaned, the sound muffled by the cushions.

"He's in quite the state," Vihaal murmured.

"He sure likes being spanked," I said, smoothing my palm over Gideon's ass again and again. It was warm and pink now.

"Yes. It's something we both enjoy from different sides."

I nodded, trying to keep my breathing steady. My legs were warm underneath Gideon's naked body. His cock pressed against my thigh in the best of ways.

"He's shaking."

"Yes."

"He's all right?" I asked.

"He's just fine," Vihaal assured me.

Gideon groaned and squirmed, then settled again with a resigned sigh.

"He loves this. Don't you, Deo?" Vihaal asked.

"Fuck," Gideon murmured. "Yes."

"Being objectified. Being at the whim of my desires. Being over your lap. He's been wanting *that* for some time."

"You're kidding," I said, trying to wrap my head around it.

"I never kid about that sort of thing." He nodded toward the bottle of coconut oil in my hand. "Use some of that and play with his ass."

My breath hitched and I zeroed in on the shadowed cleft between Gideon's cheeks. I flicked off the stopper and poured some of the oil into my hand, as directed.

"Rub it between your hands, to warm it up," Gideon said.

"Who's giving the instructions here, Deo?" Vihaal sighed.

"You are, Vihaal. I'm sorry."

I exchanged a look with Vihaal, who nodded, so I did what Gideon had asked.

When I started rubbing the oil on his rosy buttocks, Gideon sighed with pleasure.

"That feels good," he murmured, letting his thighs splay open. The sight of his sweet little hole in the hairless cleft of his ass, within reach of my lubed fingers, was too much. My fingers slid across his skin.

"Why don't you go up on your knees, Gideon?" Vihaal suggested. "That will help you to keep from rutting against Angel, and will make all of your bits accessible."

I let my hands fall as Gideon moved with the sinuous grace of a jungle cat. The position put his head and face closer to mine.

"Hi," he whispered, looking at me with glazed eyes.

"Hi," I said, with a smile. "Ready?"

"Ready all this time."

"Quiet now," Vihaal muttered. "I want to enjoy the show without any distractions."

I heard a zip and looked over. Vihaal had reached into his pants and now brought out his cock, using some lube from his own bottle to ease the way.

"Uh uh," he scolded. "Eyes on the prize. Pay attention and get started."

"Yes, Vihaal," I said, tearing my eyes from him and planting them on the beautiful ass before me.

I ran my fingers over the top of Gideon's buttock to gather some more of the oil, then traced them down between the crack of his ass. He sighed, spreading his thighs for me.

"Oh yes. Stay like that, Deo. That's perfect," Vihaal murmured.

Gideon purred like a cat, with his arms stretched out and his back arched, his ass in the air.

I found his wrinkled hole with my finger and rubbed it. I'd fingered women before, but Gideon's soft cries and frantic gasps made me hard as steel in an instant, and it all seemed so much hotter.

Gideon hissed and canted his hips.

Vihaal cursed, then said, "Stay still, my little rocking horse. Let Angel play with you."

"Yes, Vihaal," Gideon gasped, forcing himself back into the required position, as I continued to rub his entrance. It was soft and bumpy and so, so vulnerable. I slid my fingers to his testicles and spread some of the oil around them and over his taint.

He quivered and panted.

I took two fingers and rubbed them down his crack, over his hole and back, a few times, until he was gasping and moaning. I played with his balls then did the same thing again. It was fun teasing him, knowing he loved it and that he was struggling to keep control of himself.

When I slipped the tip of my finger inside him, he cursed.

"Deeper," Vihaal said, his voice husky with need.

I went deeper, gazing at Vihaal with all the heat that had built up in me, as Gideon gasped and whimpered. He was so hot and tight around me.

"Oh fuck, yes. That's lovely. Now pump it in and out. Slowly."

I did as commanded, glad to have Vihaal's direction. He knew Gideon, knew what Gideon enjoyed, and also what Vihaal himself wanted to see. I could hear the sounds of flesh on flesh as Vihaal stroked himself while he watched me fingering his husband.

His *husband*. I was finger-fucking Vihaal's husband and hard as a rock underneath him. I was the king of the fucking *world*.

I made a little sound and added a second finger to the first, stroking them in and out of Gideon, entranced by the sight and the feel of it. It was hypnotizing.

"Oh. Oh, God," Gideon moaned. "Oh, fuck. Oh please. Please."

"No, you cannot come, my Deo. Keep it together," Vihaal murmured.

"But...but..."

"Don't you fucking dare—" Vihaal had only enough time to warn him, when on another pump of my fingers, Gideon's thighs trembled and he made a soft sound, his cock spurting thick streams of jizz onto my jeans.

He let out a plaintive cry, riding the pleasure as Vihaal and I watched, then gasped a string of apologies.

"Sorry! Oh my God, I'm sorry, V. I'm sorry." He was frantic and I wondered for a second if he was scared of a beating. But I knew Vihaal wouldn't actually hurt Gideon.

Vihaal huffed a laugh and stood, his cock in his hand. He came over and gave Gideon a slap on the behind. "Bend over the couch," he said, his tone one of resigned amusement as Gideon scrambled to obey.

I stared in fascination at the jelly-like puddle of Gideon's release starting to seep into my pants then dabbed a finger in it, while Gideon got into position and Vihaal moved in behind.

My cock throbbed as Vihaal gave himself a few more strokes and pushed his cock deep into Gideon and roared as he came, jerking his hips as he climaxed, digging the fingers of one hand into the skin of Gideon's hip.

Gideon yelped as Vihaal took his pleasure, then withdrew in one quick movement.

Semen dribbled out of Gideon's ass. Vihaal scooped it with a finger and pushed it back.

"Keep it in, naughty boy. I don't have a plug at hand to do it for you."

"Oh fuck," Gideon muttered. "Oh fuck. Vihaal. *Fuck*."

"Now get over here and thank Angel for that lovely finger-fucking," Vihaal instructed. He glanced at me. "Take out your cock."

I fumbled with my fly.

"I'll do it," Gideon said hastily.

"Hurry up," Vihaal told him as Gideon stilled my hands and took over.

As I sat there, my head spinning with what had happened and was happening and was going to happen, Gideon undid my fly and released my erection, tucking the band of my boxer briefs underneath. I was so hard and Gideon looked so sweet post-orgasm. The knowledge that he was filled with Vihaal's spunk was fucking profane.

Gideon looked up at me then licked his lips and opened his mouth, watching me with those hazel eyes as his sweet lips wrapped around me.

"Oh my fucking God. *Gideon*," I gasped. "Fuck."

He took his time bringing me to the edge and back, watching me clutch the sofa cushion with white knuckles as I tried to hold off. But I was so close already, from everything we'd already done together.

"Please, please," I begged, my gaze on Gideon at first, then switching to Vihaal.

Vihaal shrugged, still with two fingers on Gideon's no-doubt swollen and leaking hole. "Whenever you like, Angel."

I opened my mouth and gasped, the orgasm launching the moment Vihaal gave his permission. I made choking noises as my body was taken over by uncontrollable spasms, the intensity of my pleasure a testament to my desire. I gaped at Vihaal, trying to breathe as I realized that the drawn-out wail echoing off the walls was from me.

Chapter Twelve

Lying awake in the guest room after we'd ordered pizza, I replayed every bit of the encounter in my mind. That had been one of the hottest things I'd ever done. Having my cocked sucked by another man was the least surprising thing about it, except I'd literally exploded and Gideon had swallowed every fucking drop.

I'd never felt more aroused, intrigued, and satisfied.

I had a queen bed to myself. After such a busy and intense day, I fell asleep in no time.

I jerked awake in the darkness. The digital clock on the dresser said it was one-twenty a.m. I rolled over and listened to the strange silence of a house I didn't know and tried to think of anything but what the three of us had gotten up to last night, because I didn't think it would put me to sleep this time. I tried to think of puppies and kittens, or lying under the moonlight in a sleeping bag, or even floating on an air mattress on the lake—all things that usually helped me to relax and drift off. None of it worked. Because Gideon and Vihaal kept appearing in my vignettes and I…missed them.

I got up and tiptoed down the hall, past their bedroom where all was silent but for someone's soft snoring. I went downstairs. There was a light on over the stove for which I was grateful. I got a glass of water and stood at the counter, taking sips and trying to decide what to do. My gaze locked on the sofa where everything had gone down before the pizza.

I had three choices.

I could write them a note and summon an Uber, so that I could sleep in my own bed, in my familiar house, which was *kind of* an appealing idea.

I could go back to the guest room and hope I didn't lie awake until dawn.

Or I could see if there was space in the king bed for one more person. It seemed strange to be apart from them, after we'd gotten so close. They'd invited me into their room for the night, but also made sure I knew that the guest room was mine if I wanted it.

At the time, it had seemed like the most sensible choice. Whatever was going on between the three of us seemed to be happening fast, and it had seemed sensible to slow things down. But now I wasn't so sure.

I heard the soft pad of footsteps and looked up.

"I thought I heard you down here," Gideon said, yawning and blinking in the faint light.

"I'm sorry. I tried to be quiet," I said. He looked adorable and sleep-mussed and younger than his twenty-six years in a pair of pink booty shorts and nothing else.

"Are you all right?" he asked.

"Yeah, of course. Just having trouble sleeping." I shrugged and smiled.

"Oh, honey. Come to bed with us!" Gideon said, giving me the sweetest smile.

"Are you sure?" I asked.

"Yes. I can't promise Vihaal won't fart or snore," he said, rolling his eyes. "But just before we settled in, he said he wished you were there with us."

"Really? He did?" The thought warmed me in places that had been cold for too long.

"Uh huh," Gideon said, yawning. "Come on."

He reached for me and I took his hand. He tugged me behind him up the stairs and into the bedroom he shared with Vihaal.

"Oh good," Vihaal murmured from the bed. "Get in here."

"You can scooch in next to me," Gideon said, climbing under the covers and shuffling over to Vihaal, who put an arm around him.

"Get in the bed and go to sleep, Angel."

"Yes, Vihaal," I said.

The sounds of steady breathing, and the warmth of our combined heat, helped me slide into a deep, restful, and secure sleep.

* * * *

I opened my eyes to a ray of sunlight bouncing off the wall through a tiny gap in the curtains. I lay there, with someone's — presumably Gideon's — back against mine. As I contemplated the multiple random occurrences that had led to me waking up in the bed of two fascinating and attractive men, Gideon sighed and rolled over, flinging his arm across my shoulder.

I blinked, so charmed in that moment, and able to feel the press of his morning erection against the top of my buttocks. I hadn't realized how lonely I'd been.

I closed my eyes and drifted in and out of consciousness, until a giggle and a moan woke me.

"He's awake," Gideon said, his voice breathy and soft.

"Well, he is now," Vihaal murmured. "Good morning, Angel."

"Morning," I mumbled, as Gideon moaned again, his breath hitching in a telltale way.

"I'm just giving Deo a little good morning handy, if you'd like to watch," Vihaal murmured.

A good morning handy? What was this utopia I'd somehow become a part of?

I shifted around, and found myself facing Gideon, whose head was thrown back and whose face was the picture of bliss. Vihaal's forearm was concealed by the coverlet, but it shifted in an obvious rhythm as Gideon groaned.

His eyelids fluttered open and locked on mine. "Good mo—" His breath hitched. "Good morning," he said.

Vihaal chuckled, his hand moving faster.

"I'm so sorry," Gideon apologized. "He just reached around and started doing it." He sighed, his pretty lips parted and his eyes closed again.

I smiled, giving him a kiss on his stubbled cheek. He smiled blissfully and pursed his lips. I bent and kissed him, then drew back so I could watch.

"It won't take long," Vihaal said. "Gideon's quite randy in the morning, and I'm looking forward to a peaceful breakfast."

"Bastard…" Gideon said, then moaned. "Oh fuck, V. That feels so good."

"Lift the covers, would you?" Vihaal said to me.

I did, of course, and had a perfect view of Vihaal's hand pumping Gideon's cock.

"Would you do me a favor and get some lube? It's in the top drawer beside you."

"Sure," I said. I got it and held it out toward him.

"Squirt some in your hand. You can help."

My eyes flashed upward to meet his gaze. "I can?"

"Well, can't you?" he asked, gazing at me with so much affection it kind of startled me. Vihaal was so self-contained and so…controlled, that when these moments of openness and relaxed authenticity occurred, it hit me right in the feels.

Vihaal angled the swollen appendage toward me.

I squirted lube into my palm, rubbed it over both hands, then took what Vihaal offered and spread the slippery fluid all around.

Gideon's eyes fluttered open again then closed. He made a resigned sound and turned his face into the pillow as I worked lube back and forth over him, speeding up and slowing down, just like I enjoyed myself.

"He'll come soon. Keep going."

"Oh fuck, oh fuck," Gideon moaned as his cock stiffened in my grasp.

A memory flashed through my brain of Tommy Cavendish in the tenth-grade locker room. I think maybe we'd jerked each other off. Yes, we had. It was coming back to me now. I slowed down.

"Shit," I said, flashing a surprised gaze to Vihaal's.

"What?"

"I, uh, just had a memory of doing this to another kid in high school."

"Really. How very interesting."

I shrugged and resumed, listening to Gideon's soft moans and gasps to motivate me.

"In tenth grade. Tommy Cavendish. He did it for me after. I don't know why I'd blanked that out. I remember liking it a lot. But maybe thinking, since I was turned on by girls too, that I should focus on that."

"Understandable," Vihaal murmured, his gaze fixed on my hand.

"Stop talking about girls..." Gideon breathed.

Vihaal chuckled. "Now go hard and fast," he told me.

I did and Gideon tried to pump himself into my hand. But Vihaal had a firm grip on him.

"You want to come, precious boy?" he whispered in Gideon's ear.

"Almost there. Please, V."

"Then do it. All over Angel's hand."

Gideon gave a tortured sound as spunk erupted over my knuckles, soaking the sheet.

"Oh, that's so lovely to watch," Vihaal said, his fingers still wrapped around the base of Gideon's cock. He aimed the tip at Gideon's belly as I stroked more jizz out of him.

"Oh my God. Oh my *God*." Gideon groaned, an ecstatic grimace on his face.

After a moment the jizz stopped spurting and Gideon sighed. Then stretched. Then gazed down at me as I held his cock and stared at the spunk on his belly.

"Lick it up, Angel," Vihaal said.

I glanced at him. "What?"

"You heard me."

I gazed at the smear of jizz on Gideon's belly, contemplating. Then I bent and lapped up the warm fluid, like a cat after drops of milk.

"Oh yes. Angel will fit in well here with us, won't he, Gideon?"

"Oh my God. Kiss me. Please, kiss me," Gideon begged, leaning forward.

I surged forward and caught Gideon's sweet lips with my own, tonguing his open mouth, sharing his spunk with him. He ate at me greedily while Vihaal watched.

"All right. Enough," Vihaal said, swatting Gideon on the hip. "Get cleaned up and be downstairs for breakfast in half an hour. No more sexy business, either. I have other plans for Angel."

Holy hell. My body tingled with excitement and my morning wood twitched. But I needed to piss.

I helped Gideon clean up. We stole soft kisses and gentle caresses here and there, but otherwise obeyed Vihaal's instructions.

When we got downstairs, there was coffee in the carafe and bacon sizzling on the stove.

"Angel, that cushion on the floor is for you."

"Pardon?" I asked, then looked to where Vihaal was gesturing.

A green throw pillow had been placed on the kitchen floor, by one of the chairs. I recalled our conversation at the theater.

I looked at Vihaal. He looked at me.

"You want me to…kneel on the cushion? Really?"

"Yes," he said, throwing me a benign smile. "Try it. You might like it."

Would I? It seemed such a bizarre thing to do, but I had enjoyed being fed at the movies. I was a guest in their home. Maybe it was the least I could do for them, considering they'd rescued me from my broken car the night before.

I took a deep breath, walked over, and kneeled on the cushion, my cheeks flaming with embarrassment. I glanced at Gideon. He placed his hands palm down on his thighs for a second. I started to place my hands properly but then the thought of my car breaking down hit me.

"Oh fuck," I said, starting to get up. "My car."

"On the cushion, Angel," Vihaal said, and I found myself obeying the unquestioning authority in his voice. I settled back on the cushion and placed my hands on my thighs.

"But it's still at the movie theater," I said.

"It's been taken care of," Vihaal said.

"I— What?"

Vihaal shrugged, pouring himself a coffee. "I had someone collect it. It's at the repair shop I use."

"Oh."

"You can call them later on and find out what the diagnosis is. But for right now, don't worry about it."

"Yes, Vihaal," I said, happy to not have to think about anything more than staying where I was.

Vihaal took a plate from the counter and placed it before Gideon. It was loaded with eggs, bacon and sausages. He grabbed the other plate and brought it over to the table. He sat down beside where I was kneeling and I averted my gaze, staring at the floor like a good submissive.

What is happening to me? Have I been abducted by incredibly sexy aliens?

"Do you need to safeword, Angel?" Vihaal asked, taking a bite of his eggs.

I swallowed. "No, Vihaal."

I liked the name Vihaal. And I liked the man. Especially as he took little pieces of his breakfast and fed me, his fingers soft against my lips. None of that sexual stuff like at the movies. He was simply providing me nourishment, at his own slow pace, while he and Gideon had a conversation that didn't include me.

Once I got used to the strangeness of it, I didn't mind being down here. For one thing, I didn't have to worry about making conversation. It was implied that I should be silent and receptive to Vihaal's dedicated feeding, and I was. The food he offered me tasted wonderful, even better doled out in little bites from his long fingers. The messy things, like bits of egg, he allowed me to lick from them, like a cat. I felt like a cherished pet, in the best of ways.

Vihaal ate with a knife and fork, but he continued to feed me from his plate, like it was his favorite thing to do.

"Can I please give our little kitty some food?" Gideon asked.

"Of course. But come over here. I think he's very comfortable where he is."

"He's such a cutie. What should we name him?" Gideon asked as he picked up his plate and came over to my side of the table.

The humiliation of being discussed this way shot a thrill right through me that made my cock hard.

"Hmm," Vihaal said. "What about Sweetie?"

Sweetie? What the fuck?

Gideon's frown matched my own. "No, I don't think so. How about Baloo? Like the bear in *The Jungle Book*?"

"Well, I guess Baloo it is, then."

Jesus fucking Christ. What had my life come to? And why did I like it?

Gideon's eyes went wide. "We need to get him some kitty ears! And a collar!"

My cheeks were aflame, but so was my whole body. I was aroused and humiliated and very fucking confused about my own reactions. But I continued to kneel on the cushion and accept bits of food from Vihaal and Gideon, my gaze moving from one to the other, until their plates were empty. I was almost disappointed when that happened. That's a lie. I was *absolutely* disappointed.

Vihaal wiped his fingers with a wet cloth and stroked my hair.

"Baloo, you've been very good. I'm so pleased."

I heard those words and objectively, they were ridiculous. But from Vihaal, they made my heart sing.

"Yes, Vihaal."

"Did you get enough to eat? Grab another piece of toast or I can make more eggs..."

I stood, feeling unwieldy and off center. "No, I'm fine. I'm full."

"Do you want to go shopping with Gideon today?"

"I would love to, but I promised my mother I'd pay her a visit," I said.

"Oh!" Gideon said, "Where does she live?"

"In a very expensive retirement home in the West End," I said. "She says she loves it. But her memory's going." I shrugged and turned to Vihaal. "Did you ask your manager about the financial records?"

"Not yet. But after I drop you off at the retirement home, I'm going to pay a visit to my store. Dominic should be there, and I will bring it up with him. See what his explanation is."

"Oh, you don't have to drive me. I can get an Uber."

"Nonsense. Gideon, are you coming or do you want to stay here?"

"Well, if it's not shopping, I'd just as well stay home, if you don't mind. But please *do* say hi to Dominic for me," Gideon muttered in a sardonic tone.

* * * *

I loved my mom, and she'd been a pretty cool person twenty years ago. She had control of most of her mental faculties — enough to keep her off the Memory Floor, at least for now.

Her short-term recall was hit and miss, and I found myself answering the same question several times, which wasn't that big of a deal. And she could surprise me. I'd be having what I'd thought was a casual conversation and she'd pick up on something important. Like today.

"So, what's the deal on the romantic partner front? Anything for me to get excited about?" she asked with a steadfast seriousness that made me sit up straighter.

"What? No!"

"Huh."

"What's that supposed to mean?" I asked.

"Seems strange that you date all these women but none ever sticks. I just wonder sometimes…"

"Mom. Seriously. Are you kidding me?"

"So you still haven't found anyone?"

"Well no. Not exactly."

"Not exactly? What the fuck does that mean?"

"Oh my God, Mom! Do you talk like that in here?"

"I say what the fuck I want, if that's what you mean. I'm not gonna start pussyfooting around just because I'm locked up in a place with do-gooders."

"You're not locked up, Mom. You can come and go as you please."

"So you say. You know how bad my legs are, Angel," she said, giving me a sad look.

"You've got your walker. And I keep asking if you want me to arrange for a scooter."

"Hmph. A hazard, those things. I almost got mowed down in the hallway the other day. Some of these people don't know how to fucking drive."

"Mom, come on," I said, sitting on the edge of the bed by the chair she was in. "You shouldn't be swearing."

"Angel," she said, leveling a look at me. "It's one of the few joys I have left."

I grinned, because, yeah, she was hilarious when she was feeling punchy.

She narrowed her eyes. "Now, back to what I asked you. What do you mean, not exactly?"

"Oh." *Fuck.* "Well, I just meant to say no. No, I don't have a steady girlfriend."

She looked at me. I looked at her.

"What *do* you have, then?" she asked.

I looked away — at the window, at the door.

"What's going on?"

"It's...it's a man," I said, my voice low. "It's two men."

Thank God her hearing was compromised.

"A man!" she exclaimed, so loudly I was worried that people in the hallway would hear.

"Shhh!" I said. "Jesus!"

"Angel Barnett, did you go get yourself a boyfriend?" she asked, as excited as if I'd won the lottery.

"Not exactly. Shhhh. Mom."

"Not exactly?" she said in a stage whisper, her face the picture of astonishment. "Are you getting plowed, Angel? My sweet little boy? *By a man?"*

I gave her a look. She was anything but sentimental.

"Oh my God," I muttered.

She chortled. "Oh, bless my sorry old bones. Well, I'll be. Although I can't say I'm all that surprised."

"I'm not getting plowed!" I said in a stage-whisper. "Jesus."

"You're *the top?* Well, that *is* surprising..."

"Mom! What the hell?" I asked, in a quieter voice. At this rate, the whole floor was going to know about my private life.

My mother waved her hand in between us. "Never mind. So, who is this man? Tell me! This is the most entertaining news I've had in months. Maybe years. I always suspected the women were a distraction from what you really wanted."

What. The. Fuck.

I gaped at her. "You did?"

"Oh, Angel. You always had a thing for good looking men."

"Oh my God. My whole life has been a lie."

"So, what's his name?"

"Um...Gideon," I said. Might as well go for the gold. *Try this for amusement, Mom.* "And Vihaal."

She stared at me and her chin dropped. "He has...two names?"

I shook my head.

"Then what do you—oh! Two men? You cheeky devil."

I couldn't help laughing at the look on her face.

"Angel! What on Earth?"

"What can I say? It just happened. I don't remember how."

"Well, what do they look like? Do you have a photo?"

"Oh, no, I don't really... It's kind of a casual thing right now."

Even though it doesn't feel casual. Not for me, at least.

"Oh. But they're nice men?" she asked, actually expressing concern for my wellbeing.

"They're really nice, Mom. You'd like them."

"When can I meet them? Where did *you* meet them? How long have you been with them?"

"It's been several weeks now. Well, the romance, at least." Romance? Was it a romance? I couldn't use the word sex-fest or she'd run with that. "We've been friends for a bit longer."

"Hmm. Are you being safe?"

She means condoms. Oh my God. "Yes, Mom."

"You know, condoms are very important for anal sex."

"Oh my God. I know. Please stop."

Listening to your seventy-nine-year-old mother say 'anal sex' was beyond uncomfortable.

"I'm not even—I mean," I scrambled, putting a hand to my head. "We're not even—never mind."

"Well," she said. "You've made a boring old woman's day very interesting."

"Good. I guess?"

"Are they younger or older?" She watched me with eyes that could still see things nobody else could. At least she'd likely forget everything I told her by tonight.

"Gideon is younger, and he's very cute," I said, listening to the words coming out of my mouth as if they were spoken by another person. It didn't seem like me, but it was. It so was.

"Not too young, I hope."

"He's twenty-six. And Vihaal is forty."

"Forty!" she said, eyes widening.

"Mom, I'm thirty-six."

"No! You're thirty-six? Really? God, the time flies when you get old." She shrugged. "I suppose ten years isn't that much of an age difference."

I'd been born when she was in her early forties. A completely unexpected pregnancy that she'd accepted with grace and always called a fortuitous accident. I'd never felt unwanted. Not like Vihaal, it seemed. I needed to find out more of that story.

"Vihaal doesn't look his age. You know, now that I think about it, he looks kind of like Rahul Kholi, the actor."

"Who?"

"He was Napoleon in *The Fall of the House of Usher*." We'd watched the series together, back when mom was still living in the house. She'd enjoyed it.

"Oh yes. Oh! Really?"

I described how sweet they were, and how I'd met them through Jacob and Sebastian. She seemed satisfied.

"Well, I'm glad that you're finally exploring your sexuality. I knew there was something else there."

"Mom. If you've known all this time, why didn't you say anything?"

She smiled at me smugly. "Because I think it's important for people to figure these things out on their own."

Chapter Thirteen

I got a text from Vihaal the next day, telling me that the Bordello had been booked for the following night and that he'd left a package in my mailbox.

Go and get it. Then come back and phone me, so we can discuss.

10, 4

I went to the mailbox. There was a white paper bag containing something inside it. After I went back in the house, I opened the bag and removed the contents, then read what was written on the front of the box — *Fleet Enema. Personal cleansing device.*

I dropped it like it was on fire and stared as it hit the floor with a thwack, causing the cats to jump.

Oh, hell no. What the fuck?

The cats were coming to investigate now, sniffing around it and carefully approaching. I stared back and forth between my phone and the box on the floor for a second or two. Then my phone started to ring. I answered.

"Angel?" Vihaal said.

"Uh huh."

"Did you get the package?"

I didn't say anything.

"Did you get the package?" he asked, his voice a bit sterner.

"Yes, Vihaal."

There was a pause. "Okay. Do you know what it is?"

"Um, is it what it says on the side of the box?" I asked, wondering how my life had devolved into this.

"I certainly hope so."

"Vihaal. I...can't."

"What?"

"I've never..." I rubbed a hand over my head. "I don't think I can do it."

There was a pause during which I could hear his soft breaths. Then, "Shall I come over and do it for you?"

My mouth went dry. "What?"

"You know, if you ever have to go for a colonoscopy, you'll have to do that and more."

"Really?"

"Yes. Ask me how I know."

I couldn't help a twitch of my lips because the thought of Vihaal preparing for a colonoscopy was somewhat amusing.

"Do I really have to?" I leaned down and picked up the box, examining the side of it and reading some of the text. *Safe and effective. Easy to use. Mild and non-irritating.*

Yeah, my ass.

I snorted a laugh.

"You don't *have* to do anything. But if you choose not to use it, you're going to seriously derail my plans for the Bordello."

I almost dropped the phone. "V, I don't think I'm ready for you...or Gideon...to, like, you know. Top me."

"Oh my darling, I know that. That isn't what I have planned."

"Oh," I said, my curiosity piqued.

"Are you telling me that none of those sexy women you've taken to bed has offered to stick a finger up your ass, Angel?"

Well... "I mean, I seem to remember it coming up. But I always said, no thanks." I turned the box over in my hand. "None of them ever told me to use one of these."

"No, I don't suppose they would have. Look, Angel, you don't have to do anything you don't want to. You can always safeword."

He waited.

I didn't say anything. Then I sighed. "Fuck."

"That's not your safeword."

"You promise...that if I use this fucking thing...that you won't go too crazy?"

"Of course I won't. I know you're new to...pretty much everything. But I'm telling you, you're missing out."

"Am I?"

"Well, you can tell me, I suppose. After I show you."

I hesitated. I closed my eyes and hefted the box up and down in my hand. I'd done scarier stuff in my life than this. I could do this.

"Fine."

"Pardon?"

I cleared my throat. "I said, fine. I'll use it."

Vihaal took a long, slow breath. "Now that's my good boy."

His voice was syrup pouring over me. I closed my eyes again and enjoyed the satisfaction of pleasing him.

"We'll pick you up at seven."

"I'll be ready."

Hopefully.

* * * *

It hadn't been that bad. Once I'd gotten over my initial shock, and past the wall in my brain that said *absolutely not*, I had to admit it wasn't that big of a deal. There was a certain sense of accomplishment and I did feel clean and fresh and ready for anything. I was probably as nervous as a virgin on her wedding night, but I trusted Vihaal and at least I knew there wouldn't be any unwelcome surprises if—*when*—he started playing down there.

Oh my God. Was I really going to let him?

Gideon and I had finally gone shopping, so I had some new clothes to wear to Molly's. This time I was dressed and ready when they arrived and he texted from the car.

I put on my fancy new cashmere overcoat—not bright blue like Gideon's, but a soft camel brown—grabbed my bag, and locked the door behind me.

Gideon leapt out of the passenger seat. "Here you go, Angel. You can sit up front."

"Thanks," I said, slipping in beside Vihaal.

"Hello, Angel," Vihaal said, his gaze assessing. "Everything go okay this afternoon?"

"Yep. Just dandy," I replied, hoping that would be the end of it.

Vihaal sighed, his gaze roaming over me.

"Did you follow my instructions?"

"Yes, Vihaal," I admitted.

"Oh good. Then I don't have to come up with another way to make you uncomfortable."

I gave him a shocked look, but he simply smiled, and the warm affection in his gray eyes made me feel so good.

Gideon's fingers curled around my shoulder as he leaned forward and kissed my ear.

"I'm glad you tried it. It's not that bad, and it means we can play harder. I used one, too."

Walking into Molly's with them felt exciting. I felt so proud to be in their company. They were widely respected here at the club and probably everywhere else they were known.

When I hung up my overcoat, and Vihaal saw me in my form-fitting, plaid wool pants, paired with a loose, linen top, he put a hand on my shoulder to get me to stand still while he took it in.

"Angel. Oh yes. I think perhaps Gideon has found his true calling." He turned to Gideon, who grinned with pride and pleasure. "You should be a personal shopper or a fashion consultant."

"Hmm. I'll have to consider it." Gideon looked me over and sighed. "It's so much fun dressing someone like Angel. And bringing out the gay that's been hidden inside all this time."

"Wait, what?"

"Sorry. I mean, bringing out the bi. Whatever." Gideon gave me a look. "If you think you look straight in those pants, your more in denial than I thought."

I laughed. "I wasn't exactly trying to look straight, even when I thought I was. But is this how easy it is to come out?"

Gideon grinned. "I guess we'll see."

"It's a shame you're going to have to take it all off once we get to the Bordello," Vihaal commented, giving me a voracious glance.

I followed Vihaal and Gideon to one of the free tables in the gaming parlor. Robin Webb, in his molly boy outfit, preened on stage, holding a microphone.

He squinted at us and spoke into it.

"Oh, hello! Is that Mr. Petrovsky and Mr. Foster?"

"Oh dear," Vihaal muttered.

Gideon patted him on the ass. "We have a reputation, V."

"I suppose so," Vihaal mumbled, giving Robin a wave and sitting at the only free table.

"But who the fuck is that with you? Wait. *Oh my God*."

The other men in the room chuckled and everyone looked over at us.

"Is that Angel? Oh fuck, sorry. I mean, is that Mr. Barnett? No. It can't possibly be."

He was so fucking dramatic.

I waved and smiled.

Sebastian, who was at the piano, said into his microphone, "Robin, aren't you supposed to be performing? Gossiping about the patrons isn't what we pay you for."

"Oh, please. That's *totally* what you pay me for," he said, giving Sebastian a look.

Sebastian shrugged. "Why don't you tell us a dirty joke? Or do that routine you've been practicing."

"Oh! Yes, well, it's not quite ready yet. But I can tell some jokes. Why not? Let's see…"

"Oh, boy, here we go," Vihaal said, sitting back and crossing his arms, gazing at Robin with mild amusement.

"Oh, you love it, V," Gideon said, adjusting his chair so he had a good view of the stage. "And he's so fucking cute! Maybe we could make it four tonight."

Vihaal's head spun around and he gave Gideon a look.

Gideon laughed and put a hand over his mouth.

I couldn't help grinning.

Robin crooked his head and put a finger to his chin.

"Ah, okay, I've got one. What's the difference between purple and pink?"

He waited while we all thought about it. Nobody answered.

"The *grip*."

Laughter and groans.

"Oh, you love it, you dirty fucking bastards. Here's another. What do Life Savers candies do that men cannot?"

Nobody knew.

"Come in five different flavors," Robin said, licking the tip of his finger and lifting it in the air.

"Ba dump, dump," someone said.

"I can come in different flavors!" a man yelled out.

"No you can't, you idiot," another man grumbled.

"But the pineapple!"

"Didn't make your spunk taste any different."

"You literally said it was sweeter!"

"Didn't want to disappoint you."

"Well, you're disappointing me now."

I snickered to myself as Gideon howled and even Vihaal smiled.

"Keep it down in the gallery," Robin piped, shielding his eyes and blinking at the audience. "You want one more?"

"That's what he said!" someone yelled.

"Oh, so funny. My, my, my, we are chipper tonight. All right, let's see." He rested his chin on his arm and scratched his cheek. "Why isn't there a pregnant Barbie doll?" He frowned. "Wait, *is* there a pregnant Barbie doll?"

Men muttered back and forth.

"Oh, whatever. Why isn't there a pregnant Barbie doll?" Robin repeated, glancing around.

"They aren't anatomically correct?" someone offered.

"Well, duh. But, no, that's not it. Anyone?"

Nobody had an answer.

Robin grinned. "Because Ken came in another box."

Lots of groans all around, except for Gideon, who laughed maniacally.

"All right, I'm done up here. Anyone need a drink? I know I do."

"I hope that's a joke," Sebastian said into his mic. "Because you're on duty."

"Oh, fuck off. Of course it's a joke. That's what you pay me for," Robin said, then laid his mic on top of the piano and pranced down the steps to the carpeted floor.

He made his way right over to Vihaal. He crossed his arms over his corset and raised his eyebrows.

"Why are there *three* of you?" He swiveled his head and gave me a once over. "Angel, are you being sex trafficked?"

I burst out a laugh, my cheeks flushing.

"Hello, Robin," Vihaal said, in that way he had of turning even the most boring statements into something sexual.

"Hello, Mr. Petrovsky," Robin replied, with a saucy lilt as he fingered the collar of his chemise so that his nipple was more visible.

"Put that away. You'll not tempt me this evening. I have four nipples to play with tonight, and none of them belong to you."

"What a shame," Robin said, sighing. He turned to me and offered his hand. "So. What on Earth are you doing with these two perverts? And why do you look so..." He gave me a once over. "*Doable?* Accountants aren't supposed to look so hot, you know."

Sebastian came up behind Robin and placed a hand on his shoulder.

"Robin. Your job is not to grill our patrons on their choice of companions. Or to tell anyone how hot or not they are allowed to look."

Robin gave Sebastian the most withering look I'd ever seen.

"My job, Sebastian, is to be my charming self. And this is who I am. So back off and leave me be."

Sebastian smiled at me. "Angel. Nice to see you again."

"Sebastian."

"Well. Now you look good enough to be on the arms of these two very particular men."

I raised my eyebrows. "Only now?"

He smiled.

"Hey, Sebastian," Gideon said. "How are things?"

Sebastian shrugged. "Good." He tilted his head at me. "Does Angel know he looks gay now?"

"Oh, for Christ's sake," I muttered.

"Yes. We've told him," Vihaal offered.

Sebastian smiled wider.

"I'm bisexual," I muttered. "Or pansexual. Wait, what's the difference?"

"Bi gives the impression of only referring to two genders, while pan refers to a multiplicity of them," Vihaal explained. "However, the term bisexual can be used to mean any gender. It's all just semantics."

"Well, anyway, the important thing to remember," I said, "is that I could have sex with a woman *tomorrow*."

Vihaal gazed at me with predatory and possessive eyes.

I withered under his gaze and backtracked.

"Well, in this specific case...not relevant," I admitted. "But I could. If I wanted to."

"And I could put on a tutu and dance on that stage. It's fairly unlikely," Vihaal said, running a hungry gaze over me."

"And that is a fucking shame, V. I'd love to see it," Gideon commented.

"Do I really look gay?" I asked Sebastian.

He laughed. "I'm messing with you. But you do look too good to be straight." He examined me again. "Very...metrosexual."

"The clothes do make the man," Gideon said.

Robin raised his hand for a high five. "Preach it, sister."

Gideon started to respond, then hesitated. "Wait, we're not supposed to touch, right?"

Sebastian rolled his eyes. "I guess I can let a high five go. Otherwise, he'll be moaning about being left hanging for the rest of his shift."

Robin gave Sebastian a malicious smile. "Oh, you do know me well."

Gideon and Robin slapped their right hands together with expressions of triumph.

"Can I get you gents anything?" Robin asked.

"You can get me the key to the Bordello," Vihaal said, standing. "It's almost nine."

"As you wish," he said, giving Vihaal a polite curtsy.

He gazed at me and Gideon, and clicked his tongue, eyeing Vihaal.

"You lucky fuck."

Chapter Fourteen

Vihaal got the key, bade adieu to Sebastian, and led the way to the Bordello.

Once we got into the room, his demeanor switched from arrogant — but charming — patron, to stern dominant.

"Gideon, strip. Angel, take this time to gather yourself because it will be your turn next," Vihaal said, sitting on the settee and crossing one leg over the other. "And don't forget that you can use your safeword at any time. Tell me what it is."

I stared at him, blood rushing everywhere but my brain, and for a moment I couldn't remember.

"Oh, wait. It's Devil."

"Yes. Gideon? What's yours?"

"Tambourine."

Gideon held my gaze as he pulled off his emerald green sweater.

My breath hitched at the sight of him. He was wearing a strappy fabric harness that triangulated his upper chest and nipples as if it were some kind of male bra, anchored by a thicker strap across his sternum. There were also narrow bands that headed down his sides and disappeared into his dress pants.

"Doesn't he look lovely?"

I swallowed. "Yes, Vihaal."

"Now, Angel, I want you to do the honors. Strip him to the straps, please."

My fingers itched to obey. I loved the gender-bending lingerie on him and found myself reacting strongly to it.

His skin positively glowed. The way the black fabric contrasted his pale skin and emphasized the areas of his body that might not draw attention otherwise, made me crazy. I wanted to lick him, and run my fingers under and over the thin straps, and stroke and pinch his nipples. Instead of challenging me, Gideon's subtle masculinity was endearing and arousing. True, he wasn't coated in thick hair or bulky with muscles, but he was undeniably male.

I stepped forward, my heart going wild at our proximity, and took hold of the waistband of Gideon's pants, then took a deep breath and tugged them down. All the way.

Gideon stepped out of them and I moved back to get a good look.

The lines of the harness extended from his waist to slim bands that circled his thighs, reminding me of a garter belt with only the tops of the stockings. Gideon's cock hung half-hard between his legs, looking pretty and seductive. He kept himself smooth all over, whether at Vihaal's request, or for his own preference, I had no idea.

"Your turn, Angel," Vihaal murmured. "But first, Gideon wants to kiss you."

I took a breath and my eyes flashed to Vihaal. I returned my gaze to Gideon, who had moved closer. He took my chin and, with a glance at Vihaal, brought his open mouth to mine

My body zinged with bolts of lightning. I parted my lips and Gideon's tongue snaked inside. He tasted like peppermint and chocolate. He was so soft and sweet, and I was a slave to him as much as to Vihaal.

I heard a grunt from the settee and imagined that Vihaal was enjoying this. I knew I was. When Gideon pulled back, he was fully erect and grinning like he had many, many secrets to share.

"Look what you do to him, Angel," Vihaal murmured. "And me."

Vihaal gestured to the very obvious tent in his pants.

"Good. I'm glad," I said. Then I remembered myself. "Yes, Vihaal."

He shrugged and pursed his lips, blinking with affection in an imaginary kiss.

I undid the top buttons on my linen shirt while I tried to collect myself. I was already so turned on and excited about what might happen over the next hour.

"I didn't even think to buy fancy lingerie, Vihaal," I said, undoing the last button on my shirt, and pulling it off. I let it drop to the floor.

"What a shame," Vihaal murmured, eyeing me with consideration.

I met his gaze as I proceeded to undo my pants and tug them past my expensive, and very tight boxer briefs. At least I'd upgraded my underwear, thanks to our shopping escapade. The royal blue briefs clung to my ass and hips and outlined my erection well.

"Mmm," was all Vihaal said.

Then I was naked. Standing in a dedicated kink room with two hot and adventurous men, who were examining me like I was up for auction. I was a little scared, a little self-conscious, and a lot turned-on.

"Follow me," Vihaal said.

He led us over to the area of the room that contained the large bed.

"Angel, I want you to get up and kneel there, facing us," he said, pointing at the foot of the mattress.

"Wait," I said, struggling for breath all of a sudden.

"Yes?"

"So…this is a lot."

"I understand."

"Is there something I can say if I need things to slow down, but don't necessarily want them to stop?"

"Of course. You have ultimate control over what goes on here, even though it seems like I do. Just tell me to go slow."

"Okay," I said, taking a deep breath. I climbed up and kneeled on the bed.

"Now put your hands behind you. I want to admire you."

I put my hands at the small of my back which made my chest push out and my shoulders go back. I watched Vihaal as he moved around the bed, eyeing me from every angle.

"Fuck, yes. You're even more of a vision than I'd anticipated. Isn't he, Gideon?"

"Yes, Vihaal. He's so beautiful."

I gave a small laugh, because it sounded so absurd. Nobody had ever called me that.

"Don't laugh, Angel. It's true."

"Yes, Vihaal. Thank you, Vihaal." I gazed at him with sudden adoration.

"Gideon, get me some rope."

"Yes, Vihaal," Gideon said.

Rope. Jesus. This is happening.

While Gideon was doing that, Vihaal stepped close and took my chin in a firm grip.

"Settle down. We have an hour." He leaned in and kissed me.

My breath hitched at the chemistry of our connection, and Vihaal made a sound as he opened his mouth and tapped at the seal of my lips with his tongue. I parted them, and was immediately swept up with my desire for this dominant man—a dancing flame that wanted nothing but to burn itself out.

Vihaal kissed me harder, and I met him with an equal hunger. He dragged his tongue over my chin and up the side of my face, ending in another breath-stealing kiss.

"Oh, fuck. I want to eat you up."

I shuddered, because I couldn't honestly think of anything better. It turned out that kissing a man was exactly the same as kissing a woman, except for subtle differences that only served to inflame me. There was more of a suggestion of restrained aggression, at least with Vihaal. I liked the feel of Vihaal's stubbled skin and rough mouth, as much as I enjoyed Gideon's plump lips and slightly smoother feel. Maybe more.

Vihaal pulled away and wiped a hand over his lips, staring at me in confusion, as if I'd presented him with an unexpected puzzle.

"See?" Gideon said, with a cheeky eye-roll. "Not just me."

"No, not just you. Now shush and give me that rope."

Gideon passed Vihaal the rope so he could bind my hands behind my back with quick and efficient movements.

"Test those knots for me."

I pulled at the ropes but they were secure.

"There are scissors if we need to get you out of them in a hurry."

He left me to gather some things, which he placed on the mattress behind me. I didn't really pay attention because I couldn't take my eyes off Gideon on his knees on the floor in front of me.

Then Vihaal stood beside Gideon and started to strip. I watched with fascination as he took off his clothes—all of them—and stroked his erection while gazing at me out of hooded eyes.

"Gideon."

"Yes, Vihaal," Gideon said, glancing up.

"Come."

Gideon shuffled over and positioned himself in front of Vihaal.

"Open your mouth," he commanded.

Gideon did so, as wide as he could, resting his hands on his thighs and extending his tongue.

"Brace yourself."

Vihaal grabbed a handful of Gideon's hair, and his own erection, and pulled Gideon's head back. Then he slid his cock into Gideon's open mouth.

Gideon made a garbled noise as his muscles tensed. He grabbed hold of Vihaal's thighs to avoid toppling over.

A white-hot spike of arousal hit me, and fluid surged over the head of my dick and dripped onto the mattress as I shivered with erotic hunger.

Vihaal met my gaze as he fucked Gideon's mouth. Subtle emotions played on his features even as he attempted to remain unmoved. Gideon choked and gasped, but did his best to accommodate Vihaal.

"I'm going to come. Swallow it."

Vihaal thrust twice and closed his eyes, barely making a sound as he came. Gideon's eyes bulged and his face turned red. Then Vihaal pulled out, dragging a string of jizz over Gideon's lower lip. He gave Gideon a controlled slap to the cheek.

"Good slut."

Gideon whimpered at those words.

"Thank you, Vihaal," he gasped. His gaze flashed to mine with desire and hunger.

"Get up," Vihaal said.

Gideon stood, a little shaky, his lips puffy and swollen.

"Give Angel a kiss. Make sure to share the results of your face-fucking," he said.

I waited with bated breath as Gideon approached. He bent to kiss me, his lips shiny with saliva and spunk.

I gasped as our mouths met and desire surged in me. The bitter taste of semen combined with the sweetness of Gideon's mint-laced saliva. I opened wide to his plunging tongue and tried to control my breathing.

Fuck. Fuck.

"Enough," Vihaal said.

Gideon gave me one last tongue-fuck then retreated. I leaned forward, desperate to stay connected, and heard Vihaal chuckle. I kneeled there, gasping and wide-eyed and hard as a plinth as I watched Vihaal lick his palm and wrap his fingers around Gideon's erection.

Gideon groaned and clutched Vihaal's arm as Vihaal stroked his cock with violent, quick movements.

"I'll come, I'll come..." Gideon gasped, his gaze moving from me to Vihaal as his breath hitched.

"Good," Vihaal said.

Gideon's eyes widened then closed as he gave himself up to it. His hips jerked as he cried out, jizz shooting from him like water from a spigot. He seemed completely overcome and a slave to Vihaal's wishes.

"There," Vihaal said. "That's you and me taken care of."

He smiled at a dazed and astonished Gideon.

"Now we can concentrate on Angel without any distractions. Although I don't think it will take either of us long to get hard again. Not with what I'm planning, anyway."

"Yes, Vihaal." Gideon's voice was rough from Vihaal's treatment, but he seemed content enough.

Now they looked at me and my cock throbbed.

"Stand there, Gideon," he said, pointing to the foot of the bed.

Gideon obeyed, moving to stand before me, his cock beginning to deflate, still shiny with the remnants of his release.

Vihaal climbed onto the bed behind me and leaned close. He smelled of expensive bath products and a hint of citrus.

"Move your knees apart," he said in my ear.

I closed my eyes and did as he asked, his power over me undeniable.

"Gideon, I want your cock hard again in a minute. I'll have use for you soon enough."

Electricity zinged along my nerves as Vihaal touched my lower back, right where the crack of my ass began.

I took a deep breath. I'd had women touch me just about everywhere, but none had gone further than a few benign tickles in that area. I wondered if they'd been holding back, out of fear of how I'd respond.

I knew Vihaal wasn't going to do that.

He started to move his fingertips down into the cleft between my cheeks, and my breathing caught as anticipation gripped me.

"Oh, fuck, such a pretty little arse on you," he said.

My eyes flashed open and I saw Gideon touching himself in front of us. I wanted to say something funny—make a joke—to defuse some of the tension. But I couldn't think of anything.

"Such a shame no-one's ever played with you here, before," Vihaal said, the tip of his finger glancing over my hole. I gasped and forced myself to stay still as a thrill of pleasure went right through me.

"Steady..." Vihaal said, taking hold of my wrist. "Let me touch you in this soft and secret place. Please, Angel."

"Y—yes, Vihaal," I breathed, shuddering from the vulnerability of it. This place on my body that I had never touched or probed, even though I'd thought about doing so more than once. There was humiliation and fear, but also a rising conflagration of desire.

He touched me there again, and this time I pushed the shame away.

No, that's not right.

I reveled in the shame. I let it flood me and engorge me even more. It was my offering to Vihaal.

"Such a pretty little hole," Vihaal murmured, teasing me in that hidden place. "Look at him, Gideon. He loves it."

"I knew he would, Vihaal," Gideon gasped. He was teasing himself and half-hard already, watching me come apart in front of him. Vihaal's touch disappeared and the lid of the lube bottle snapped open. Then he resumed, his finger slick and cold, and I melted inside.

My lips parted and my eyes closed as spikes of pleasure traveled from his touch to my inner parts and up my standing cock.

"Push out, as if you're trying to shit."

"Fuck," I said. "Oh fuck."

I did what he'd told me, gasping as the tip of his finger went in. "Oh…Jesus…"

It was such a strange, intense sensation, but I didn't hate it. I'd even say that I liked it.

"Feel good?" Vihaal asked, cupping my chin with his free hand and sliding the finger in my ass deeper.

A heartfelt whimper was all I could give him.

He tapped at my lip and I opened my mouth, sticking out my tongue.

"Good boy." Vihaal's finger slid into my mouth as he skewered me at both ends, like a piece of meat on a spit.

I groaned and tried to breathe, my heart going like gangbusters. All I could do was stay still and take it, and that thought sent waves of heady lust through me.

My heart was going to fly out of my chest it was beating so hard. My cock was a rod of desire and I didn't know what to do with these feelings. I pulled at my bindings and whimpered again.

"You're so lovely and soft. You're doing so well," Vihaal murmured, his breath hot on my ear.

He circled my torso with his arm and held me tight. His erection nudged my back with a hot pressure and his tongue traced the shell of my ear. "So fucking hot. You are precious. And you are mine."

"Yes, Vihaal," I said, my words garbled by his finger, a breathless testament to how I felt in that moment. I was. I belonged to both of them.

He slipped his finger from my mouth but pushed the other one so deep I yelped. Then he twisted it and nudged a spot inside me that felt so good I almost cried. My cock surged and pleasure coiled in my balls. I let my head fall back on his shoulder as his other hand slipped over my belly and his fingers closed around the base of my cock, angling it forward.

"All right, Gideon. I want you sucking this fine example of a cock while I play with a nipple."

I made a sound that came out like a sob, and my breath hitched. I was done for. I prayed that Vihaal wouldn't demand that I hold off because I wouldn't be able to.

"I—" I stuttered. "I'll come!"

Vihaal chuckled and kissed me sweetly on the cheek. "I know. Whenever you're ready."

I caught a glimpse of Gideon parting his lips and leaning forward, but closed my eyes before I felt the warmth around my cock.

This wasn't real. Having two men to pleasure me with such thoughtfulness and care, was a fantasy and a dream.

Gideon's tongue teased the weeping head of my cock, and Vihaal's body was solid behind me, his breath in my ear, and his fingers drifting up my abdomen leaving actual goosebumps before they closed on my nipple.

Gideon swallowed around me and I choked on air as waves of intense pleasure took me over. Vihaal's words echoed somewhere outside of me as my body spasmed in his grasp. "So sweet. So sexy. So delicious."

The noises I made were obscene and too loud. Gideon growled around my cock. He kept on devouring me, even as I came. I must have unloaded gallons into his throat. I had the presence of mind to open my eyes, to see him there, his forehead creased with effort and concentration, eyes closed, and hands gripping my thighs.

Vihaal's cock pulsed against my lower back, as he pinched my nipple, hard.

"Oh, honey. You're done for." Vihaal whispered. My orgasm continued and I gave a helpless shout, Vihaal's tight hold the only thing keeping me steady.

Fuck, fuck, fuck.

"Good boy," he whispered in my ear. "Good boy."

Gideon climbed up on the mattress and leaned in, covering my mouth with his, sharing what was left of my release. Then Vihaal took his chin and kissed him over my shoulder, with so much passion I felt it radiating against me.

Chapter Fifteen

Vihaal untied my wrists and I brought my arms forward, rubbing the skin where the ropes had been. Gideon was back on his knees, his cock still hard and his chest moving with his breaths, as he fixed his gaze on the floor.

"Has anyone ever bound your wrists before, Angel?" Vihaal asked.

I shook my head. "No."

Vihaal seemed surprised. "Blindfolded you?"

"Uh. Nope."

Vihaal made a shocked face. "Where on Earth were you finding these women?"

I shrugged. "Mostly at clubs. Bars."

"Ah. Still, it's a little strange that none of them wanted to experiment with bondage or sensory deprivation."

"Isn't it the other way around, though? Normally?"

"You mean, doesn't the man usually tie up the woman? Not in my circles, but perhaps in the straight world. Did you ever?"

"Well, no. I'm too much of a feminist for that." I offered a weak laugh. "Or, I think I am."

Vihaal regarded me with a strange expression. "Yes, well that's one more thing I enjoy about same sex relationships. No gender politics."

"I'm only now realizing how fucking boring my life has been."

"Well, I'm glad I can liven it up for you." He smiled. "I have plans for Gideon. Would you like to watch?"

"Oh, my God. Yes," I said, gazing at the sweet young man who kneeled so obediently beside us, practically vibrating with tension.

Vihaal went to the rack of clothes and brought back one of the vintage kimonos for me to wear. I wrapped the soft and silky fabric around my nakedness and tied the sash.

"Lie against the pillows. I'll try to keep him in view," Vihaal said. "Now where did I put that rope? Aha. Gideon, can you please get me two more lengths?"

Gideon nodded and stood, padding over to where the rope was kept, his svelte muscles straining against the thin straps of his harness. He brought back what Vihaal had asked for.

"Now. Up on the bed, and face that way," Vihaal said, pointing to the side of the bed.

Gideon obeyed, his eyes like dark licorice as he glanced at me, his chest rising and falling as Vihaal tied a length of rope to a convenient grate bolted to the ceiling above the mattress. I'd not noticed it before, or had possibly dismissed it as some kind of decoration, but it framed a squared area about three feet above my head, to facilitate just this kind of thing.

"Hands up and crossed."

Gideon raised his hands, and Vihaal knotted the rope over both wrists, then secured them to one of the bars of the grate. Gideon was held in position, kneeling with his arms stretched upward, his left side to me, so that I had a good view of both his ass and his cock, and of anything that Vihaal might do in either of those places. He looked like some kind of androgynous prince in the lingerie-like body harness. I couldn't stop staring.

Vihaal left us to get more equipment.

Gideon turned to me.

"Angel," he whispered, when Vihaal was at a safe distance and probably wouldn't hear. "Did you like having your cock in my mouth?"

"Yes."

"Will you fuck me one day? I'd really like you to."

I could only nod my head.

He glowed with happiness, then lowered his gaze as Vihaal returned with several things that he laid out.

"Once you've recovered, Angel, I might ask for your help. But for now, simply observe as I bring Gideon to a state of ridiculous desperation."

"Oh fuck," Gideon muttered. "Typical."

"Yes, and you love every minute of it."

Gideon shrugged as best he could with his arms pulled up by the ropes. "Maybe not every *single* minute."

"Oh, Deo. You know I can make it so much worse for you," Vihaal muttered, giving Gideon's ass a hard slap.

"Fuck," Gideon cursed again. "Yes, Vihaal," he said through clenched teeth.

But the look he gave me was blissful. I recognized this for a dance they liked to play together.

Vihaal pulled on a nitrile glove and snapped it, making me jump.

"May I talk, Sir, or do you need me to be quiet?" Gideon asked.

"You may talk. For now."

Gideon turned to me. "When he puts on the glove, I know I'm in for it."

I nodded, licking my lips, eager to find out what *in for it* meant.

Vihaal's lips curled in a half smile as he coated his gloved fingers with lube. With no preamble, he inserted his forefinger into Gideon's anus up to the knuckle.

Gideon cried out, perhaps not prepared for the suddenness of the invasion. But as Vihaal pumped his finger and twisted his wrist, prodding Gideon from all angles, Gideon made desperate and ecstatic exclamations.

Vihaal met my gaze as he turned his hand the other way and probed Gideon roughly, then angled his wrist to access him better, making him mewl and gasp. He went back and forth between motions, as Gideon hung helpless before me, responding dramatically to it all. Gideon's slim body contorted in his bindings, with the narrow harness straps emphasizing every curve as his muscles.

Vihaal reached around and gave Gideon's cock a few hard pulls, eliciting a series of agonized gasps.

"Oh, Vihaal," he panted. "Can I come? I think I might come…"

"Oh no, you certainly cannot," Vihaal muttered, as if the very idea was ludicrous. "Why are you so close already? You finished about fifteen minutes ago."

"I don't know," Gideon moaned. "It's just, you know how much I like a good finger fucking. And with Angel watching… Oh fuck. I need to stop talking."

"Yes, you'd better."

Vihaal added a second finger and Gideon grunted, moving his knees further apart on the mattress in order to accommodate.

"Good boy. Open up for me. Let's show Angel how many you can take, hmm?"

"Oh fuck. Oh fuck. No. Vihaal…"

"Are you safewording?" Vihaal asked, pumping the two fingers in and out of Gideon in rough movements that caused Gideon to groan and pant and grimace.

"No!" Gideon assured. "But if you're adding more, you're going to have to go easier."

Vihaal chuckled and withdrew his fingers from Gideon's ass, walking away and discarding the nitrile glove.

Gideon watched him. "Wait. Where are you going?"

Vihaal glanced back at him. "If you don't want my fingers, I'll need to find something else to stick up there." He winked. "Or maybe that was the plan all along."

Gideon sighed and hung off the ropes as if he wanted a nap more than anything. But his whole body was flushed and his cock was still hard, with a bubble of moisture at the tip.

I wanted to taste it. I wanted to crawl over there and suck Gideon's cock while he was bound this way. But I'd need permission and I didn't know if I was prepared to ask for it.

Vihaal returned with something long and black in his hands. The sight of it caused a shiver of delight to go through me. I had no idea what it was, but I had a feeling it was going into Gideon somehow.

"See something you like?" he asked, tossing the rubber item on the bed beside Gideon, who saw it and made a desperate sound.

It was a smooth black piece of rubber or PVC with a pointy plug on each end, like a snake with a large head and a smaller tail, about four feet long.

"If you can wait a moment, Angel, I will ask you for some assistance."

"Yes, Vihaal," I said.

I watched as Vihaal squeezed lube onto the top of Gideon's crack and smoothed it down between his cheeks.

"Spread your knees. Open up for me."

Gideon leaned forward, giving the rope his weight as the metal frame creaked. He spread his thighs and pushed his ass out.

"Good boy."

Vihaal teased the tip of the snake's tail, which was the smaller of the two plugs, against Gideon's opening.

I watched with fascination as Vihaal pushed it slowly into Gideon, who took deep breaths and groaned as it invaded him. Finally, the plug slipped in and disappeared, so that only the rubber body of the snake was visible, with the larger plug — the head — dangling at the end.

"There we go. Doesn't that look nice?"

I didn't know if he was asking me or speaking rhetorically, but I answered anyway.

"Yes, Vihaal." Fuck, it looked depraved and delicious. I couldn't stop staring.

"Do you know what it's called? This conveniently invasive rubber snake?" Vihaal asked as he gently pushed the plug further into Gideon, as Gideon panted and made tortured facial expressions.

I shook my head.

"It's called a devil's tail." Vihaal lifted the other, thicker, end to show me. "See?"

"Oh. Yes."

"All right, my pretty boy," Vihaal murmured to Gideon. "Do you want more?"

"Yes," Gideon moaned, his cheeks flushed and a thick sheen of sweat on his forehead. "Oh, God. Oh God."

"He loves this thing. Well, probably hates it a bit, too."

"Oooh," Gideon groaned, twisting in the ropes to ease the pressure inside him.

"All right?" Vihaal asked.

"Yes," Gideon said, sounding as if he was in pain. But I didn't think he was.

"More?" Vihaal asked.

"More," Gideon whispered.

Vihaal pushed the tail further as Gideon panted and gasped.

Vihaal paid close attention to Gideon's reactions as he nudged the object further. "Mmm," Vihaal murmured. He used a finger to tease Gideon's entrance where the rubber went in. He slapped Gideon's ass — one side, then the other.

Gideon's groans echoed off the walls of the Bordello, his hole clenching around the invading snake as Vihaal spanked him in a slow, steady rhythm.

I couldn't tear my eyes away.

Vihaal gazed at me as he sucked on his index finger. He pulled it out of his mouth then teased Gideon's hole and pushed it in alongside the glistening black rubber.

Gideon whimpered as Vihaal probed him. Then Vihaal withdrew.

"Now, watch this," he said, as if I could possibly tear my eyes away.

He grabbed the tail just beyond where it emerged from Gideon's shiny hole and tugged it.

Gideon groaned as the plug moved through him. I watched more of the shiny rubber appear as Vihaal pulled. It stopped coming easily so Vihaal gave it a quick tug. Gideon cried out as the slippery tail end of the snake popped out, then he gasped lungfuls of air as his whole body shuddered.

"Again," Vihaal said, rubbing the tail end at Gideon's entrance and making him accept it again.

Gideon moaned and twisted. "Oh my God. Oh fuck."

"More?"

"More. Oh...God," Gideon moaned. "More. *Fuck.*"

Vihaal uttered a dramatic sigh. "If only my cock was as long as this devil's tail. Then you'd be in for it, Deo."

Gideon whimpered and groaned as the plug traveled further into his bowels.

"All right," Vihaal said finally. "Let's give Angel a bit of a show."

Vihaal squirted more lube into his hand and coated his cock with it, jerking himself and making sure he got good and wet. He met my gaze as he positioned himself behind Gideon, took hold of the rubber snake to keep it still, and eased his cock in.

Gideon's breath stuttered and his head lolled against his arm. His pale skin shone with sweat and his cock dripped with his arousal. I couldn't take my eyes off him.

"Angel. Get in front."

Gideon must have felt the dip in the mattress. His eyelids fluttered open and he made the softest sigh as his glazed eyes shifted my way.

Vihaal grunted and gasped, his eyes locked onto the spot where they were joined. After a few moments, he thrust deep and squeezed his eyes shut, letting a long puff of air out of his nose and jerking slowly against

Gideon's ass. He came with a grunt and stayed motionless as the orgasm went through him. Then his features relaxed, and he kissed Gideon on the shoulder and nodded to me.

"You want to taste him, Angel?"

I stared at Gideon's erection and licked my lips. "I do. I really do."

"All right. Suck him. Make him come."

I planted my hands on either side of Gideon and bent to his arching, dripping erection.

"I give you permission to come, Deo," Vihaal said, still lodged in Gideon's ass and holding the rubber snake as he pumped with his still-hard cock.

"If you don't want to swallow, Angel, just spit it out," Vihaal suggested.

I wrapped my fingers around the base of Gideon's dick and tentatively extended my tongue to swipe the head. Then something took over, and I parted my lips and got to fucking work. Gideon's excited moans went straight to my balls. I found myself slobbering and sucking and teasing and tasting, as if I'd been doing this my whole adult life.

Then Gideon threw his head back and wailed, his cock stiff and hot as it emptied. And I swallowed it down like a pro.

I kept Gideon in my mouth until Vihaal told me to release him. I pulled off, feeling protective as Gideon's softening cock slipped out. I used a corner of my kimono to wipe my lips, wondering how I'd ever recover from this — from them — and if I even wanted to.

* * * *

Walking back to the gaming parlor without revealing on my face everything that I'd done and witnessed was a challenge. The molly boys could probably see everything in my dazed and satisfied expression.

Sebastian smiled when he saw me.

"Ah. Did you have fun?"

"Not telling," I replied, miming a zipper closing over my lips.

"What happens in the Bordello, stays in the Bordello," Vihaal said.

"I think that was Sebastian's rule to begin with," Gideon muttered.

He was tired, and ready to go home. Vihaal had removed the devil's tail and wiped him down with great care, then kissed us both in thanks for a memorable evening.

In the car, Gideon said, "You don't know how long I've waited for that."

"For the devil's tail?" Vihaal asked with confusion.

"No, although that was lovely. I meant, for the opportunity to go down on Angel, and for him to do the same to me," Gideon confessed.

"Hmm. I'm feeling left out," Vihaal grumped, but in a good-natured, teasing way.

"Oh, V, you know you're the central part of everything, don't you? Angel and I would never have gotten anywhere without you."

"Well. That makes me happy."

"I'm sure." Gideon, who was sitting in the back seat again, leaned forward and kissed Vihaal on the cheek, then did the same to me. "Now let's get home and hang out. I doubt we're ready for bed yet, are we?"

"Not at all," Vihaal murmured. "But a bourbon and a movie would be nice, if we can agree on something."

* * * *

There were two full bathrooms at Gideon and Vihaal's place. Gideon offered to use the one downstairs because he kept some of his products there. Vihaal let me take my shower in the en suite bathroom first.

There was a double vanity topped with marble, and the shower enclosure was tiled in slate, with a rain showerhead and a bench. It would have fit all three of us, to be honest. I had half expected Vihaal to join me but I wasn't upset to have the gorgeous room to myself.

The water pressure was sublime and I closed my eyes, enjoying the pounding of the wet heat on my muscles. The liquid soap that I pumped from a fancy-looking bottle in the little alcove smelled like pineapple and reminded me of him.

There was a knock on the bathroom door. "Can I come in?"

"Sure," I said immediately. It was Vihaal's and Gideon's bathroom after all, and he'd already seen me naked.

He came into the room in only his boxer briefs. Vihaal was an incredibly good-looking man. In a completely different way than Gideon, but not any less affecting. They were like two sides of the same card — one small and pretty, the other tall and imposing.

Vihaal was much more masculine-looking than Gideon, and possessed an air of confidence in his own physical attractiveness that was highly alluring. Gideon didn't seem to care what anyone thought of him, whereas Vihaal was proud of his physical stature, and he had every right to be. His smooth skin was the color of burnished bronze and had reflected the lamplight of Maverick Molly's so beautifully. He had aristocratic features, and dark black hair with a bit of a wave. The hair on his body was light in weight, but dark in color.

"Well look at you. All wet," he said with a grin, as he leaned against the vanity and crossed his arms over his chest. He watched me as I stood there with a palm full of body wash, not knowing how to reply to that comment.

It was a shower. So yes, I was definitely wet.

"Well? Aren't you going to use that soap, Angel?" he asked, gazing at me with an indefinable expression. "Or would you like me to do it for you?"

Chapter Sixteen

I stared at Vihaal for a long moment, unashamed of my nudity, knowing that this man had taken me in hand in the best of ways, when I hadn't even known that was what I'd craved.

"Yes, Vihaal," I said, giving myself up to him.

I wanted him close. I wanted to feel those rough and skilled hands on my body. I'd waited years and years for this kind of attention and I was greedy for it.

Vihaal smiled. It lit up his face like he was a kid with an ice cream cone. I figured I was the ice cream cone.

With one movement he pushed his undershorts down and off, tossing them into the hamper. I was transfixed and caught up in the newness of the experience. Of looking at another man in this hungry and appreciative way. Of *allowing* myself to do it.

He was half-hard. My mouth went dry as I looked at him. His cock was thick enough, ruddy and leaned slightly to the right as it swelled, which it did now. I'd never really noticed men's cocks before, and even now, what Vihaal's and Gideon's cocks looked like—their size, girth, and attitude — was irrelevant. It was the men they were attached to. My only interest lay in how they indicated arousal, and the skill with which they were used to give pleasure.

"It's always done that," Vihaal muttered, opening the glass shower door and stepping in as I made room. "Gideon calls it the Jolly Roger."

I snorted a laugh and Vihaal's eyes sparked with amusement.

"He calls your dick the Jolly Roger?"

Vihaal grinned. "Sometimes."

He wrapped his arms around my waist and pressed his dry body against my wet one. "It's got that pirate angle. Makes me feel like a *right scoundrel*," he said, in a perfect Cockney accent.

I grinned and offered my palm full of body wash to Vihaal, even as it slid through my fingers.

"Oops," I said.

"I'm exercising a great deal of restraint," Vihaal said, gazing at me as hot water cascaded over us. "But I can see that you're definitely *not straight*."

He gestured to my now full erection.

I looked down at myself. "I've come to terms with it."

"Mmm. I'd love to come to terms with *that*," Vihaal murmured.

He hooked a finger under my chin and turned my face so he could kiss me. It was tender and greedy at the same time. He took his time, and when he pulled back finally, it was like I'd woken from a dream.

"I've been waiting to kiss you that way," he said.

"Really?"

"Well, yes. A real, non-performative, kiss. Without an audience." He gazed at me with such affection and warmth, I almost felt guilty. He was another man's husband.

"Um, so how does this work, exactly?" I asked, gazing into Vihaal's blue-green eyes.

He smiled again. "Well, I get some body wash, and I use it to—"

"Cute," I said, kissing him softly on the cheek. "I mean, how does this thing with you, and Gideon, and me, work? How do I know what's allowed and what's not allowed? Or what's polite and what's rude? I feel like I've been thrown into a game I've never played and handed…the ball."

We both grinned at my double entendre.

Vihaal gave me a look as he reached around me and pumped some body wash into his hand. Then he slid his palm up my chest, over my collarbone, and cupped the top of my throat, forcing my chin up. I stared at the top of the shower stall, wondering what was going on in his head.

He kissed the lobe of my ear and licked a line along my jaw.

"Don't worry so much. We'll let you know if you're stepping on anyone's toes."

"Okay," I said. "I don't want to interfere with what the two of you have."

"Oh, Angel. You already have, but in the very best of ways," he said, smoothing his hand down my throat and rubbing the body wash over my chest in slow, sensual, circles. "You enhance our relationship, you know."

"Even when it's just the two of us? Like now?"

"Yes."

"Okay," I said. "And Gideon won't be jealous?"

Vihaal laughed. "I doubt it. And if he is, he'll tell me. And we'll figure out some new guidelines. Communication is the basis of everything we do together, Angel. The kinky stuff. The unconventional relationship. Really, everything. So, please do speak up, like this, if you need clarification, or you have emotions you want to express. We need to be open and transparent if this is going to work."

"I'll do my very best."

"Oh, I know you will. You're a very good boy, Angel," he murmured, smoothing the body wash over my shoulders and down my arms.

"Fuck. Why does it feel so good when you say that? And so fucking hot?"

"I think you've been waiting for that kind of validation for a very long time. You seem to have slid right into the kinky side of our relationship without a problem."

He grinned against my neck and pressed his lips just below my ear, his breath a warm puff against my wet skin.

"You like me to take over."

"Yes."

"You like to be told what to do."

"Yes."

"You like to please me."

I sighed. "Yes. Fuck yes," I said, turning my face toward him.

He caught my lips with his and kissed me like he had all the time in the world. My heart, that vulnerable organ that I'd guarded so fiercely for most of my life, thumped in my chest and loosened, drumming to the beat of Vihaal's.

When he released me, I closed my eyes as he spread more body wash over my chest and belly. My hands lay on his forearms as he washed me all over, even in the most intimate places, and I let him, my desire rising.

I caught his face between my hands, and guided his mouth to mine, surprised at how malleable he was. Not always the stern Dom, Vihaal relaxed under my kiss and let me explore him, responding to my gentle probing that soon became hunger and a rampant need. Then he matched me, kissing me back hard, breaths hastening, slippery limbs colliding.

"God," I gasped, eating at his lips as if they were the sweetest candy. I wasn't surprised when Vihaal took my wrist and forced my arm behind my back. In fact, it only made me harder.

"Turn around."

I obeyed without question, my cock so hard it throbbed in time with my beating heart. He let go.

Vihaal went to his knees and I gasped with the shock of it. His broad hands traveled down my back, his thumbs slipping between my cheeks and spreading me as he nuzzled between them.

"Fuck," I gasped. "Fuck, fuck, fuck."

"Anyone ever eat your ass before?"

"No. *Fuck*. No," I stuttered.

"You poor baby," he said, then his tongue was on me.

I splayed my hands against the tiles and rested my forehead on them, gasping and groaning as Vihaal— *Vihaal!* — used his entire fucking face to eat me out. I never thought it would feel as good and as dirty as it did. I almost protested, because it made me feel so damn vulnerable, but then his tongue was working its magic and I was lost to the intensity of the pleasure.

"Oh my God," I groaned.

Vihaal chuckled then hummed, and the vibrations added to the bliss of it.

"Vihaal. Fucking *Jesus*."

He transformed me into a writhing, gasping mess, with water dripping down my face and fluid dripping down my cock. Then he pulled off, gasping, and told me to turn around again.

As soon as I faced him, he grabbed my cock and went to town. My back started to slip so I splayed my arms out on the wet tiles, trying to stay upright. I gazed down at him through the curtain of water and tried to breathe.

"Fuck. Fuck. *Fuck!*" I yelled as I came, overtaken by him again. This man had my fucking number.

My shouts echoed off the walls of the shower as Vihaal swallowed everything and pulled off finally with a very satisfied smirk.

"There we go," he muttered, wiping his lips.

I gaped at him as he stood, my arms still spread on the cold tile, my body trying to recover from…everything.

He came close and kissed me on the mouth, hard, then drew back. And there was stern, Dom Vihaal once again.

"Now dry off, get dressed, and go downstairs."

I didn't answer right away. I was still trying to herd a few brain cells. I breathed and swallowed. Then I nodded weakly.

"Yes, Vihaal."

When Vihaal joined Gideon and I downstairs, he told Gideon—with my permission—about our little détente in the en suite.

"I was hoping that would happen," Gideon admitted, grinning. "Angel, don't look so surprised. Vihaal and I share everything. Even you."

I blinked. "I feel like I'm in some kind of alternate universe."

Vihaal shrugged. "You mean, one where people are honest with each other and don't try to take away another person's agency?"

"Yeah. That one."

"I'm the first to admit that poly relationships won't work for everyone. And I honestly don't know if this thing with you will be a success or not. But I have very good feelings about it," he said, with candor.

"Yeah. Me too," I said.

"Me three," Gideon agreed. "Now, let's pick out a movie."

* * * *

We slept together in the big bed. This time, I went in the middle, and was surprised to wake up with my arm thrown over Vihaal. I carefully extricated myself before noticing that Gideon wasn't in bed with us.

"He went to work," Vihaal mumbled, reaching behind him, finding my arm, and bringing it back to where it had been before, tugging me closer.

I smiled and cuddled against him, closing my eyes and drifting off again.

* * * *

"I didn't think he worked weekends."

"He doesn't usually. It's only a six-hour shift. Not so bad."

We were down in the kitchen, drinking coffee, and Vihaal was regarding me thoughtfully.

Does he want to feed me again? I put down my coffee and gazed at him expectantly.

"I want to take you car shopping."

"You want to *take me* car shopping."

"Sorry. Let me rephrase that. I would be happy to join you while we look at a few options. You need a way to get around. As much as I enjoy driving you places, you need your own car, Angel."

I blushed. "Yeah. You're right. And I'd love your help."

"Money isn't an issue?"

"Well, I mean, I have enough for a car payment, as long as it's reasonable."

"What's reasonable?"

"Like...something around four hundred a month. Maybe five?"

"All right. And what else are you looking for in a car?"

I had to think about that for a minute. "Well, reliability most of all. I don't really care about looks."

Vihaal scoffed. "Don't be ridiculous. The car he drives says a lot about the man driving it."

"You think?"

He gave me a look. Maybe it was time for an upgrade in that department.

"I've got some ideas," Vihaal said. "Car shopping is something I enjoy, so I'm quite willing to help."

"Sure. You're probably a much better negotiator than I am. You can use your whole Dom vibe."

He smiled. "I have a Dom vibe?"

I gave him a look. "Of course you have a Dom vibe. Everyone can see it and you fucking know it."

Vihaal seemed inordinately pleased with my remark and I was glad to have said it.

We ended up going to three different dealerships and looking at a variety of cars. I finally chose a Hyundai Sonata, blue, from the lot. It looked sporty and slick. I'd never had such a sexy car.

Vihaal did all the negotiating and got me an amazing deal. This was not a surprise.

I signed off on the paperwork, gave my banking details and arranged to pick it up in two days. I was oddly thrilled about it. I didn't normally get excited about cars — they were a pricey necessity — and the entire process of negotiating a good deal and making sure you didn't get taken advantage of was a pain in the ass. This had been a dream.

"Thank you, V," I said as we left.

"Of course. I'm so glad you accepted my help."

"My instincts were right. You killed it."

"Thank you. It was highly entertaining, especially when he tried to trick me into getting an enhanced service plan, when the regular one covered everything you'll need." He clapped his hands together. "Now. We need some lunch, and then I'm going to take you to see my store. I'm in the mood for a fast-food burger. What do you say?"

"Hell, I'm always in the mood for a fast food."

We ended up at A&W and, since Vihaal didn't want to risk staining the leather seats in his Audi, we ate inside. It seemed strange for Vihaal to be in a fast-food joint, especially because he had worn his business suit to look intimidating and professional at the dealerships. I had to fight my amused smile as he ordered us two Cheddar Bacon Uncle Burgers and fries.

By the time we got to a table, I couldn't help the laughter bursting out of me.

"What?" Vihaal asked, the beginning of a smile on his face.

"Nothing. I've never seen you acting so ordinary."

"I don't understand the ridiculous names they give these burgers," he said, starting to unwrap his. "But they are fucking delicious."

He got a few looks because, yeah, he had a Dom vibe, and he looked incredibly hot. It didn't seem to matter what he was doing or where he was, Vihaal had this calm competence and sense of power that made people give him automatic respect.

When we got back in the car, before he started driving, Vihaal looked at his phone and started tapping.

"Gideon's home," he said. "I'm just letting him know where we're going."

"Sure."

Once Vihaal had pocketed his phone and started the car, I got a text from Gideon.

You got a car!

Yep. Vihaal is an ace negotiator.

Lol. Good at negotiating me out of my pants. Everyone's scared of him. What color?

Metallic blue.

When do you pick it up?

Monday.

Cool cool. Have fun at Tarnish. Watch out for Dominic. He's a dick.

Ok

Vihaal's blind when it comes to that guy. I think he's a creep.

Okay. See you later.

Are you coming back here?

Maybe? I don't have a car yet, and my laptop's at your place.

Maybe you should just move in. laughing/smiling emoji.

I didn't know whether it was a joke or if he was making a dig at my presumption. My thumb hovered over the keys as another message popped up.

It was a joke. Kind of. I love it when you're with us.

My heart fucking melted again. What were these two men doing to me? I was turning into a marshmallow.

Same, same. Smiley face.

Vihaal's antique store was near Main Street, on a little side avenue. He parked in the lot behind the historic Victorian house with *Tarnish* in bold brass letters over the door.
"This is it?" I asked.

"This is it," Vihaal said, as we rounded the corner to the front façade. "What do you think?"

"It's pretty."

"Yes. I was lucky to secure the space for the price I did. Of course, rent's gone up over the years, but it's still reasonable."

I followed Vihaal up the steps and inside, as the clanging of a bell on the door announced our arrival.

A young woman with shoulder-length blue hair looked up. "Vihaal! Hey!"

"Alice," Vihaal said. "How are you?"

"Ah, can't complain. And who is this?" she asked, gazing at me with curious and twinkling eyes. She had a silver ring in the center of her lower lip that sparkled under the fluorescent lights.

"This is Angel Barnett," he said, putting his arm around me. He leaned in to speak softly to Alice. "He's a new acquisition."

Both Alice and I gaped at Vihaal.

"For the...store?" Alice asked, assuming I was a new staff member.

Vihaal smiled. "No, no. For me. And Gideon. A new romantic partner."

Alice blinked slowly. "Oh, my. Well, that's fantastic. Ever the overachiever."

"Well." He shrugged.

She came out from behind the desk and offered me her hand. "Mr. Barnett. I'm Alice Henderson, Assistant Manager."

"Wonderful to meet you. So, this is Tarnish," I said, looking around.

"How are things going, Alice?"

"Great! I mean, I think? Dominic doesn't tell me anything. We've been busy lately, though. Of course, it's dead when you come for a visit." She laughed. "But I swear, we've been hopping."

"Good. I'm glad to hear it. Is Dominic in today?"

"Yeah, he's in the back," Alice said, her expression somewhat less exuberant.

The bell jangled and two customers came in, talking together and laughing.

"I'll let you deal with them," Vihaal said, "we won't be long. Come on, Angel. I want you to meet my manager."

Chapter Seventeen

The store was packed with antique and retro items, most of them seeming to be high value and unique. From what I'd seen in the accounting books, Tarnish specialized in pieces that couldn't be found just anywhere.

Vihaal led me along a narrow hallway and through a room with larger pieces of furniture, then knocked on a door with a sign on it that read Staff Only.

"What is it, Alice?" an irritated-sounding voice said from within.

"It's not Alice," Vihaal stated, in a tone that I recognized as one not to be messed with.

In a moment the door opened. A man in jeans and a ratty sweater stood there, his hair messed, as if he'd just gotten out of bed. He was shorter than both of us and the thick stubble on his face added to his unkempt appearance. His eyes flashed to me and back to Vihaal.

"Vihaal. You didn't tell me you were paying us a visit."

Vihaal shrugged. "I didn't plan it. Thought I'd pop in. This is Angel Barnett. He's going over the books for me."

Dominic turned a suspicious glance to me. "Oh."

"Angel, this is my manager, Dominic Pineda."

I held out my hand. "Nice to meet you."

Dominic gave me a fake smile. "Well, come in. Sit down."

He opened the door wider and beckoned us into an office that was in a state of general disarray. He tidied up some papers and moved a box of supplies out of the way.

"Sorry, I didn't know you were coming."

"I wanted to show Angel my store. He's never been here." Vihaal gestured for me to take one of the empty wood chairs.

I sat. Vihaal took the chair beside mine. Dominic sat in the chair behind the desk.

Vihaal gave the top of the desk a critical look.

Dominic laughed nervously. "I would have tidied up if I'd been expecting you."

Vihaal didn't reply.

Dominic turned to me. "Are you an accountant?"

"I am."

"A *certified* accountant?"

I blinked. "Yes, I'm certified."

"Angel is perfectly qualified to look over the books. And he's working for me, so you can ask me any questions you have."

"Is there a problem?" Dominic asked.

"That's what I'm hoping to find out," Vihaal said.

"You know, Vihaal," Dominic said, steepling his fingers and leveling a look of confidence at Vihaal. "Your father recommended me because of my vast arena of skills with antiques assessments and accounting."

"Yes, I'm aware."

"Mm hmm. So I take a slight offense to being second-guessed," Dominic said.

I glanced at Vihaal. I was already agreeing with Gideon. This guy was a dick.

"Noted. But irrelevant. This is my store, isn't it?"

"Well, yes but your father —"

"I'm well aware that my father helped me set the place up. But his name is not on any of the ownership documents. He recommended you and so I hired you."

"Yes. Do you think he would recommend someone who was incompetent?" Dominic asked.

"No, of course not. But he might have recommended someone who was a little *too competent*."

They regarded each other again. I knew what Vihaal meant by that remark, and I think that Dominic did as well.

Dominic smiled and shrugged, sitting back in the chair. "I think you'll find everything in order. I'm simply surprised that you'd take on the expense of double checking everything."

Vihaal returned Dominic's smile, but there was no warmth in it. Having received many of Vihaal's warm smiles by now, I was kind of an expert on them.

"Since the store's profits have been in decline, it's well worth Mr. Barnett's time and my money."

Sweat beaded on Dominic's forehead.

"The economy is not the best at the moment."

"No. That's true. But it makes sense to check things out, in any case. It's possible that you made a mistake," Vihaal said with calculation and suspicion.

"I suppose that's true," Dominic muttered. "Although I sincerely doubt it."

"In any case, I wanted to speak to you personally, and let you know that I may be asking specific questions about the accounts. Depending on what Mr. Barnett discovers."

Dominic couldn't hide his unease. He glanced at me. I gave him a cool, detached smile, inwardly cheering for Vihaal, who was being so incredibly intimidating.

"Does your father know?" Dominic asked.

"I beg your pardon?" Vihaal said.

"Have you told your father that you're hiring someone to go over the books at Tarnish?"

"It's none of his business."

"I see," Dominic said. "Well, I hope you won't mind if I let him know."

"I'd prefer that you didn't," Vihaal said. "This is between the two of us."

"Hmm. I think that he would be quite disturbed to know you doubted my abilities."

"Is that so?"

Dominic looked less sure in the face of Vihaal's challenge.

"I think so," he mumbled, glancing at me.

"Well, I suppose we should find out. Because if my father, bless his cold, calculating heart, has any underhanded influence on my store, it ends now."

Dominic looked shocked. Then he looked angry. He stood.

"How dare you accuse me of being underhanded!"

Vihaal blinked slowly and remained seated.

"I didn't accuse you of anything," Vihaal said calmly.

"By hiring this man to go over the accounts, you're as plain as stating it outright."

Now Vihaal stood. Tension simmered inside him as if it were a tactile energy field.

"This *man* has a name. It's Angel Barnett. And he is a Certified Public Accountant and also a close personal friend," Vihaal said in a low, threatening tone. "If either you or my father do anything to thwart Mr. Barnett's examination of the accounts from the past three years, I will not be pleased. I could fire you this minute, Dominic."

"But your father—"

"—is *not* running this *business*!" Vihaal said, his voice raised. "I am! And I would ask you to remember that."

I'd never seen him this angry, and boy, was it something. My pulse skyrocketed and my cock swelled in my pants. He was magnificent—blazing with barely contained fury—and I could see the effect it had on Dominic.

The manager sat down. He picked up a pen, then started writing on a piece of paper with furious motions.

"What are you doing?" Vihaal asked.

"I'm making note of this unfair treatment. I won't be intimidated in this manner," he stated, although his red face and trembling hand belied that assertion.

"Are you able to give my father a message, since you're so close to him?"

"I suppose..." Dominic said, somewhat appeased. He put down the pen.

"You can tell him that I will be looking into the management of this store, and if I find anything that stinks of embezzlement or mismanagement, that you will be out the door. And I don't give a fuck what he thinks."

Dominic's mouth fell open. Vihaal stood.

"Angel. Let's go."

Dominic stuttered a laugh and repeated my name in a jeering way.

Vihaal leaned forward and planted his hands on the desk. Dominic clutched the edge of the desk as if ready to propel himself back, if needed.

"I'll fire you on the spot for insulting him. Apologize to Mr. Barnett, or you're done," Vihaal growled, a taut wire of restrained rage.

I sat there, eyes wide and genuinely frightened for Dominic.

Dominic stared at Vihaal. He hesitated a bit too long, and Vihaal slammed his hands on the desk, making Dominic's things rattle and Dominic himself start.

"Apologize to Angel this instant," he said, his voice alarmingly calm and quiet.

Dominic licked his lips and turned to me, summoning a very insincere smile.

"I'm so sorry for that remark, Mr. Barnett. Please accept my apology."

I nodded. "Fine."

Vihaal straightened, pinning Dominic with a withering glare.

"Come on. Let's go," he said, turning to usher me out of the office. I stayed close, not wanting to remain with Dominic a moment longer than necessary.

As we passed through the main part of the store, Alice, who was with a customer, glanced over with a worried look. It was entirely possible that she'd heard some of that.

"I'm so sorry to interrupt," Vihaal said to the customer — a middle-aged woman wearing an expensive-looking wool coat. "I need to talk to my associate for a moment."

The woman blushed and stammered, faced head on with Vihaal's considerable charisma. "Oh, of course! Take as long as you need, I'm still trying to decide."

"Thank you so much," he replied with a smile.

He led Alice over to the checkout desk.

"Yes, Mr. Petrovsky?" she asked.

"I only wanted to say that I'm very pleased with the job you're doing here as Assistant Manager. Please let me know if Dominic is out of line in any way."

She nodded. "Thank you."

"Have a wonderful day."

"You as well. It was great to meet you, Mr. Barnett."

"Likewise," I said.

On the way home, Vihaal cursed and hit the steering wheel with both palms, then sat back against his seat and looked at the roof of the car.

"That fucking snake."

"I think Gideon's right about Dominic," I said. "Do you think he's stealing from you?"

Vihaal turned to me and raised his eyebrows. "Do you?"

"I think it's possible. He rubbed me the wrong way entirely."

This caused Vihaal to slowly smile, and I felt an answering cheerfulness in my pants, even after such a stressful encounter. Vihaal, in business mode and on the warpath, was something to see.

"Mmm. I'd like to rub you the *right* way."

I swallowed, suddenly breathless. "You're pretty fucking hot when you get angry."

Vihaal's smile got wider. "Am I?"

"Thanks for standing up for me and my weird name." I grinned.

"Your name isn't weird. It's lovely," he said. "And if this is a competition, my name doesn't exactly roll off the tongue."

"True. I love your name, though. It suits you. What does it mean, anyway?"

Vihaal gave me a genuine and astonished smile.

"What?" I asked, breathless at the look in those eyes.

"I've only had one other person even ask me that question."

"Gideon?"

"Yes. Anyway, it means something like imposing, and grand," he said, smiling. "But also, beautiful."

"That's pretty fucking accurate."

"Thank you. That's what Gideon said."

I shrugged, tracing the edge of the glove compartment with my fingertip, and giving Vihaal a coy look. "Well, to be fair, we're both trying to get into your pants."

And that made him laugh. A huge, tension-relieving, chortle from deep in his chest.

"I liked Alice. A lot," I said.

"Yes. She's wonderful."

"How long has she been the assistant manager?"

"Oh, gosh, it's been...four years now. No, five."

"Maybe she should be the manager."

It was an offhand comment, but I meant it. My impressions of them had been diametrically opposed. Alice had come across as competent and sincere, Dominic as ineffectual and shady. I wondered why Vihaal had left him in charge for so long.

"You said your father recommended Dominic to manage the store?"

"Yes. I thought, at the time, that he was helping in his own particular way. But now I'm starting to wonder if Gideon is right about my father possibly sabotaging me."

"Do you think your father would do something like that?"

"I'm not sure," he said, then went quiet. After a few moments, he started talking again. "My father sent me away to boarding school when I was six. I didn't want to go. What eight year old wants to leave the only home they know to stay at school night and day for eight months?"

"Not many."

"I certainly didn't. I begged my mother to let me stay, but she said that it was my father's prerogative to send me. I didn't even know what that word meant." He sighed. "But by then it had become obvious that my autistic younger brother would likely never speak or function in a normal way and I think that was a big blow to them, especially my father. He didn't want me brought down by my younger sibling's disability. Which in retrospect seems even more hideous than it did at the time." He shrugged. "Or perhaps, they simply had their hands full."

"Oh jeez. That's pretty rough. Was it terrible?"

"Angel, those first few weeks were hideous. I missed my mother and my home so much. Not my dad, particularly. But everything else that was familiar. I got used to the place. It wasn't a bad school — they did their best for us — but I'd have preferred not to have lived there. And I didn't understand why you'd go to the trouble of having a child if you didn't want them to live with you. It didn't make sense." He offered me a sad smile. "So, I figured it must have been because I wasn't a very good child, and they regretted having me."

"Oh, V," I said, my forehead creasing with sympathy. "No."

"I was very young, and confused, and homesick. I decided that I would do everything in my power to prove my worth. I put everything into my education. I maintained excellent marks across all subjects. I was determined to show my father how valuable and accomplished I was, so that he'd let me come back home."

Vihaal frowned and shrugged.

"Of course, all that served to do was confirm to him that he'd made the right choice to send me there. Because to him it looked like I was thriving." He gave me a somewhat more cheerful look. "I suppose, in a way, I was. But in other ways I was seriously deprived. I didn't have many friends, because the other students were intimidated by me." He laughed. "Even at eight, I was a bit of an ass."

I grinned, trying to picture him that young. He continued.

"I don't think I bullied anyone overtly. But I'm sure there were some contemptuous glares at opportune moments. And perhaps some unkind words."

I gazed at him, trying to imagine it. "Did you eventually figure out a way to be happy there?"

He thought for a moment, staring out of the windshield at the back of his store.

"Happy? No. But I found a way to survive, and I did become popular, eventually, although I held most of my cards close to my chest," he said, waggling his eyebrows.

"The gay thing, or the kink thing? Or both?"

He gave me a cheeky smile that made my heart ache. "Oh, Angel. You do ask the most entertaining questions. Well, I figured all of that out by the age of fourteen, I suppose, one way or another."

"You little devil."

He actually seemed a bit embarrassed. "It's amazing what you can get away with if you motivate people properly. I won't say anything more, but just know that I had partners at school, and we had fun, and we parted on good terms. But it was all on the QT. From other boys and from the staff, obviously." He shrugged and traced the steering wheel with the tip of his index finger. "I'm sure there were rumors."

"I can imagine," I said.

"Can you?" He smiled at me in a coy way. "What do you think the rumors about me were, Angel Barnett?"

"That you were a sex god with a pair of handcuffs under your pillow," I stated, without having to think about it.

He smiled wider.

"Well. Maybe not a sex god...but a lesser, equally as compelling, entity."

Vihaal sighed and leaned toward me, taking my chin in his fingers and kissing me hard on the mouth, then pulling back.

"Am I a sex god, Angel?" he asked, in such a serious tone of voice it gave me shivers.

"Well," I said, trying to quell the excitement in my gut. "It's easy to get on my knees for you."

And there was that smile again, the one that took over his face and made fireworks go off inside me.

"We should get home. Gideon's probably waiting," Vihaal said, still staring at me with intense emotion.

"Yes," I said. "What are you going to do about Dominic?"

"I don't know yet. That comment about Alice has got me thinking. Even if we don't find anything definitive, I'm not sure I'm comfortable with Dominic in that position anymore."

"No. That's fair."

"I'll have to give him some notice and a decent severance package. It might be worth it for the peace of mind. I can't believe I've trusted him as long as I have."

* * * *

Gideon was waiting for us at their place.

"So? How did it go with Dominic?"

"About as you'd expect," Vihaal muttered.

"Huh. What did you think of him, Angel?"

"Not much, to be honest. He gives me the creeps."

"Nobody likes Dominic," Gideon affirmed. "I don't know how you've put up with him so long, V."

"Yes, I'm starting to wonder that myself," Vihaal said, patting his knee. "Come here. I want to kiss you."

Gideon smiled and rushed over, seating himself on Vihaal's lap and throwing his arms around him. They kissed with passion and lots of tongue as I watched, Gideon giggling and Vihaal trying not to smile.

"Well, you're in a good mood," Gideon murmured, glancing at me. "How on Earth did you manage it?"

I shrugged. "Vihaal told me about being sent to boarding school."

"Oh, yes, the *woe is me, my family is so rich that I was cast aside,* story. Please. You had it pretty good, V."

"I was very homesick."

"Oh, baby, I know. I'm sure you were. But then you became the hottest, queerest, and kinkiest member of the school, and the rest is history." He got off Vihaal's lap and gave him a formal bow.

Vihaal gazed at Gideon for a long moment.

"Be honest with me, Deo. Do you think my father deliberately put someone in charge of Tarnish who would steal from me? From us?"

Gideon's expression sobered. "Honestly? I wouldn't put it past him."

"I'm starting to wonder."

"I have good instincts about people, you know. I was right about Angel."

"Yes. You were."

"What?"

Gideon glanced at me, then returned his gaze to Vihaal.

"I told V that I thought you were at least bi, or maybe pan, or maybe even mostly gay but suppressing it. And that once we got you to see it, all that repressed sexuality would come pouring out, hopefully over us both."

"Wow." I laughed. Because he'd been right. He'd been so, so right.

Chapter Eighteen

"Did you bring the cookies?" Mom asked.

I pulled them out of my bag.

"How is it you can remember that I'm bringing you cookies, but you have trouble with what I said a few minutes ago?" I asked, putting my satchel down and taking a seat on the edge of her bed.

She shrugged. "Priorities. Also, if I didn't get you to repeat everything three times, you'd be out of here after ten minutes."

"That is not true."

I watched as she opened the package and took out a cookie. Before she bit into it, she gazed at me with sudden curiosity.

"How are those two men you told me about? I forget their names."

Honestly, I was impressed she remembered them at all.

"Gideon and Vihaal. Yeah, they're good."

"Hmm. Is it just hot sex, or do you actually like them?"

I choked on my own saliva. "What? Oh my God. Mom."

"It's a legitimate question."

"It's a little personal."

"I'm your mother."

"Exactly!"

She chewed a piece of her cookie thoughtfully. "I just want to know if they're your boyfriends or if you're all just getting down and dirty with each other."

"You know that's really none of your business, right? You've never been interested in my sex life before."

"It was never this exciting."

"Fine. They're more than hookups. Satisfied?"

"I don't know what a hookup is."

"It's when you— Never mind. I guess you could call us all boyfriends. Man, that is the weirdest thing I've ever said."

She snorted a laugh that blew cookie crumbs onto her lap. "Oh no it's not. You've said some very strange things over your lifetime, Angel Barnett. Like when you told your father he'd have to drug you and kidnap you if he wanted you to join the neighborhood soccer team." She grinned.

"Did I really tell him that?"

"You hated soccer."

"I still hate soccer."

"Well, I'm glad you've found someone. Two someones, in fact. Who would have thought."

"Yeah, well, it was a complete surprise to me. It's still a surprise. Every single day."

"Would you like a cookie?"

"Oh, no thanks. I just had lunch." I decided that two could play at this game. "So...any romantic prospects for you?"

She froze with the cookie halfway to her mouth. "What do you mean?"

"Well, it's not too late for you to have some fun, you know."

"Please. I've barely got any time left, do you think I'd waste it on trying to get a romance going with one of these old losers?"

I laughed.

"When are you going to bring your men to meet me?"

"Oh...I don't know. It's only been a few months, Mom. I don't want to jump the gun."

"On what?"

"On asking them to meet my mom. That's something that you do after, you know, six months. Maybe even a year."

"A year! I might not be here in a year!"

That was a distinct possibility. Still, I wondered how Vihaal and Gideon would respond to being invited to visit my aging mother.

"Okay, okay. I'll ask them. Eat your cookies."

She grinned and took another bite.

* * * *

It took me the better part of two weeks to go over the Tarnish accounts for the previous two years. The same shady transactions kept popping up, and the same Divine Treasures supplier was mentioned with no detailed listing of items purchased.

I went through everything, taking notes and writing a report for Vihaal. It was clear to me that there was something fishy going on. And I was sure that Dominic was at the root of it.

When I told Vihaal my suspicions and returned the files, with my notes and comments in a document that I put on a flash drive, he gave a world-weary sigh.

"I'm so sorry, V," I said. "This is a shitty situation to be in."

He nodded. "Thank you so much, Angel. You've helped me immeasurably. Send me an invoice for what I owe you."

"I will."

"How's the new car?"

"Fantastic. I love it."

Vihaal stood there silently for a long moment.

"I think we need to go to Molly's."

"Oh," I said. "Well, I'd love to."

"I get horny when I'm stressed. And Gideon's always horny."

I laughed. "I mean, he's got to get sick of us at some point, right?"

Vihaal shot me an appalled look. "I certainly hope not. I want both of you in the Bordello with me this weekend." He looked me up and down. "Yes. I need to get you into those ropes again."

I cleared my throat, trying not to get hard.

"Look, can I ask you something?" I said. It was now or never. "Not related at all to what we just spoke about."

"Of course."

I hesitated, smiling nervously because it was so awkward to invite your new boyfriend—one of them, anyway— to meet your aging mother right after he'd expressed a detailed interest in tying you up with rope.

"My mom. She's in a retirement home and I— She gets bored and I never know what to talk about, and I might have mentioned you and Gideon."

Vihaal regarded me with amusement. "And?"

"And now she wants to meet you. And him. But you don't have to. Of course, you don't have to. I mean, she wanted me to ask if you would…"

"Angel, we'd be delighted to meet your mother. When?"

"Oh fuck," I said. "I hadn't thought that far in advance. I thought you wouldn't want to."

"She's your mother, Angel. Of course I want to meet her, and thank her for giving you such a wonderful, and accurate, name."

I narrowed my eyes.

Vihaal continued. "I'm going to tell her what a sweet young man you are. The perfect exemplification of the moniker."

"She's not going to believe you, but okay."

He laughed. "Should I tell her how much of an angel *you're not?*"

"No! God, no. Just let me prove to her that I didn't make you guys up!"

"Does she think you did?"

"It's possible."

"Well, we can't have that. Why don't we all go on Saturday morning? Would that work? I'll try to reserve the Bordello for that evening."

I gaped at Vihaal in disbelief. "You're going to introduce yourself to my mom, and Dom me in the Bordello the *same day?*"

Vihaal smiled. "Yes. Gosh, now, that does sound rather depraved."

* * * *

214

"Now, look, her short-term memory is going. So she might say the same thing a few times. Or ask the same question," I cautioned them.

"Understood," Vihaal said as we walked to the elevator.

"Hi, Mrs. Carter," I said to a woman I recognized.

"Hello, Angel," she replied, looking at Vihaal and Gideon with much interest. "Did you bring Natalie more cookies?"

"Actually, I've got cherry turnovers today. From the bakery."

"Oh! Lovely. You're such a good son."

"Ha, ha. Thanks." I blushed as I pressed the elevator button.

I glanced at Vihaal who regarded me with a satisfied, almost smug, expression. Then I looked at Gideon, who leaned in and patted my arm.

"Oh my God, you're so cute! Do you know everyone here?"

"God, no," I said, as the elevator doors opened.

"Angel!" Mr. Al-Moodi said as he stepped off with his cane. "Good to see you!"

"Thanks, Mr. Al-Moodi. You're looking good!"

"Who are these fellas? Narcs?"

"No, they're just..." I coughed. "They're my friends. Mom wanted to meet them."

"Oh! She gets around, that woman. Barely remembers my name but she wants to meet *everyone*." His eyes went wide. "Oh, she's out of cookies!"

"I'll get some more."

"Yeah, yeah. Tell her I said hi. She won't remember me."

We got into the elevator. I was pretty sure my face was beet red. Vihaal and Gideon watched me with surprise and way too much enjoyment.

"What?" I said, trying to hide in the corner of the elevator. "She likes cookies."

"So do all her friends, apparently," Vihaal said, smiling.

I looked at the bag in my hand. "I should have brought cookies. I thought she'd like something different for a change."

"And it's a special occasion," Gideon said, bumping me.

"Is it? I'm starting to wonder," I said with a sardonic lilt.

"Why are you embarrassed? Is this some holdover from pretending to be straight?" Gideon asked.

I laughed. "Maybe. I don't know. It's just that I've put a lot of energy into impressing you both. And this is kind of…well, it's just sad and boring."

"Honestly, Angel. What's more impressive than a man who's not afraid to do nice things for people?" Vihaal asked. "Kindness in general is underrated."

"You're the coolest," Gideon said, leaning in to kiss me.

I practically combusted with fear that the elevator doors would open and we'd cause some kind of medical incident.

"Hey, can we keep the PDA for Molly's?" I whispered, even though we were the only ones in the elevator. "Some of these folks have delicate coronary systems."

Gideon burst out a laugh. "I'll try to keep my hands off you."

"And I'll make sure he does," Vihaal said, winking.

I'd already told them that my mom knew we were more than friends. And that she was cool with the whole bisexual/gay thing. But I wasn't sure about any of the other residents.

"This is it," I said, pointing to number three-one-eight and taking a deep breath before I knocked.

"Mom, it's Angel," I said in a loud voice so she'd hear me.

"Angel who?" she asked from inside the room.

"Very funny. I've brought some people to meet you," I said. "Are you decent?"

"Not at all. But come in anyway."

I glanced at Vihaal and Gideon.

"Hold on," I said.

I pushed the door open a crack and saw her sitting up in bed with a sweater on over her nightgown and the covers pulled up around her waist.

I beckoned Gideon and Vihaal to follow and went in.

"Mom, how come you're in bed?" I asked.

"Didn't feel like getting up. Give me a break, I'm seventy-nine."

"Hey, remember I told you I was bringing Vihaal and Gideon to meet you?"

"Who? What?" she said, looking at Vihaal and Gideon like they were leprechauns or aliens.

Oh fuck no.

"I, uh...the men I told you about? Remember? Gideon and Vihaal..."

"I have no idea what the fuck you're talking about. Who are these people?"

Oh my God. Why? Why today?

"Hello, Mrs. Barnett," Vihaal said. "It's so lovely to meet you." He held out his hand to her. "I'm Vihaal Petrovsky, and this is Gideon Foster."

"Hey," Gideon said, smiling at my mom while I tried not to have a nervous breakdown.

"Oh!" she exclaimed, putting a hand to her face in sudden—but very fake—realization. "Yes! Angel told me all about you both! I'm so glad to finally meet you."

I'm going to kill her in her sleep.

"That's very funny, Mom. Pretending you forgot. Ha ha," I said, as the blood returned to my brain.

"Look, honey, I don't have that many amusements anymore. I take 'em where I can find 'em."

Vihaal looked at my mom like she was a rock star. Gideon put a hand to his mouth to keep from laughing, his eyes dancing with mirth.

My mom looked at the two of them like she'd forgotten her age. "My, aren't you handsome. Both of you. Well, well."

I put a hand to my forehead as Gideon failed to contain himself and burst out laughing. Mom smiled at him.

"And aren't you adorable," she said. "You're Gideon?"

"Yes, Mrs. Barnett. It's so nice to finally meet you!"

"Oh, please call me Bridget."

"Okay, Bridget," Gideon said.

My mom cackled.

"That's not your name," I said, my voice tired. "It's Natalie."

"Well, Bridget is the name I've always wanted."

"Bridget is a beautiful name," Vihaal said, throwing me a look before turning back to my mom. "May I call you Bridget also?"

"Of course." She turned to me. "What's in the bag?"

"Oh. I brought you some cherry turnovers," I said, handing it over.

"Oh, damn, I was hoping for cookies. Thank you, though. You're always so thoughtful."

"I can bring you some cookies, Mom. I'll bring some tomorrow."

"Nonsense," Vihaal said. "I'll send some. What kind do you like? Chocolate chip? Oatmeal raisin?"

"Oh my!" My mom blushed and fidgeted with the edge of the blanket. "Well, I do like a good chocolate chip. Or chocolate chunk. Or even *double* chocolate."

"Done. The bakery we picked these up from has a delivery service. You'll receive some tomorrow, Mrs. Bar—I mean, *Bridget*."

"Oh, my, thank you," she said, reaching out for me.

She grasped my arm and tugged me in close, her gaze fixed on Vihaal.

"This one is very sexy," she said in a voice not as quiet as she supposed.

"Mom!" I whispered, shocked and embarrassed.

"Are you getting up to some nasty things with these men, Angel?" she asked, in an excited and eager voice.

"I'm not telling you that!"

"Bridget," Vihaal said. "I can assure you that Gideon and I are treating Angel very well." He lowered his chin and sobered his gaze. "Very, very well."

My mom let go of me and smiled. "That's all I wanted to know. Now, let's eat. Get the plates, Angel. I want *that* man to have the biggest turnover," she said, pointing at Vihaal.

I got the plates, dying a little on the inside.

* * * *

Afterward, on our way to the cars, I apologized.

"I'm *so* sorry."

"About what?" Gideon asked, popping the last of his turnover in his mouth and licking his fingers.

"About my mom and her failing memory. Also, she doesn't have much of a filter anymore. She was rude and I'm sorry."

"Angel, she's a very old woman," Vihaal remarked. "I think we can forgive her that."

"I thought she was lovely," Gideon said. "And hilarious. I think she did it all on purpose."

"Well, the first part, when she pretended not to know who you guys were, yes. That was a joke on me. For sure."

"It was a good one," Vihaal affirmed. "She's got a spark, your mom."

"Yeah. Lucky me," I joked.

"Angel," Vihaal said, turning me around and giving me his stern look. "You *are* lucky. She's incredibly open-minded for someone of that generation. And sex-positive. My own mother cursed me and sent me to the Devil when she found out I was gay."

I gaped at him. "Really?"

"Yes. But it's all right. Satan and I are on very good terms."

I smiled. "Yeah, okay. That's true. She's pretty awesome. I'm just...I'm embarrassed."

"I know. And it looks good on you. Remind me to embarrass you more often."

Gideon laughed with glee as we parted to go to our cars.

* * * *

In the Bordello, Vihaal got right down to business.

"Both of you, clothes off. Fold them neatly and put them on the settee," he said. "And Angel."

"Yes, Vihaal?"

Vihaal nodded at the St. Andrew's cross. "You're going up there."

I gaped at him. "On that...on the *cross*?"

Vihaal smiled.

"Isn't that a little..." I swallowed. "...hard-core for someone just starting out?" I asked, my voice in a higher pitch then I'd intended.

"I think you can handle it," he commented. "It's more for keeping you in one position for an extended period. You'll find it quite comfortable, I'm sure."

I wasn't convinced.

"Yes, Vihaal."

"It will also give you a good view of what I'm about to do to Gideon."

Oh, well in that case... "Okay. Sure."

He raised his eyebrows in a way that sent desire shooting up my spine.

"Yes, Vihaal," I corrected myself.

We stripped and folded our clothes while Vihaal gathered a selection of items at which I didn't dare look too closely. I was anxious, as I always was in this room at the beginning of a scene. I was also pretty fucking into it.

"Come and kneel at my feet, both of you." For once, Gideon was completely naked, without any kind of adornment. I wondered if Vihaal had expressly asked for it.

We kneeled at Vihaal's feet. He'd taken off his suit jacket but otherwise was dressed like a wealthy entrepreneur. I had a good view of his shiny brown dress shoes.

He put his hands in his pockets and gazed at us.

"Hmm. Neither of you are fully hard. I expect more from you in this room, you know."

I swallowed. I looked down at my cock and saw that it was almost standing straight up. I was pretty close to being fully hard.

"Perhaps you should entertain each other for a bit before we start. Gideon, take Angel over to the spanking bench."

"Yes, Vihaal," Gideon said, excitement in his voice.

I wasn't sure I wanted to be spanked, but it wasn't the worst thing that could happen in this room, so I followed Gideon over to the bench. Vihaal grabbed a straight chair and set it at a comfortable viewing point, then sat and leaned forward with his elbows on his knees.

"Angel, I want you bent over the side — it should be at just the right height for you."

Gideon showed me how Vihaal wanted me and helped me to fold myself over the padded bench, and stretch my arms out to each side. I did so, feeling like a piece of meat or a sex toy. My cock was definitely hard now.

"Excellent," I heard Vihaal say, his voice low. "Gideon, show me Angel's hole, will you?"

Oh my God. My face flamed with humiliation but my cock throbbed with arousal.

A puff of air exited Gideon's lips. "Yes, Vihaal," he said.

In a moment, Gideon's hands were on my buttocks. He slid his thumbs down my crack and spread my cheeks apart. I tried to breathe and figure out why being put on display so pragmatically for Vihaal's pleasure was such a huge turn-on. He sure knew how to drive me mad.

"Oooh, yes. So pretty. You have a beautiful asshole, Angel."

More shame. My insides roiled with it, but my arousal level was white hot.

"Yes, Vihaal," I whispered.

"Do you want to play with that pretty hole, Gideon?"

Oh my fucking fuck.

"Of course I do, Vihaal. Thank you."

I pressed my cheek to the bench and closed my eyes as Gideon stroked a finger over my hole. By now, I knew how good it felt to be teased there, but it still made me feel soft and vulnerable and off center.

"Mmm. So sweet. What a good boy you are, Angel," Vihaal said.

I heard him get up. Then the sound of his footsteps.

"Am I doing it right, Vihaal?" Gideon asked in a sweet, coy voice that I hadn't really heard him use before.

"Oh yes. Just like that. Pet his pretty hole while I watch. He's making such lovely sounds."

Gideon stroked and teased me, as I lay spread over the spanking bench, alternately dying of embarrassment and gasping with excitement. It was a heady mindfuck.

"A fine slut for you, Vihaal."

My brain went numb and checked out. I heard everything but I'd stopped reacting to it with my mind, and only did so with my body.

"Suck on your finger," Vihaal said.

I heard slurping noises, then something pressed against my hole.

"Let him in, Angel."

I made a strangled noise as Gideon's slick digit breached me.

"Oh," Gideon said, going deeper as I made ridiculously vulnerable noises. Why did that feel so fucking good?

"Soft?" Vihaal asked.

"Like velvet, Vihaal," Gideon said, pushing his finger further as I lay helpless against the bench.

"Oh fuck. Fuck," I gasped, unable to stop myself from pushing my ass up to meet him.

"Do you like that, Angel?"

"Yes, Vihaal." I managed to get the words out past my humiliation.

"Mmm. I could watch Gideon fingering you all night."

I squeezed my eyes shut as the pleasure spread and consumed me. I didn't know how much more I could take. I was hard and leaking, my body hanging off that one profane invasion.

"Take your finger out now, and use your tongue. He likes a good tongue laving. Ask me how I know." Vihaal sounded so smug, and I flashed back to the shower we'd shared.

"I don't have to. You've obviously tasted him," Gideon said. "Now it's my turn."

His finger slipped out, and he spread me again. The flat of his tongue slid over my hole and I choked on air.

Chapter Nineteen

I kept flashing back to being in the shower with Vihaal, when he'd done this to me for the first time. Then I came back to the present. Then I returned in my mind to the shower. My overwhelmed brain couldn't decide what was happening or where I was. But my body reacted to Gideon's tongue as if it wasn't mine to control.

Gideon spread me wide as he ate at me, using his tongue, his lips, and sometimes his whole face, in a way that defied comprehension. But it was so fucking good.

He gasped and sighed and rubbed himself against me as he drove me into a state of euphoria, while Vihaal looked on.

I grasped the edge of the bench in order to ground myself to the current moment—to keep myself from flying up, up and away—and from sliding to the floor in a boneless heap.

"Yes, that's right, Deo. Have him for *fucking supper*." Vihaal's voice hovered in the air of my consciousness as I almost died on that spanking bench. I came close to losing complete control and splashing the floor with my jizz, but somehow, I held off.

"All right. Enough," Vihaal said, the words hovering just on the edge of my awareness.

Gideon didn't listen. The bliss continued as I fell into incoherent madness, gasping and almost sobbing.

"Enough!" With one word Vihaal commanded our attention.

Gideon pulled back.

"I'm sorry, Vihaal," he said as I clutched the edge of the bench, trembling and blinking, and trying to collect myself.

"You did well, Deo. He can barely stand."

I heard sounds of movement.

"Now help me," Vihaal said.

I was pulled to my feet.

"You can walk, Angel. One foot in front of the other," Vihaal encouraged.

By the time I'd realized what was happening, they'd got me to the St. Andrew's cross.

They spun me around and Gideon pinned me to keep me upright while Vihaal buckled me into the cuffs — attaching me, spread-eagled, to the contraption.

"Hold on to the grab bars," Vihaal said, and showed me the small posts that jutted out where my wrists were shackled. I wrapped my fingers around them and gazed at Vihaal. I was panting as if I'd run a race. My body was a conflagration of desire. They could have strung me up anywhere — I was a rag doll to their manipulations.

Vihaal ordered Gideon to his knees.

"Open your mouth."

I watched, rapt, as Vihaal fisted Gideon's hair to keep him still as he buried his cock in Gideon's open mouth.

"That's it," Vihaal said as he fucked Gideon's face with brutal and commanding motions. Gideon coughed and drooled but did his best to accommodate Vihaal's vigorous actions. My eyes went wide at the sight and my balls ached with desire.

After only a few moments, Vihaal went deep and groaned as he climaxed. I watched as Gideon's eyes bulged and he swallowed Vihaal's release, then gasped when Vihaal withdrew.

"Such a good slut. Such a good boy."

Gideon braced his hands on his thighs as he struggled to recover, swallowing and licking his lips while Vihaal tucked himself away.

"Well done," Vihaal said. "Now over to the bench, my dear."

"Yes, Vihaal," Gideon said, with a torrid glance at me that sent bolts of lightning up and down my spine.

I watched as Vihaal stripped off his clothes, slowly, so that Gideon and I could enjoy the reveal. Had I ever stood a chance of resisting him? I'd been a goner from the start.

Gideon climbed onto the spanking bench, his cock bobbing as he moved, and lay face down on the padded top. There was a space at his hips for his dick to hang, so that Vihaal had full access. Vihaal attached cuffs and wrapped a collar around Gideon's throat, fixing him at multiple points so that he was well restrained.

"Comfy?" Vihaal asked.

"Yes, Vihaal," Gideon sighed. "Thank you, Vihaal."

"Mmm. Don't thank me yet. I want to fucking wreck you. I'm going to drive you absolutely insane before I have you."

Gideon whimpered, comprehending the seriousness of his predicament.

"I want Angel to see how much you love being at my fucking mercy."

"I'm yours, Vihaal," Gideon murmured. "I've always been yours."

"And now there's two of you. Aren't I the lucky one?"

Vihaal looked like a god, standing there beside Gideon, making free with all of that restrained flesh. He gave Gideon a slap to the ass and Gideon thanked him for it. Then the other side. More words of gratitude.

"Mmm. You aren't going to thank me for what I do next."

A thrill passed through me at those words.

"Gideon likes a bit of pain with his pleasure, even when he doesn't. And he has his safeword. Don't you, my dear?"

"Yes, Vihaal."

"Tell me what it is."

"Tambourine."

"Excellent. Let's get started."

Vihaal flashed me a devilish smile as he walked the short distance to the bed where he had laid out supplies. He picked up something and came toward me.

"This one's for you, Angel," he said, holding up a braided cord with a sliding bead to clasp it together. "To keep you hard and keep you from spilling too soon."

I'd never worn a cock ring, but I trusted him.

He held my gaze as he wrapped it around the base of my dick and balls, then tightened it so it was snug.

"Thank you, Vihaal," I said. It was instinctual now, my response.

Vihaal grinned and cupped my chin, then kissed me hard on the mouth, breaching me with his tongue and leaning his body against mine.

A wave of euphoria washed over me. Then Vihaal stepped back, released my chin and bent down. I had a second to think — *What the fuck?* — before he took the head of my cock in his mouth and swirled his tongue around it as I gasped and groaned in sudden delight.

He pulled off then, a string of saliva connecting his lower lip to my cock for a brief moment before it broke. He straightened and gave me the most incendiary look as he turned and walked away.

He picked up a paddle from the bed — a serious-looking, leather one — and positioned himself behind Gideon.

"Ready, my sweet little pain slut?"

"Yes, Vihaal. Always," Gideon murmured.

I had a good view of Gideon, and of Vihaal standing behind him. Gideon's gaze met mine as Vihaal landed the first swat. Gideon's eyes closed and he whimpered. He cried out as Vihaal landed heavy blows to his poor, sweet ass.

After several blows, it became obvious that Gideon was struggling. I tried to remember that he had a safeword that he could deploy if he wanted Vihaal to stop, but it was both difficult and hot to watch him writhing and moaning. But I knew by now that, sometimes, the struggle was the whole point. The wish to please your Dom, fighting the urge to give in to your own weaknesses.

I glanced at Vihaal, and something about his face flashed alarm.

There was blood. Blood on his face.

"V," I said. "V, you're bleeding."

Vihaal landed another blow to Gideon's flesh as bright red blood seeped from his nose, coursed over his lips, and dripped onto his bare chest.

"Fuck," Vihaal swore, dropping the paddle and moving to the bed where he grabbed a towel, and pressed it to his face. "*Tarnish.* Fucking *Tarnish.*"

I remembered that it was Vihaal's safeword. It meant that we had to stop the scene. But Gideon and I were both trussed up, and we'd need Vihaal to release us.

"V?" Gideon said, his voice sounding panicked. "Vihaal!"

"It's all right. A nosebleed. For fuck's sake."

Gideon started laughing.

"Are you all right, V?" I asked, worried.

"He gets them a lot," Gideon said. "He's fine. But we'll have to stop."

Vihaal stood, the towel pressed to his face, and walked over to me first, unfastening the wrist and ankle cuffs and helping me to get down.

"You can take off the cock ring yourself."

I stood there, fumbling with the braided cord, while Vihaal did his best to release Gideon using one hand, then went to sit on the edge of the bed.

Gideon walked over to him, his cock softening, his ass a rosy pink.

"Is it bad? Let me see."

Vihaal was pinching the bridge of his nose with one hand but moved the towel away so that Gideon could have a look. There was a lot of blood.

"Ooh, this is a bad one."

"It'll stop in a minute," Vihaal said. He gestured to the two of us. "You might as well get dressed. I'm so sorry. We were having so much fun."

"Jesus, V," I said. "Don't worry about us." My arousal had vanished at the first sight of the blood and I was happy to put my clothes on.

Gideon met my gaze and shrugged. "I'm sure Sebastian will refund us some of the fee."

"I'm not worried about the fee, for fuck's sake," Vihaal muttered. "This was not how I'd intended to spend the evening."

"He always gets grumpy when he has a nosebleed. So this is normal," Gideon advised as we got dressed.

"Particularly when it interrupts something important," Vihaal said.

"Hey, it was fun while it lasted. We can pick it up again sometime," I said.

Vihaal grunted.

A sudden thought gripped me. "What if Vihaal had keeled over unconscious? How would we have gotten free?"

Gideon glanced over. "Well, someone would have come to check once our hour was up, if we hadn't returned the key."

So we'd have been stuck until then. Thank God that hadn't happened.

We finished dressing and brought Vihaal's clothes to the bed.

"Is it stopping?" Gideon asked.

Vihaal lifted the towel, and more blood dripped down.

"Shit," I said. It didn't look good.

"It usually stops by now. Doesn't it?" Gideon said, gazing at Vihaal with some concern.

"This does seem rather excessive. But I'm sure it will stop."

"Maybe we should get you dressed," I suggested.

"Fine," Vihaal said, strangely pliant. "How's your ass, Gideon? Did I go too hard?"

"No, it's just fine. And don't try to distract me."

Gideon and I glanced at each other. He was obviously worried about Vihaal. But nosebleeds were so common. I was sure the bleeding would stop soon, maybe by the time Vihaal was dressed.

It didn't.

"V, I think we need to go to Emergency," Gideon said. The towel was almost completely soaked with blood at this point. Gideon took it from Vihaal and passed him another.

"Don't be ridiculous," Vihaal said, pressing the fresh towel to his face, but not before a splash of blood landed on his white shirt. "I'm fine."

Gideon threw me a look, then took a clean corner of the saturated towel between his thumb and forefinger.

"This has never happened before," he said, spreading it open.

"It's fine."

"We need to go," Gideon said.

"It's more likely to stop if I stay still."

"It's *not stopping*. We need to go to the ER." Gideon turned to me. "Back me up on this."

"Vihaal, I think Gideon is right," I said.

"I think you're both overreacting."

"Vihaal. Please," Gideon said. "If you don't come with us this minute, I'm calling nine-one-one and you'll have that humiliation to add to everything else."

"So fucking embarrassing." Vihaal looked at me, then at Gideon, then rolled his eyes. "Fine."

"Good," Gideon said. "Let's go."

Gideon and I led Vihaal, still holding a bloody towel to his face, through the gaming parlor to the bar. Sebastian's face, when he saw us, went white.

"Jesus Christ. Did one of your subs rebel and punch you in the face, Vihaal?" he asked, coming out from behind the counter. There were gasps as other people saw us.

"It's a nosebleed," Vihaal muttered. "Bad one."

"We're taking him to the ER," I said. I handed Sebastian the key. "There may be some blood on the floor. He's already soaked one towel."

Sebastian's face paled further. "Oh shit."

"Sorry," Vihaal said.

"No, no, it's fine. Can I help in any way? An ambulance?"

Vihaal started to shake his head.

"Stay still!" Gideon said.

"No ambulance," Vihaal grunted. "For fuck's sake."

"We're driving him," I said. "But thanks."

We settled Vihaal into the passenger seat.

"I can put on my own fucking seatbelt," he said when I tried to do it for him.

"Fine," I said, irritation replacing my fear.

"Just start the car. I've got the fob in my pocket."

Gideon pressed the start button and Vihaal's precious Audi roared to life.

"For God's sake, drive carefully. If you damage this car I'll—"

"You'll what, V? Paddle me within an inch of my life?" Gideon snapped.

I grinned from the back seat. What on Earth did you threaten a pain slut with, I wondered.

"I'll ignore you for two days," Vihaal mumbled. "How about that?"

Ah.

"Empty threat. You never could," Gideon stated.

"Try me." Vihaal's voice sounded strange, with the towel pressed to his nose.

"Do you think V could ignore me for two *hours*, Angel? Let alone two *days*?"

"Not a chance," I said. "No way."

"Well, isn't this nice. Now there's two of you."

"Yes," Gideon said. "Thank God you're here, Angel. I don't know if I'd have been able to convince him on my own."

Even though I was worried about Vihaal and all the blood, which terrified me in a visceral way, Gideon's words hit in a place I'd ignored for a very long time.

Gideon stole glances at Vihaal as he drove.

"Keep your eyes on the road, Gideon. I'd rather not end up in a car crash."

"Oh, ha ha. This is what happens when you pick your nose."

I looked at Vihaal, who gave Gideon a steely stare.

"Slander doesn't look good on you, sweetheart. You know I don't do that."

"Okay, fine. But how come you get nosebleeds so often?"

Vihaal sighed and shrugged. "Who knows? I've never had one this bad."

"Well, at least you admit that this one's unusual," Gideon said.

We were close to the hospital now and I started to feel better about everything.

"I don't know if it's *going to the ER* bad," Vihaal mumbled.

"Well, we're fucking here now. I'm going to pull up to the Emergency entrance. Angel, can you help Vihaal in and I'll park and come find you?"

"Yep. Got it," I said, trying to remember the last time I'd had to bring anyone to the ER.

"You'll need the fob," Vihaal said, searching in his coat pocket while Gideon drove onto the hospital grounds and found the ER drop off. "Here."

"Thank you," Gideon said.

He pulled up to the curb and I got out, then helped Vihaal out of the passenger seat. I moved to take Vihaal's elbow.

"Angel, you don't have to lead me. I'm not fucking blind."

A flash of anger flared. "Excuse me? I'm just trying to help."

His eyes widened and softened above the bloody towel. "I'm so sorry. I'm...not very good at accepting help."

"You don't say?" I replied dryly.

"I know you had something else in mind for tonight."

"Vihaal, don't worry about it," I said.

There was a nurse at Reception who took one look at Vihaal, then glanced at me.

"Nose injury?"

"Nosebleed," Vihaal said as I shook my head. "It won't stop."

"Okay. I'm going to need you to fill out this form, please."

"Can we get a fresh towel or something, please?" I asked. "This one's going to start dripping soon."

She acknowledged the bloodied towel in Vihaal's hand with professional detachment. "I'll have somebody bring one. Please take a seat and fill out the form."

I took the clipboard and pen from her and found two empty seats in the corner, where we could still be seen.

"Can you do it and I'll dictate?" Vihaal asked.

"Of course."

He spelled his last name for me, then helped me fill in the rest of the form. By the time we'd finished, Gideon had found us.

"They didn't give him a fresh towel?"

"I asked for one. She said they would."

Gideon rolled his eyes and held his hand out for the clipboard. "Here, I'll take that to Reception."

I handed it to him, with the pen.

When he returned, he was carrying a clean towel.

"Got one. Had to promise to give her my firstborn child, but…that shouldn't be an issue." He winked and passed it to me, then held his hand out for the bloodied one.

When Vihaal pulled the soaked towel away from his face, blood was still trickling out of his nose. I passed him the clean one.

"Thank you."

"I think it might be slowing down," I said.

"Then we can leave?" Vihaal asked, his eyes hopeful.

It was strange seeing him so pliant and vulnerable, and amusing to watch him follow Gideon's directions, in a complete turn-around from the usual circumstances.

"No way. You need to be seen," Gideon stated. "I'm not getting you all the way home and then having to come back."

Gideon held the bloody towel gingerly between his fingers and grimaced, then turned to me.

"Do you think Sebastian wants this back?"

I shook my head. "Doubt it."

I pointed in the direction of a biohazard waste receptacle.

"Ah. Yeah, that's a better idea," he said, heading over.

Gideon returned. "I should have asked her for some gloves. I'm going to go wash my hands."

"Bathroom's over there," I said, showing him.

"Wow, you're pretty good in a crisis, Angel," Gideon said, grinning at Vihaal. "I guess we should keep him."

"I guess we should," Vihaal said, in a shockingly affectionate way for someone holding a towel against their bleeding face.

He reached for my hand and I gave it.

"I'm glad you're here," he said, as Gideon made his way to the washroom.

Chapter Twenty

We waited about four hours for Vihaal to be seen. I think the nurse at Reception got tired of getting us clean towels so she sped things up.

I stayed in the lounge while Gideon accompanied Vihaal to the exam room. I tried to relax, even though an ER was not the place to do that easily. Although I supposed it was better than the Intensive Care Unit.

According to Dr. Google, it wasn't particularly unusual for someone who frequently got nosebleeds to find themselves in this situation. At least we'd insisted that he seek medical attention, so things could be resolved. Hopefully he wouldn't need to be admitted.

After checking out the probable prognosis online, I had nothing to do but play games on my phone while they were gone. It could have been worse. At least no-one was screaming. A baby cried now and then, and at one point a little kid was running around cursing randomly until someone stopped him. But other than that, it was peaceful.

A shadow fell across my phone. I looked up.

Gideon stood there, looking green.

"Are you okay? Where's V?"

"They're packing his nose. I couldn't handle it."

I looked past him to the exam area. "What does that mean?"

He sighed and collapsed in the chair beside me, making a face.

"It means they shove all kinds of shit up his nose…like, way up. To keep the bleeding at bay, I guess." He threw me a disgusted glance. "So gross. He's lucky I'm so fucking in love with him. They cauterized the bleed first, but it didn't stop. So they're packing it." He gave me a wry look. "V is not amused."

I laughed softly and shook my head. "No, I bet he isn't. So, he gets these a lot?"

"Not like this. I've never seen one this bad," Gideon muttered. "Usually he just pinches his nose and sits still for fifteen minutes and it stops. Like he said, he's had nosebleeds all his life. I think his dad gets them too." He put a hand on my shoulder and looked at me with gravity. "Are you okay? Not getting super squigged out, are you? Or figuring we're more hassle than we're worth?"

"Fuck no. I'm upset that we had to stop our scene. I, uh, didn't actually mind being so vulnerable. I was enjoying myself."

"Oh yeah?"

"Yeah. Couldn't wait to see what he had planned for you."

"Is that so?" Gideon said, gazing at me with a familiar look in his eyes. Then he looked over my shoulder.

"Here he comes."

I followed Gideon's gaze and saw Vihaal walking toward us. He looked exhausted and displeased.

White packing gauze bulged out of one nostril with a string hanging down. He was carrying his coat and a bunch of papers. Gideon and I walked to meet him.

"I'm so sorry. I look disgusting." His voice sounded even stranger now and he did look ridiculous. But he was still Vihaal and the Dom vibe was still there, somehow.

"It's not that bad," Gideon said. He took Vihaal's coat. "Are you free to go?"

"Yes. At least we can go home. I'm so sorry about all of this."

"Hey, you know what, V?" Gideon said, with a grin. "Sometimes it's good to remember you're human."

"Very funny." He gazed sheepishly at me. "How are you doing, Angel? Fed up with us, yet?"

"Nah. You won't get rid of me that easily."

"Well, then. Let's go home, shall we?"

* * * *

"Oh my God, it was horrible. Blood everywhere. It wouldn't stop!" I said, describing the scene in the Bordello to Jacob and Sebastian, at a lunch spot in the Byward Market the next day.

"Sucks that it was right as things were getting good," Sebastian said.

"Yes! I was raring to go and then—blam! Bright red blood on V's face. I didn't know what was happening."

"Sebastian and I have discussed installing some kind of sound-activated emergency call device. I think we're going to do it. That was a close call," he said. "We did warn the cleaner."

"Yeah, I don't think there was much on the floor. But we got out of there so quickly, I don't know."

Jacob and Sebastian glanced at each other. It looked like they were trying not to smile.

"What?" I asked.

"You, uh, call Vihaal, 'V', do you?" Jacob asked.

I blushed. *Dammit.* "Sometimes."

"Well," Sebastian murmured. "That is just adorable."

"It's Gideon's nickname for him. I kind of picked it up. Anyway, it's easier to say than Vihaal."

"And quicker," Sebastian said, with a leer. "'Oh, V, can you pass me the poppers?'"

"They don't use poppers," I said, giving Sebastian a critical look. I'd only recently learned what poppers were, and why some people liked them.

"Okay. Then, 'V, can you pass me the cock ring? So I can stay nice and hard for you?'"

"Honestly, how old are you guys? Wait. Do you guys use poppers?"

Jacob started laughing.

"Sometimes," Sebastian admitted. "Never mind."

"I think it's wonderful that you three are, uh, getting along so well," Jacob said.

I nodded. "Yeah, it is. Anyway, V's—*Vihaal* is miserable right now because he's got gauze stuffed way far up his sinus cavity. I feel so bad for him," I said, taking another gulp of my beer. "Anyway, the packing comes out day after next."

"That's good," Jacob said, watching me carefully. He took a French fry from the plate we were sharing. "Things are getting serious between the three of you."

I traced a crack in the top of the Formica tabletop with my finger. "I mean. Yeah. I think so."

"So, are you calling yourself bi, or pan, or gay now?"

"Fuck if I know. Definitely not straight."

"Have you, uh, you know... How far have you gotten?" Sebastian asked.

I blinked. "Sebastian, really? Are you trying to find out if someone's popped my cherry? Is that the initiation?"

Sebastian held up his hands. "Sorry, sorry. That was inappropriate. And no, that doesn't matter." He cleared his throat. "Penetration isn't the definition of sex. Especially queer sex."

"Trust me, I felt properly 'initiated' the day that I kissed them."

"Awe!" Sebastian said, glancing at Jacob. "That's so cute!"

"Oh, stop it. It's not cute. It's fucking amazing. They're so fucking hot I don't know what to do with myself."

"Looks like you don't have to do *anything* with yourself," Jacob joked, leering.

I rolled my eyes. "Very funny."

"Look, we're thrilled about this. Can't you tell?" Jacob said.

"Yeah. We told them you were worth the effort," Sebastian said.

"Wait. How long have they been...like...thinking about me that way?" I asked, intensely curious.

"Oh Christ, since that day we introduced you to them at Johnny Farina's. Remember?"

It took me a minute. "Oh fuck, that was *ages* ago!"

"They've been pining."

"No, they haven't."

"Oh yeah. We told them you were probably straight but that there might be some wiggle room. If anyone could find it, it was those two."

"Wow," I said, well and truly stunned.

Christ, they *had* been courting me.

* * * *

Vihaal had to put up with the nose packing for two days. Gideon fussed over him when he wasn't at work and got angry when Vihaal pushed him away. It was apparent that Vihaal did not like being in such a vulnerable condition, preferring to look after himself. But Gideon couldn't help himself, especially since he was trained to be a support person.

I had to spend some time at my place anyway, as I had client meetings and didn't want to be a disturbance, but I did offer to drive Vihaal to have the packing removed, since Gideon would be at work at the time of his appointment.

"You didn't have to do this, Angel. I could have driven myself."

"Oh no. You're supposed to have someone bring you," I reminded him.

He flashed me a look. "You always do things by the book, don't you?"

"Not always," I said, giving him a look. "But when it comes to your health, I do."

Vihaal sighed.

"You know," Vihaal murmured, staring out of the window, "Jacob once told me that you find out the true mettle of people during a crisis."

I nodded. "That makes sense."

He regarded me soberly.

"What?" I asked, glancing at him as I drove.

"I've missed you, Angel."

"What?" I said, laughing. "It's been two days."

"I know."

I glanced over and he was regarding me with a wistful expression. With his nose packed, he looked like a love-struck, accident-prone, kid. My heart about melted.

"I missed you guys, too. My cats, however, were thrilled to have me home."

"Oh yes. What are their names again?"

"Toff and Rummy."

"Adorable. I bet you are a wonderful cat dad," Vihaal stated.

"I mean, lately...I've been neglecting them. Because I've been so caught up with you two," I admitted. "Thank goodness they can keep each other company."

Vihaal hummed. "I hate to take you away from them. But I enjoy having you stay with us. Very much."

"Yeah?"

He grinned. "Yeah."

I sat in the waiting room of the ENT's office for a half hour while they tended to Vihaal. Eventually, he came out of the office with more papers.

At least his nose looked normal now. But his face had gone a bit sallow.

"You okay?"

"I think so. Despite the fact that I almost passed out during that vile..." He shuddered. "Procedure."

"Oh no!"

"Doctor said it's not uncommon."

I gave him a curious glance.

He shook his head. "You really don't want to know the details."

"Okay, then."

"I hope I never have to go through it again." He held up a small box. "The doctor gave me this spray that I can try if I have another bad one. It might work and it's a lot easier than going to the ER." Vihaal put the little box in his pocket and got out his phone. "And I have about fifteen texts from Gideon. He's mad because I haven't been answering them."

"You want me to let him know we're done?" I asked.

"Thank you."

Vihaal went to speak to the receptionist while I got out my phone and texted Gideon.

V is done. The packing is out.

Why isn't he answering me???

He was having the packing removed?

All fucking morning?

He said he almost passed out.

Omg. Shocked face.

Doc said that's common. He's okay now. Just a bit grumpy.

eye-roll emoji. I hope we can go back to the Bordello soon. We all need a bit of a stress relief. And to finish what we started.

Yes!

Vihaal was advised to forgo any strenuous activity for a week after the incident. They were both glad to have me return to the house. Vihaal was in a better mood, at least, until the end of the required sex fast. On the last day of his week-long abstinence, he came downstairs with his hair mussed and a determined look on his face.

He clapped his hands together when he saw Gideon and I watching the news.

"Okay. You and you," he said, pointing at each of us. "On the floor, getting busy. I want to see cocks in mouths and fingers in asses. Chop chop."

Gideon and I looked at each other then at Vihaal.

"What?" I said.

"But you're not supposed to —" Gideon began.

"Yes, exactly. Which is why you and Angel will be doing all the work. *On each other*." Vihaal sat himself in the armchair and looked at us expectantly. "Well? What are you waiting for?"

"But…this is going to turn you on, V," Gideon said.

"Yes, I'm sure it will."

"And you're going to want to join in. And the instructions clearly say —"

Vihaal put a hand to his head. "I know what the instructions say. What they *don't* say is that I can't sit in a chair and watch my two partners get each other off."

"Well, no, it doesn't say that," Gideon admitted. "But —"

"Gideon," Vihaal said, in a tone that we both knew well. "If you don't start doing something sexual with Angel in a moment, I'm going to put you over my lap for a spanking. And I think *that* would count as a vigorous activity, wouldn't it?"

"V, we're not in a fucking scene right now," Gideon said. "You can't just come down here and demand that we start going at it." He crossed his arms over his chest. "So rude."

Vihaal looked at me. I mean, I was game for it. But I could also see Gideon's point.

"I mean, yeah," I said.

"I'm sorry. I don't know what's wrong with me," Vihaal said, putting his head in his hands.

Gideon's expression softened. "Oh, V. I don't think you've ever been forced to abstain before."

"No. It's cruel and horrible."

"Anyway, you could have just asked," Gideon said, his eyes softening.

Vihaal nodded, then lifted his head from his hands.

"Do you think," he said, gazing back and forth between us. "That the two of you could perhaps do something incredibly depraved together…that I can watch? Please?"

I'd never seen Vihaal looking so contrite.

He continued. "It would mean the world to me."

Gideon stepped forward and leaned down, bracing his hands on Vihaal's parted thighs, and meeting his gaze.

"Has there been any more bleeding? Tell the truth."

"No. None. I promise."

"And you're feeling okay?" Gideon asked.

"My nose feels great. My dick and balls, on the other hand…"

Meanwhile, amused by Vihaal's desperation and, to be frank, not a little pent up myself, I ogled Gideon's ass. He was wearing a pair of baby blue yoga pants that hung low on his hips. I'd always been an ass man. Now I was even more of one.

I had already gotten up from the sofa. I moved in behind Gideon and laid my palm on his cloth-covered ass cheek.

He swiveled his head as my gaze met Vihaal's.

"What the fuck are you doing?"

I took my hand away and smiled.

Vihaal chuckled.

"Nothing," I mumbled.

"Don't play innocent with me, you depraved fuck," Gideon said, deadpan. Then he winked. "Pull down my pants and get busy."

"There you go," Vihaal said.

Gideon turned to face him as I slid my fingers under the waistband of the yoga pants.

"Settle down," Gideon told Vihaal. "Don't you dare move from that spot, and if I see any fucking blood, we're calling this off."

It was hilarious to see Gideon making threats and demanding obedience, as Vihaal sat placidly in the chair. Talk about a role reversal.

For me to take the initiative was unprecedented, but I was absolutely ready.

"Go for it, baby," Gideon said, giving his hips a wiggle.

"Does anyone mind if I take over the direction of this little détente? Safewords are available," Vihaal said, getting comfortable.

"Hmm," Gideon agreed. "Somehow I doubt they will be necessary."

"Unless I get another nosebleed."

"Oh fuck, you'd better not. I don't know what I'll do if—" Gideon gasped as I pulled his yoga pants down to his thighs.

"No underwear?" Vihaal gasped. "Cheeky."

I stared at the globes of Gideon's ass and smiled. "Very."

"Give him a slap, will you? I need to hear that sound."

Gideon wiggled again. "Do it, Angel. *Hard,*" he said.

I gave him a playful slap then a stronger one right after. Oh, hell yes. I did it again, watching his ass jiggle and the rosy mark my hand left.

Gideon moaned and surged forward, his mouth finding Vihaal's. Vihaal's fingers slipped into Gideon's hair as he devoured him with a searing kiss, the sounds of their breathing loud in the room.

I could have stared at Gideon's ass for an hour, especially now that it had my pink handprint on it. But the mark was fading, and instead of putting it there again, I leaned forward, licking and kissing the warm skin of Gideon's behind, as he lost himself to Vihaal's kiss.

He smelled amazing and tasted even better. He widened his stance and arched his back.

Vihaal kept Gideon in place and plundered his mouth like he'd never stop. The sounds of breathing and the slurping of tongues and lips had taken over. I was hard and desperate as I spread Gideon's ass and licked along his crease.

His reaction was everything I'd hoped for.

He made a frantic sound and broke away from Vihaal to curse, then Vihaal coaxed him back, reaching for Gideon's erection.

"Oh fuck," Gideon mumbled against Vihaal's mouth, as I licked him everywhere I could reach—his balls, the base of his cock, his sweet, small hole. He tasted of soap and tangy sweat, and his own particular essence.

"Oh, fuck yes," Vihaal muttered, breaking away from the kiss and bringing Gideon forward, to tongue his nipples and play with his cock, while I kept up the ass-eating.

"You're not..." Gideon gasped, "supposed to be...involved, V."

"Oh, for fuck's sake, I'm fine. Besides, I think Angel has found something he likes."

I groaned against Gideon's wet skin and pushed my tongue against his hole, then swiped it up and down his crease, holding his cheeks wide.

"Strip, Angel. I want to see you." Vihaal ordered.

I pulled my face off Gideon with some reluctance. I stroked a finger over his glistening hole, then tore off my clothes in record time, throwing them to the floor.

"He's been waiting for you to fuck him. A long time," Vihaal said.

"Has he?" I already knew that. Today was his lucky day, then.

"Mmm," Vihaal breathed. "Do it now. Right over my lap. Just the way we are right now."

My cock jerked at the thought of it. All of a sudden, every glance and silent message I'd ever received from strange and familiar men over the course of my life flashed through my mind. Why had I never explored this side of myself? Laziness? Cowardice? A blind obedience to the thing I imagined society expected from me?

"You don't have to," Vihaal reminded me.

But it was too late.

"Are you kidding me?" I said, stroking Gideon's lower back. "I think it's about time I did, don't you?" I glanced at Vihaal. "Lube?"

He grinned, excitement shining in his eyes. "Side table drawer."

Thank God. The last thing I wanted to do was run upstairs, naked and hard, to get some.

Vihaal took Gideon's mouth again, at the same time teasing his cock and squeezing his balls, making Gideon cry out and curse and moan with excitement.

"Hurry, Angel. He needs you."

"Yes, Vihaal," I said.

I found the bottle of lube and brought it to where Gideon was hunched over Vihaal's lap, his legs spread and his ass pushed out for me. I slicked myself up, while Vihaal pulled away from the kiss and stroked Gideon's face with the utmost tenderness.

"I'm going to enjoy watching," he murmured.

"Don't you always?" I said, giving him a look.

Once my dick was nice and wet, I swiped some over Gideon's hole and got down to business. I spread his cheeks and bumped the head of my cock at his entrance, thankful for the handful of women who had been willing to give me some practice. But nothing could have prepared me for how it felt to slip inside the man I'd been getting to know over the past few months.

"Oh...fuck...me..." I muttered, the pleasure going to my head and making me dizzy. The intimacy of this act, with someone I admired and...yeah, probably loved...affected me deeply, even as the familiar sensations of it took me over.

From the look of unadulterated lust on Vihaal's face, and the sounds issuing from Gideon, the feeling was mutual.

"Oh fuck. Fuck," Gideon moaned, clutching Vihaal's biceps as he bounced off his chest in time with my thrusts. "Angel..."

Hearing my name from those cherished lips, and feeling Gideon's body surround me — it was everything I'd ever wanted. Why had I waited so long to fuck this beautiful man?

"Harder, Angel. Wreck me. I want Vihaal to see you pound me. Please..." he gasped, malleable and so fucking sexy.

My brain shut off and my body took over. I gave Gideon what he'd asked for. I met Vihaal's gaze as I realized the significance of what was happening.

Vihaal gripped Gideon's hips and held him steady. "Jerk your cock, Deo. Come all over me."

"Oh, V. Fuck. *Jesus*. Yes, yes, *yes*." Gideon took his cock in hand and jerked it, as I fucked him quick and hard, my eyes rolling back from the bliss of it.

He made a choking noise, then a loud wail as he came, his ass squeezing me as his body spasmed.

"That's it, my Angel. Fill this slut up with your spunk. *Own him*," Vihaal grunted, his face a picture of rampant desire and heady voyeuristic enjoyment. "I want to watch your face when you come."

He grabbed my chin and held me as I slammed against Gideon, his intense gaze boring into mine. I cried out as the orgasm took over, stuttering gasps and groans as I emptied my balls.

As the waves of pleasure lessened, and my movements slowed, I noticed that Gideon had his head buried in Vihaal's lap and was sucking his cock. I looked at Vihaal's ecstatic face as Gideon brought him over the edge.

The sturdy armchair creaked in protest, my heart pounded, and the grandfather clock counted time as we recovered.

Chapter Twenty-One

Life went back to normal, if that word could be used to refer to my wonderful existence. I still felt daily wonder at what it had become.

I divided my time between their place and mine, with weekly visits to see my mother—who always asked about them—and occasional get-togethers with Jacob and Sebastian. My life was full and I'd never felt so grounded.

The guest room had become my home-away-from home at Gideon and Vihaal's, where I kept a few things and which I used as an office if there was too much going on downstairs. But I slept in the main bed.

We'd spoken about the possibility of making it a more permanent arrangement, but my cats had to be taken into account. Gideon didn't seem to think that would be a problem, and I got the impression he was excited at the thought of it. But I wasn't sure about Vihaal, who enjoyed his meticulously clean and tidy home.

And, to be honest, it was nice to have my own place, where I could walk around and do nothing, stare out of the window, or sit in a favorite corner and read a book, without the distraction of the two men with whom I'd fallen head-over-heels. I had my little corner of the world that was mine and mine alone, and it was a conscious decision to share our time together. It worked well for us and I couldn't see it changing anytime soon. Although I did feel guilty about being away from the cats so much.

My blue Sonata was a joy to drive, and I was more motivated to gain new clients. With the versatility of online work, I could get stuff done no matter where I was sleeping.

Vihaal didn't have a day job — an advantage of being independently wealthy. He was on some oversight boards at a couple of places, and he did do some volunteer work for an LGBTQ+ charity — mostly online.

And although Gideon worked part-time, his job was physical and demanding, so he was often tired when he got home.

"Hey, how was your shift?" I asked one afternoon when he came home and found me sitting in the living room, working on my laptop.

He sighed and kicked off his shoes.

"Busy. Tiring."

He padded over to me.

"What are you doing?" he asked.

"Oh, you know. Charts, numbers, financials."

"Blech."

I laughed. "You want a massage, baby?"

"Oh my God. Yes!" He gave me a look. "Like, a real massage. No funny business."

I laughed. "I promise. Where do you want to do it?"

"Your room? That way we don't have to disturb the main bed." He rolled his eyes. "You know how Vihaal is."

Vihaal made the bed every morning, and didn't appreciate it being disturbed until we went to bed in the evening. It was one of his little quirks, and it didn't bother me. But this was one situation where the guest bed came in handy.

We headed up there, and Gideon stripped off his scrubs.

"Oh shit. When did that happen?" I asked, gesturing to his caged cock.

He looked a bit guilty. "Well, I asked for it."

"You...you asked Vihaal to lock you up?"

"Yes."

"You like to be...in that thing?"

"Angel. You can call it what it is. It's a cock cage."

"Yeah, I know. Remember the first scene I watched in the Bordello?"

"Oh yeah." He sighed and looked down at himself. "How do I explain it to someone who's never tried it?"

"Oh fuck no. No way. That does not look fun to me."

"Oh, Angel. Just wait. I bet one day you'll give it a go."

"No more fucking bets, Deo. Come on."

He giggled and cupped his junk, admiring how it looked. He shrugged. "I like it when V has complete control of...all of me."

"I didn't realize you had to wear it to work."

"It's really not a big deal. You get used to it." He shrugged again. "It's only for a week this time."

My mouth opened. "A week!"

"Psht. Sometimes he has me in it for months. You know what a control freak he is," Gideon said, a dreamy look in his eyes.

I held up my hand. "Okay, I don't want to know. That's something you and he can play without me."

"Fine."

"Okay."

"Whatever."

"Good."

"Anyway, someone mentioned a massage?" He tugged a pillow to put under his hips and splayed himself out on the bed, propped on his elbows. He regarded me with curiosity. "Seriously, can you handle it?"

"Can I handle what?"

He wiggled his ass. "You know. Seeing all of this alluring flesh on display. Without going into a horny trance."

I grinned. He did look good, but I wasn't an animal. Not all the time, anyway.

"I'll do my best."

He snorted a laugh, then folded his arms and rested his head on its side, gazing at me lovingly. "Thank you for this. It was a shit day."

"No worries. What was shit about it?" I asked, pouring oil into my palms and rubbing my hands together. The scent of orange blossom and camphor filled my nostrils.

"Well, there was *actual* shit involved, but I won't go into that. I'm a professional. It was a lot of physical stuff and I'm fucking tired. You know?"

"Sure." I didn't half know how Gideon did that job, but I knew I wouldn't have been able to.

I rubbed the sweet-smelling oil into Gideon's shoulders and his upper back. The sounds he made reminded me of other times he'd made those noises, and I did get a bit hard. It was difficult not to, but I savored the arousal without looking for a solution to it.

The sound of the front door slamming startled me. I heard Vihaal muttering curses, then his hurried steps on the stairs.

"That fucking asshole. That fucking, duplicitous, *asshole.*"

"Oh God," Gideon moaned, and I wasn't sure if it was a good 'Oh God' or a bad one. He hid his face in his arms.

I turned to see Vihaal stride past the open door then backtrack.

"What the fuck is going on?"

"Massage," I said. "Gideon had a rough morning."

"A regular massage? Or a sexy one?"

"Does it matter?" Gideon asked.

"Not really. I'm just curious," Vihaal muttered.

He sighed, as if seeing us having a relaxing time was the *last* thing he needed.

"What's wrong?" I asked.

"I think my father sabotaged my antique store."

"Huh. Told you," Gideon said, his voice muffled.

"Yes, that makes me feel so much better," Vihaal said sardonically. "I'm going to call and fire that skank manager."

"Vihaal. You can't fire him over the phone," Gideon mumbled, then groaned as I dug my fingers into his calf. "Fuck, you're good at this."

"It's all the typing. Strong fingers," I said.

"You've been asking me to fire the bastard for years. Now you don't want me to?"

"Yes, fire him for God's sake. But do it in person. And preferably, with *me* there," Gideon said, then moaned again. "Oh, fuck me. This is better than sex."

"I think Alice would make a good replacement," I said, throwing it out there.

"Yes. I'm going to promote her. But we need to find someone to fill Alice's job," Vihaal said.

"Would you like me to draft a job posting?" I asked. "I'd be happy to."

"Yes, Angel, that would be wonderful. I'll email you the qualifications and requirements. Thank you."

"Oh my God, Angel. I'm in Heaven," Gideon moaned, lifting his head.

"Keep it down or I'm coming in there with a paddle," Vihaal said, but it didn't sound like a threat.

* * * *

The following evening, Vihaal drove us to Tarnish. He wanted an audience in case Dominic gave him any trouble.

"What do you think he's going to do, V? Hit you?"

"He'd better not go anywhere near this nose or I'll fucking flatten him."

"You would, too. Okay, Angel, we need to protect V's nose. I am not going through another out-of-control nosebleed."

"I didn't particularly enjoy it either," Vihaal muttered icily.

"Well, it was seriously gross. You're lucky we love you."

"Certainly."

Gideon glanced at me and rolled his eyes.

When we went inside the store, a young man with nerdy glasses and a nose piercing, in jeans and a white button down, welcomed us.

"Hello, Soresh. Is Alice here today?"

"Hey, Vihaal! Great to see you. Yes, she's in the back, talking to—" He adjusted his glasses and looked in the direction of the back office. "Well, *arguing*, with Dominic." He shrugged. "About *something*."

"Hmm," Vihaal said. "I'm here to speak to Dominic as it turns out. And afterwards, to Alice," Vihaal said. He cocked his head at Soresh. "How long have you been working here? I'm afraid time passes so strangely these days..."

"Oh, I've been here for about six months now. But I only work three days a week."

"Hmm. Are you interested in more hours?"

Soresh blinked. "Absolutely. Yeah."

Vihaal smiled. "I'd love you to work for me full-time. We can draw up the paperwork next week. Alice will let you know your exact schedule."

"Thank you. That's fantastic. Oh, wait...not Dominic?"

Vihaal only smiled. "Are there any customers in here?"

We couldn't see any but there were a couple of other rooms to the space.

"Not at the moment," Soresh replied.

"Excellent. Can I please get you to put a sign on the door that we are closed, and will reopen at the usual time tomorrow?"

"Yes. Of course," Soresh said, gazing back and forth between the three of us.

"Once I leave, please take the rest of the day off. You'll get paid for your entire shift, of course."

"Oh, okay. Thanks." Soresh gazed at me and Gideon, so many questions in his eyes.

"Come on, gentlemen," Vihaal said to us.

I thought about the conversation Vihaal had had with his father, and the things the man had said to him. It had taken three tumblers of good bourbon for V to open up. It seemed that his father was jealous of Vihaal's success and also angry that he hadn't married and provided grandchildren. The homophobic slurs that had wounded Vihaal over the phone had been vicious and Vihaal had ended up cutting off the call and severing all remaining ties. He was obviously deeply hurt, although he tried to shrug it off. I figured it would take a while for him to come to terms with the betrayal.

We followed him through the store to the back room, where we could hear Dominic and Alice arguing with rising irritation on both sides. The door was ajar. Alice could be seen standing with her hands on her hips and a fed-up expression on her face.

"The store has to be kept at that temperature and humidity for valid reasons, Dominic. You can't turn the furnace down because you're too hot. Roll up your sleeves or something."

"Do you have to be so fucking controlling? The furniture isn't that sensitive," Dominic muttered.

Alice saw us out of the corner of her vision. She turned and blinked in surprise.

"Vihaal. Dominic and I were just discussing temperature and humidity," she said. "Which is very important when it comes to antique furniture, wouldn't you say?"

"Hello, Alice. Yes, vitally important, in fact. Why?"

"Well, you see, Dominic keeps turning the temperature down because he's too hot. And I'm trying to convince him that that isn't a good idea," Alice said.

"As a matter of fact, I need to speak to Dominic."

Alice smiled. "Of course." She moved to leave, but Vihaal shook his head.

"Please stay."

She nodded and moved further into the room to give us space. Dominic gave a muttered curse and Vihaal went in, beckoning to us to follow. Dominic was sprawled behind the desk, his golf shirt stained and wrinkled. He was holding an antique coin of some kind and rolling it between his fingers.

"Vihaal," Dominic said, an undercurrent of irritation to his tone and hatred in his eyes as he stared at my lover. "Your father called me."

"Oh yes? And what did he tell you?"

"He said you'd probably be coming to fire me."

"How perceptive he can be when he tries," Vihaal said in a deceptively calm tone.

"He doesn't think you should, of course. Just that you probably would."

"Well, for once, my father is right. I'm here to tell you that I no longer need you as the manager of this store. You're fired as of this moment. You'll receive a settlement package that is very, *very* generous, considering my suspicions that you've been siphoning funds over the past several years."

"That's ridiculous," Dominic asserted. "You can't *prove* anything."

Vihaal's voice, when he spoke, was calm.

"I'm not trying to prove *anything*, Dominic. I don't have time to fuck around with lawyers and legal procedures. Even though a part of me does want to see you end up in jail, or forced to pay all the money back, I don't want to go through the hassle. You're not fucking worth my time."

Dominic looked at me. Then he looked at Gideon. Then he shook his head.

"This isn't fair. Your father wanted *me* in charge of Tarnish. I've taken good care of this store for so many years!" Dominic sputtered.

The sound of Alice's muffled laughter came from the hall.

"That's debatable," Vihaal stated. "But I don't have the time or the will to argue." Vihaal stepped back and motioned to the door. Gideon and I got out of the way.

"Get out. Now," Vihaal said. "I'll email you the settlement papers and a transfer of your final earnings."

Dominic stared at Vihaal, not moving. He looked at Gideon. He looked at me.

"Your father's right about you, you know."

"Dominic. If you don't get the fuck out of my store, I'm going to call the police." The tone of Vihaal's voice sent chills up and down my spine. He was magnificent. I was in awe of his command and presence, and the way his anger made him seem ten times as big as he was.

Dominic stood. "I need to get my things."

Vihaal only nodded. "You have five minutes."

"Are you going to stand there and watch me?"

"Yes."

I'd never seen Vihaal seethe with controlled rage before. As a Dom he was stern and strict, but never angry.

"Them too?" Dominic asked, gesturing to Gideon and me.

"Yes."

"For fuck's sake. You've got them well-trained."

"You have no fucking idea."

"Jesus Christ. No wonder your own father wanted you to fail."

Vihaal's expression didn't waver, but I saw the hurt in his eyes as Dominic kept talking.

"I don't even want to think about what the three of you do in private. I'm sure it's disgusting and perverted."

Vihaal gave a small nod. "So disgusting. And very perverted."

Dominic threw me a look and I glared back. Gideon snorted with derision. Vihaal was a thousand times the man Dominic was, and so was Gideon.

And, maybe I was, too.

"You're a fucking head case, Vihaal. I hope your father disowns you and stops giving you money."

"My father hasn't given me anything except a headache for the past ten years. And the headache's name is Dominic."

"Nice," Dominic commented, grabbing his briefcase.

"I need your laptop and all your passwords, Dominic."

"Oh, for fuck's sake." He opened the briefcase and handed his work laptop to Alice. We waited while he wrote down the passwords with an angry scrawl, then grabbed an umbrella, a pair of gloves and his jacket.

"Am I okay to take this stuff, or are you going to confiscate them, too?"

"We'll escort you out," Vihaal stated.

"Fucking fine. Whatever," Dominic spat.

Alice looked shocked but not overly upset as Dominic strode past her.

"Alice, when we come back, we need to have a chat in the office. You might as well take a seat."

"Okay," she said, looking alarmed, but Gideon smiled at her and gave her a thumbs-up.

We followed Vihaal and Dominic through the main part of the store. Soresh watched with curiosity as Dominic carried his things out of the door, and Vihaal closed it behind him.

"We'll need to change the locks," Vihaal muttered.

"Good idea," Gideon agreed.

"And cancel his security code."

"Alice will know what to do and who to contact," Gideon said.

"Yes. I'm going to ask if she wants to be Manager. I'm certainly hoping she does."

"We'll just hang here," Gideon said. "You did amazing. It was so satisfying to watch. I almost came in my pants."

A laugh burst out of me at Gideon's comment and Vihaal smiled.

"It was satisfying to do it. You have good instincts, Gideon."

"Yes. You need to remember that," Gideon said with an arched eyebrow.

Vihaal's smile broadened into a relieved, triumphant one.

"I'll do my best, from now on."

He tugged Gideon close and kissed him hard on the mouth, then pulled back.

"Do you know how much I owe you, my love, for...everything that you give to me, that you do for me? And you," he said, grabbing me into the hug.

"Where on Earth did you come from and how did you end up with us?"

"Um, that was me," Gideon said, smugly. "Again. See?"

I held on to them both, not worried about Soresh seeing us, because it was who we were, and what we wanted. And this was Vihaal's store, and he was everything.

I saw him glance at the young employee before he leaned in and kissed me, then whispered in my ear. "You are the best thing to happen to us in ages, Angel. I hope you realize that."

"V," I muttered, choked up. "Really?" I looked at Gideon. "But…"

"But what? Don't argue with me."

I didn't.

Vihaal let us go. He stepped back, and it looked like he wanted to say something else. Then he sighed and grinned.

While Vihaal was speaking to Alice and offering her a promotion and a raise, Gideon and Soresh showed me around the store. I'd never been in the place long enough to have a good look at all the incredibly valuable furniture and sundry other items, so it was a thrill to be able to walk around for a bit. There were lamps and bed frames and textiles and fine wooden escritoires, wardrobes and dining hutches. There was even a section with antique bicycles and clothing.

"That's how we got to know Sebastian and Jacob," Gideon explained. "We helped them gather what they needed for the club. And we recommended a seamstress, who we hire to repair things before we put them up for sale, to make the bloomers and chemises. The corsets and leather shoes are *actual* antiques, though. We generally have enough of them in stock in to find the perfect fit."

He gestured to a rack that held a selection of shoes just like the ones the molly boys at Maverick Molly's wore. Some were brown and some were black, some had buttons and others laces. But they were all authentic.

"Oh, wow," I said, moving closer to a piece of furniture that had caught my attention. It was an antique wooden armoire—mahogany, most likely— with scrollwork details and etched vines all over the front. "That's gorgeous."

"You like that?" Soresh said. "It only came in last week. But, yes, it's so lovely."

I stepped forward and turned over the tag that was hanging on the tiny black knob. And almost passed out.

"Jesus. That's...expensive."

Gideon smiled. "Well, you won't find anything like it anywhere else. And it'll last another lifetime, I wager."

I laughed. "It's too rich for me."

There was no way I was spending upwards of five thousand dollars on a piece of furniture I didn't actually need. Even if the stunning piece made my heart ache when I imagined how lovely it would look in my living room.

Soresh didn't seem perturbed to have seen Vihaal, Gideon and I kissing earlier, and pointed out quite a few interesting objects. He seemed to know what he was doing, and had an expressive way of speaking about the things he showed us. I was glad that he would be working here full time, now that Dominic was out. Assuming, of course, that Alice would want to take over as manager.

We needn't have worried. Alice was thrilled to be offered the position, and relieved to be rid of Dominic, even though she'd had no clue he'd been trifling with the accounts.

"That little *shit!*" she said, whenever his name was brought up. "I knew he was an ass, but I had no idea he was doing anything so brazen!"

"Well, my father, who is the one who basically appointed Dominic to the position, back when I actually *cared* what my father thought, admitted that he'd tried to sabotage me."

"Vihaal! My God!" Alice said, putting a hand to her chest. "That's terrible."

"My father *is* terrible. Seems I keep forgetting, and giving him the benefit of the doubt. Never again."

I remembered what I'd learned about Vihaal's stint at boarding school and his mother's attitude toward him when she'd learned of his lifestyle.

"Will he keep trying to ruin your life, do you think?" Gideon asked, running his fingers along the edge of an upholstered settee.

"He can try as much as he likes. I won't let him." Vihaal shrugged. "After the things he said to me, he's lucky I don't try to get revenge. But I'm not that kind of a person."

"Vihaal, can I talk to you for a second?" Gideon asked, beckoning Vihaal over and proceeding to walk with him to the armoire I had so vocally admired.

"Oh fuck," I said, glancing at Soresh, who looked excited.

When Vihaal and Gideon looked in my direction, I held up my hand.

"I only thought it was pretty. I'm sure someone will buy it for the price on the tag."

Gideon said something to Vihaal, and Vihaal smiled then nodded. He gazed at me.

"You want it, Angel?"

"I— What?" I said, my voice quiet. Was he suggesting what I thought he was suggesting?

He pointed to the mahogany armoire that was currently priced at exactly *five thousand, four-hundred and thirty-nine dollars.*

"Do you want it? It's yours, if you'll promise to look after it."

"Vihaal. No. I couldn't!"

He raised his eyebrows and turned to Gideon. "Methinks the lady doth protest too much."

Gideon walked up to me. He took my elbow and led me to the armoire.

"Touch it. Go on."

I looked at Gideon. I looked at Vihaal. I looked at Soresh then at Alice.

I turned back to the armoire and reached out, sliding my fingers along the varnished wood.

"Fuck," I said, very quietly. "V, you can't. It's too much."

"Nonsense. It's yours. Now come along, it's been a trying afternoon. I'll arrange for the service to have it delivered to your house next week."

"I—I—" I choked on my words.

"You're welcome. Now come on, I'm taking you both to supper." He gathered us with his outstretched arm as he looked over his shoulder at Alice.

"Make up a full-time schedule for Soresh, will you? And I'll have someone hired to be your assistant within a week."

"Thank you, Vihaal," Alice said.

Chapter Twenty-Two

Although we knew he was relieved to have got rid of Dominic, and excited about growing the business with Alice and Soresh, Vihaal was subdued over the next couple of weeks. Learning that his father had deliberately put someone in charge of his business to undermine it, and steal from him, must have been a sobering thing. Not to mention the terrible things that had been said.

Luckily, our number came up at Maverick Molly's. The Saturday evening we'd booked came around, and we were determined to make up for our interrupted session. Vihaal wanted to pick up exactly where we'd left off, so I found myself once again bound, spread-eagled, on the St. Andrew's cross, naked except for the braided cock ring.

Flashes of the way Vihaal's face had looked that day, with blood pouring out of his nose, came back to me, but I forced it from my mind. It was unlikely to happen again in the exact same circumstances in which it had occurred before.

Vihaal had been to a follow-up appointment and the assessment was that everything looked good, and that what had happened had been one of those rare events that life was full of. Vihaal had brought the nose spray with him, just in case.

I was surprised that none of the staff made any comments or jokes regarding what had happened, but seeing as we'd ended up at the hospital, they probably figured it was a sensitive topic. Maybe Sebastian had warned them not to mention it. The event had been upsetting but easily resolved, thank goodness.

I was back on the cross, just as I'd been that fateful day. However, it seemed that Vihaal had something else in mind for Gideon.

Vihaal had moved the stocks and the padded bench to the wall to create space. He had just spent thirty minutes wrapping Gideon in red ropes, lashing his arms together behind his back and knotting them around his chest. Then he'd run the rope up to a metal ring that hung from the ceiling, and now Gideon was held in place with one knee bent and wrapped with rope to the thigh, so that he was standing on the ball of one foot, balanced by the ropes that held him upright. If he lifted that foot, he'd start to spin or sway, so he kept it on the ground, ready for whatever indignity Vihaal had in mind.

Vihaal had gagged him, too, with a thick band of black silk that looked incredible between Gideon's pink lips. Gideon blinked, his soft eyes gazing at me with a satisfaction that could not be denied. He seemed at home in the ropes, clutching in his hand a round bell that Vihaal had instructed him to drop if he needed to safeword.

"Now that's a trussed-up boy, just the way I like him," Vihaal murmured, winking at me over Gideon's shoulder. "My, my, my. Whatever have I done to deserve this? Two beautiful men at my mercy."

Gideon made a noise and Vihaal slapped his ass, making him sway and start to spin, except that Vihaal stopped the motion with a hand on Gideon's pale hip. I loved the way Vihaal's darker complexion contrasted against Gideon's lightness.

"Let's start with some finger fucking, shall we?"

Vihaal, naked except for a pair of dress pants, grabbed a black nitrile glove from a box and tugged it on. Gideon jerked in the ropes, almost losing purchase. He closed his eyes as Vihaal squeezed lube from a bottle into his hand.

I licked my lips, my mouth going dry as Vihaal's hand disappeared and Gideon made a drawn-out groan. The muscles of Vihaal's forearm strained as he showed Gideon exactly what he'd meant.

Gideon grunted and groaned, as Vihaal's gaze met mine.

"He's beautiful like this, isn't he?"

"Yes, Vihaal," I said.

Gideon was stunning in the ropes, soft and vulnerable and offering himself to us in this way, and I couldn't get over it. How lucky we were, and how strong Gideon was to be able to do it. And how far I'd come in the space of a few months.

Vihaal reached forward with his ungloved hand and lifted Gideon's chin as he continued to finger him.

"Look at Angel, Gideon. He's watching you. Watching me have my way with you. Can you tell that he loves it?"

Oh, they could tell I was entranced with them. My cock was hard, my body stiff in its bindings as my muscles clenched and unclenched at the sight before me. Gideon's eyes were dark and full of desire.

Vihaal ran his hand down Gideon's throat and over his chest, rubbing at a nipple as he passed. He cupped his hand over Gideon's caged cock and jiggled it roughly. Gideon made a sound of frustration against the gag.

"Poor baby. Can't get hard. Even as I tease you from the inside out. Poor, poor, thing," Vihaal murmured with mock sympathy, tracing his fingers over Gideon's trussed balls and along his inner thighs.

Vihaal met my gaze again and gave Gideon a few more thrusts with his fingers, then withdrew them. He walked over to a table where he had placed the things he needed.

A surge of arousal took me as he picked up the shiny metal instrument, shaped like a hook, with a medium-sized ball on one end. He brought it to where Gideon hung from the rafters.

"Ready, my boy? You're going to like this," Vihaal said, pressing the object against Gideon's hip so that Gideon could get a sense of what it was. Gideon's eyes widened. He groaned as Vihaal slid the implement along his skin, teasing him.

Gideon had waxed poetic about the anal hook in some discussions we'd had about what he and Vihaal liked to do together, and how fond Gideon was of being subdued and defiled by whatever toy Vihaal decided to use. This one was a favorite.

"Mmm, you ready to be captured like a slippery and helpless trout, while Angel watches from up there?"

Gideon made desperate sounds, his gaze finding mine, then darting away. Perhaps the humiliation of me watching was too much.

But he didn't drop the bell. He didn't safeword.

Vihaal took his time, rubbing the cold metal ball against Gideon's hole, putting pressure on it, then sliding it back and forth, teasing the hell out of his desperate supplicant.

Finally, he spread Gideon with one thumb and pressed the ball of the hook firmly against Gideon's hole, until Gideon gasped and it started to sink in. A sheen of sweat glimmered over Gideon's brow, and his hair stuck to his head around his ears, where the silk gag was tied.

Vihaal kept up the gentle pressure, and his gaze met mine with blazing intensity. I struggled in my bindings. I wanted to help, but I was kept from doing so.

Gideon's sphincter stretched impossibly wide to admit the steel ball. As Vihaal kept up a steady pressure, it slowly disappeared until in one quick movement, Gideon's ass swallowed it up. I couldn't even describe the noises he made.

"Good boy. Such a good little slut." Vihaal wiggled the cruel-looking device to make sure the ball was firmly in place.

"There. That's in. Now…" he said, grabbing another length of the red rope.

I watched as Vihaal looped the rope through a hole in the handle, then tied it to the ring to which Gideon's wrists were bound. This would keep the hook in place and free Vihaal's hands for other tasks.

"There now," Vihaal said, pleased with his handiwork. "Just a piece of sexy meat now, aren't you?"

Gideon mumbled something against the gag.

Vihaal barked a laugh. "And you can't even speak. Completely at my mercy. Just the way you like it."

Gideon whimpered as I fought my restraints. I'd never witnessed anything so arousing in my life. Gideon, his pale flesh bulging between the red ropes, his body pierced by a metal ball and hook, his mouth split by the black gag, and his will overridden by the focus of one man.

Except for the bell, Gideon had no power here. No, that wasn't true.

Vihaal was laser-focused on Gideon right now, and I was convinced that if Gideon showed any signs that he wasn't getting off on this, that Vihaal would check in, or stop, or change the course of his plans. I trusted Vihaal, Gideon trusted Vihaal, and Vihaal trusted *us* to communicate if something was wrong.

But as of this moment, everything seemed very, very right.

"Now," Vihaal said. "I need to see if Angel is paying close attention to what I'm doing."

Fuck, can't he see that I'm riveted?

I struggled as he approached. What would he do? I tried to get away, even though I knew it was useless and I didn't want saving.

The shame was there, but it was a decadent and daring treat, swirling in my belly like a fish that had escaped its tiny pond, and could thrash and leap with a strange kind of glory.

"Are you paying attention?" Vihaal asked, in that growly Dom voice he used in this room, and sometimes other places.

He wrapped his slick fingers around my cock and stroked me, hard and fast, while I made helpless noises. He could have brought me off that moment if he'd kept going, but he didn't. Just as I started to think he meant to get me there, he let go and I was left hanging, in mid-air, as misery choked me.

"*Please*," I moaned.

And Vihaal laughed.

"It's too soon. And I want you to watch what I'm going to do next. Because soon it will be your turn."

My eyes widened. *My turn for what?* I gaped at the metal hook in Gideon's body.

"Not with the hook, don't worry. I'm saving that for some unspecified date in the future, when you beg me for it."

And I would, I was sure of it.

"You're going to help me fill that slut with spunk," Vihaal muttered.

Gideon made a strangled sound as my ears started to ring.

"Settle down," Vihaal said to Gideon.

He came back to me and stroked my cheek. "I'm going to fuck him with the hook inside him. Then I'm going to fill him up, and then *you're* going to do it. And then…then I might let Gideon come. I haven't decided yet."

He gazed into my eyes, still stroking my cheek with his gloved hand.

"Can you fuck Gideon that way? Hmm? Do you think you can do that for me? He's been such a *good boy*."

Fuck yes, I can. I nodded. "Yes, Vihaal."

He slapped my cheek gently, enough to startle me, and gave me a smug look. "Figured you could. You're such a people pleaser. And I love it when you want to please *me* in particular."

"I do want to please you, Vihaal. So much."

"I know. Watch now, because when doing this sort of thing, one has to be very careful and gentle. We don't want to hurt Gideon, do we?"

"No, Vihaal."

"All right. Then watch."

I did. I saw Vihaal ease his cock into Gideon alongside the metal of the hook. I watched Gideon's frantic eyes go side to side above the gag, and his breathing stutter, and his cheeks flush.

When he was well seated, Vihaal met my gaze. "So warm. So tight. So perfect."

He made short, slow thrusts, and Gideon groaned, his eyes rolling back in his head. More fluid pushed out of his captured cock and strung from the bars of the cage in gossamer threads.

"You all right, my sweet?" Vihaal asked, making soothing motions on Gideon's hip with his thumb.

Gideon nodded frantically.

"Fuck, yes, you are. You're fucking incredible," Vihaal said, keeping up his shallow thrusts. "Oh fuck, fuck, fuck. You feel amazing. Am I making the ball move, Deo? Is it rocking inside you?"

Gideon gasped and nodded.

"My cock bumps it every time. That heavy ball in your guts," His breath came in gasps and his thrusts into Gideon sped up. He was careful not to thrust too far, but his movements sped up—short, quick thrusts—

as he held on to Gideon and made soft sounds of enjoyment.

Gideon groaned and cursed against the gag, and Vihaal uttered a soft, vulnerable cry as he climaxed.

I almost came too, watching it happen, and seeing Vihaal's tense muscles contract and tremble as he emptied into Gideon.

"That's so good," Vihaal said, as he continued to pump in and out. "It's Angel's turn now, my sweet little Deo. We're going to fill you up with it, and if you're very good and don't complain, I'll think about taking that cage off and have you finish."

Gideon whimpered, his breaths coming at a frantic pace, chest moving back and forth, as Vihaal cleaned himself and fastened his pants, then walked toward me.

He kept stealing incendiary glances at my face as he worked on my bindings and I had to catch my breath. He helped me down and led me behind Gideon.

"Look at this," Vihaal said, spreading Gideon and teasing his hole, as white spunk trickled out.

"Sink your cock into that lusciousness. Just go slow and be careful. Shallow. Don't move the ball too much."

"Yes, Vihaal."

I'd never done something so depraved but so fucking sexy. I watched my cock move in and out of Gideon, alongside the steel hook. In my heightened state of arousal, and with Vihaal holding the implement to keep it still, I climaxed quickly and hard, struggling to stand as the delicious throbs undid me.

"Oh, fuck yes," Vihaal muttered. "Now he's full of it. Soft and sticky and sweet. Sweetheart, you did so well," he said to Gideon, as he undid the rope holding the hook and tugged. Gideon groaned and leaned forward on the ropes as his hole stretched wide. The metal ball, shiny with fluid, came out in a rush. Milky white semen dripped onto the floor — mine and Vihaal's combined.

"Oh!" Vihaal frowned. "What a mess."

He passed me a soft towel. I half expected him to tell me to lick it up. I would have done it.

I wiped myself off, trying to calm my breathing, and watched Vihaal undo the catch on Gideon's cage. Even as he drew the metal contraption off, Gideon's cock erupted in his hand, spunk oozing in bursts, as Gideon gasped and choked on his groans.

"There you go, my darling," Vihaal crooned, holding his hand palm up beneath the head to catch some of it and let it drip obscenely through his fingers. "How lovely. And I barely had to touch you."

Then Gideon started sobbing, and I glanced at Vihaal for reassurance.

"He's all right," Vihaal said, as he gathered Gideon into his arms. "It was intense."

Yes. It had been.

He took Gideon out of the ropes and wrapped him in one of the robes from the clothing rack, bundling him up onto the bed for a cuddle. I got dressed and went to join them, crawling in between to kiss them and show them how grateful I felt to have been included.

Gideon clutched me close and whispered, "Thank you," over and over.

Chapter Twenty-Three

Gideon wanted to buy Vihaal a gift.

"That whole thing with Dominic and Vihaal's dad. It was a long time coming, but poor V. It's not fun to realize you've misplaced your trust in someone. In two people, actually."

"I think a gift is a great idea. You want to go to St. Laurent?"

"Nah. Let's go to Rideau. If we don't find anything there, we can check out some of those cute stores in the Market."

"Sure," I said. "I'll drive."

The Rideau Centre wasn't crowded, seeing that it was a Tuesday evening. We went into several shops, looking for just the right gift for the man who had everything.

"We could get him a gag gift," Gideon suggested.

"A sex toy?" I suggested.

"Hmm. But he has *us*."

I laughed. "True. Something to wear?"

"I don't know. Vihaal likes to pick out his own clothes."

"Tech?"

Gideon frowned. "Now hold on, I was thinking our budget would be a couple of hundred. I can't afford to buy him a laptop or a phone. Besides, he always gets himself the *best* stuff, and there's no way I can afford that."

We walked past a Laura Secord shop and Gideon put a hand on my arm.

"Wait, maybe an ice cream would help me think!" he said.

I got out my wallet. "You want me to get you an ice cream, little boy?"

"Jesus, Angel. Fuck. You just gave me a hard-on. In the Rideau Centre."

"Oh, what a shame. I'm so sorry," I said with mock concern. "You want one or not?"

"Please buy me an ice cream, Daddy!"

"Fine. What kind?"

"Vanilla, baby. That's my flavor."

"Wow, you are just full of surprises."

"I know!"

We sat on a bench and ate ice cream cones, watching people go by.

"This was a good idea," I admitted.

"Yep. So good."

"Okay, so a gift for V," I reminded him.

He shrugged. "Honestly, maybe this is a stupid idea. He's got the two of us. What else does he need?"

I laughed and shrugged.

Gideon sat up straight. "Wait, wait. That's it!"

"Huh?"

He stood and looked around for something. "Do they still have those cheesy portrait booths in malls these days?"

Oh! "Maybe?"

We finished our ice cream and went looking. And we found one.

"I don't fucking believe it. I would have thought these would have gone the way of phone booths," Gideon said.

"I guess they still make money."

"Oh shit. You got any coins?" he asked.

Turned out, the photo booth took credit. We went under the curtain, giggling like kids.

"Okay, okay. What do we want to do here?" I asked him.

"Let's do a sweet one, and two dirty ones, and a silly one."

"Fine."

"Okay."

By the time we left the booth, I thought I was going to piss my pants, we were laughing so hard. The photos were perfect. We looked like a couple of horny idiots in most, but the sweet one had turned out better than expected.

"Oh my God. He's going to cry!" Gideon said, with a hand to his heart.

"Vihaal?" I asked, doubtfully.

"You know he's a real softy underneath all of that restraint and bluster."

"Yes, but...has he ever cried?"

"You'd be surprised," Gideon remarked.

We argued about cards at the pharmacy but finally chose one, then used a pen at the bank to sign it, and sealed it into an envelope.

"All right," Gideon said, checking his phone. "I just got a text from Vihaal."

He frowned, reading it.

"Huh. Weird."

"What?"

Gideon looked up, a confused expression on his face. "He wants us to meet him at the Chateau Laurier."

"Right now?"

Gideon gazed at his phone again.

"Oh!" He chuckled, then gave me a mischievous look. "Yes. Right now. Come on."

"The Chateau Laurier? Are we having afternoon tea?" I remembered the tiny sandwiches and the first time Vihaal had kissed me.

Gideon shrugged and lifted his eyebrows. "Maybe?"

We left the Rideau Centre and crossed Sussex, then headed up the hill to the Chateau, passing tourists and business people who were headed West on Wellington Street.

"I've never even been to the Chateau Laurier. Not inside it, anyway," I admitted.

"Oh yeah? We come to see the Christmas trees over the holidays. And we've eaten at Wilfred's," Gideon confessed. "The architecture of the building is so beautiful. Vihaal's even supplied some of the furniture."

"That's so cool," I said.

The Chateau Laurier Hotel was a fixture in Ottawa. It was where all the official dignitaries stayed on their visits to the city, since it was directly beside the Parliament Buildings and a renowned destination in and of itself.

Walking into the expansive lobby through the revolving doors, I craned my head to look up to the second-floor balcony that edged the large space and wondered which famous people had stood in just this spot. I almost bumped into a woman coming from the elevator bay.

"Oh, I'm sorry," I apologized, looking up and into the eyes of Rebecca, my red-haired hook-up from the bar, what seemed a lifetime ago.

"Angel?" she asked. "What are you doing here?"

"Oh, hey!" I said. "We're just meeting a...friend."

"It's great to see you!" she said, glancing briefly at Gideon but focusing on me.

"Oh, yeah, thanks. It's nice to see you, too."

This is so fucking awkward. How do I make this not awkward?

She laughed and put up a hand. "Don't worry. I can take a hint, you know. I'm not going to ask you out again."

"Oh fuck," I said. "Thank God."

Then I realized how that sounded as Rebecca frowned. Gideon was trying hard not to laugh.

"I'm sorry. I didn't mean that the way it sounded."

"Really."

"Yeah, no, it's not that you're not cool. It's only that I've started seeing someone." I turned to Gideon. "This is my boyfriend, Gideon."

She blinked. "That's amazing! Hello!" She held out her hand and Gideon shook it.

"Hi," Gideon said with a grin.

She looked at me with real affection. "I'm so sorry I texted you all those times. I just...I had a good time that night, but I guess you were looking for something else."

"Yeah. Sorry."

"No, no. It's a good memory. Really."

"Yeah, well, it turns out I wasn't as straight as I thought," I said.

Gideon grinned. "But he was *exactly* as straight as I thought."

Rebecca examined Gideon, then looked at me. "I'm not surprised you switched sides."

I blushed.

"You should see our other—" Gideon started to say but I grabbed his wrist and pulled him along.

"It was nice to see you, Rebecca!" I said.

"We should go for coffee!" she yelled. "Platonically, of course!"

"Sure," I said. "Bye."

"Holy. Shit." Gideon muttered.

"Yeah. I wasn't expecting that."

"Anyway," Gideon said, ushering me toward the restaurant. "V told me to get a table at Wilfred's and order some drinks. He'll pay. He always does."

I followed Gideon, wondering what on Earth Vihaal was up to. Knowing him as I was learning to, it could be any number of things. My body went into anticipation mode.

As we entered the mostly empty dining room, I spotted a familiar person sitting at the bar.

"Hey, that's—"

Gideon grabbed my elbow.

"Shh. Pretend you don't see him."

"What the fuck?" I asked, lowering my hand. "Why?"

"Hello there," The well-dressed host greeted us. "Table for two?"

"Yes, please," Gideon replied.

We followed as she led us to a spot by the window.

"Is this all right?" she asked.

"Yes. This is perfect," Gideon said, motioning me to sit, which I did.

"A server will be with you momentarily."

"Thanks," I said.

When she'd gone, I glanced at the bar. I leaned forward.

"What's going on?"

Gideon stared at me for a moment, then blushed and looked down. When he glanced back up, his eyes were full of mischief.

"V and I like to play this game," he said.

"Oh no," I said, resisting the urge to look at Vihaal again. "I'm afraid to ask."

But it was a *good* kind of afraid — *a skin tingling, heart-beat-quickening, cock hardening* kind of afraid.

"Well...just play along, and you'll find out," Gideon said, checking his phone. "Oh."

"What?" I asked, my mouth going dry.

Gideon showed me his phone.

Order drinks.

My gaze flew to Vihaal before I could help myself, but he was in the same position, staring at his iPad, not looking in our direction.

He was dressed in a fancy suit, as if he'd just come from a stockholder meeting or something equally as important. But because of the way he was seated, his dress pants revealed socks with pictures of candy on them, which made me smile.

I turned back to Gideon. "Is this like a role play kind of thing? Do I need a fake identity?"

Gideon stared at me. "Yes, it's role play. No, you don't need a fake identity. We're *us*, he's *him*, but we're going to pretend we're a couple and we've never met V before. Can you do that?"

Can I do that? "Yes," I said.

"Excellent," Gideon said, as the server came and introduced himself.

"Can I get you gentlemen a drink?"

"Yes, thank you. I'll have a rye and Coke," he said. "Angel?"

"Oh, um, a rye and ginger, please."

"Back in a moment."

"So, what do we do?" I asked, once the server had gone. "Just have some sips of our drinks? Then what?"

"Don't worry, he'll text me instructions. I'm used to this but usually I'm on my own. This is the first time I've had a lover to bring him."

Oh hell. I was so on board with this already.

Our drinks arrived, and we sat there chatting about nonsense. Gideon looked down at his phone again.

"He wants us to come over."

"To the bar?"

"Yeah. Like, pretend we saw him and we want to introduce ourselves. As a prelude to, you know, *introducing ourselves.*"

"Jesus. You two have this down, don't you?"

"Yeah, it's fun. And super fucking hot."

"I'm getting that vibe."

"Ready?" Gideon asked.

"Wait," I said, downing the rest of my drink. "Now I'm ready."

Gideon stood and picked up his glass. I followed him to the bar, glad there weren't many people in the restaurant, and nobody at the bar but Vihaal.

When Gideon was close enough, he said, "Excuse me," and Vihaal looked up.

I grinned to let him know I was in on the joke. But he stared at me as if I was a complete stranger. As my smile faded, my cock swelled and fireworks started going off in my belly.

"Can I help you?" he asked, checking us over with an obvious interest.

"Oh, I really hope you can," Gideon replied. "My, uh, partner and I just came for a drink at this lovely hotel, but we don't know anything about Ottawa. We were hoping you could show us around...maybe starting with a room in this hotel." Gideon asked, with that cheeky way that I loved so much.

"But..." Vihaal stated, gaze moving back and forth between us. "I don't have a room."

Gideon grinned and sipped his drink, taking my hand in a subtle gesture that only Vihaal could see. "Maybe you should *get one*."

Vihaal's gaze roamed over him again, and he smiled. "The rooms here are very expensive."

"It'll be worth it. Trust me," Gideon said, stroking my fingers in a way that made it feel like he had his hand down my pants.

Vihaal regarded us carefully, as if he really was trying to judge whether paying for a room would be worth it. I leaned in and whispered in Gideon's ear, flashing a quick glance at Vihaal.

"What did your friend say?" Vihaal asked.

"He said we should tell you that we're extremely obedient. If that was something you might like."

Vihaal didn't say anything at first, but he pushed his drink away and shut his iPad case.

"As a matter of fact," Vihaal muttered, standing and looking us over even more overtly. "It's something I might like very much."

My body hummed with energy. I'd never done anything like this before, in a public place. It seemed risky and scandalous and very, very exciting.

"Wait here," Vihaal said.

"Yes, Sir," Gideon replied, and Vihaal smiled briefly then left us.

"Is he getting a room?" I asked.

"Fuck, I sure hope so," Gideon muttered. "You did great! Keep it up and we're going to have the *best* time!"

Vihaal came back with a room key and grabbed his jacket off the stool. "All right. I have a room. Perhaps we should introduce ourselves."

"Oh, fuck, yeah, that's a good idea. I'm Gideon, and this is Angel."

"Hi, Gideon. Hello, Angel." He frowned. "How old are you?"

"Oh, I'm not a day over twenty-two," Gideon lied, "and Angel just turned twenty-one."

My eyes went wide and I managed to hold in a laugh. In no universe did I look younger than Gideon. But this was so much fun.

Vihaal smiled. "I see. Well, I'm Vihaal, and I'm not a day younger than forty-eight. That's quite the age difference." His eyes sparkled with amusement as he chose a pretend age for himself.

"Yes," Gideon agreed. "We do hope you don't mind. And I, uh, hope you've had a recent physical. No heart problems?"

I almost did laugh and Vihaal smiled.

"No worries there."

Vihaal motioned to the bartender and laid a fifty on the counter. "That's for their drinks and mine."

"Perfect. Thank you."

We followed Vihaal to the elevator.

"We're on the twelfth floor," he said.

"Oh. There should be a nice view from there," Gideon said.

"Yes, well," Vihaal said, looking him up and down. "I don't give a fuck about the view."

"I was simply making conversation. I don't give a fuck about the view either."

"Then we understand each other." Vihaal turned to me. "And you? Did you say your name was *Angel?*"

"Yes."

"Hmm. Do you care about the view?"

"No. Fuck the view," I said, adjusting my pants.

The elevator doors opened.

"In you go," Vihaal said, ushering us into the mirrored car.

Gideon and I moved toward the back of the elevator as Vihaal pressed the button to close the doors. Then he turned around.

"All right. Here are the rules once we get into that room. You don't speak, unless it's to say *Yes, Sir,* or *No, Sir.* The safeword for everyone is *Prime Minister.*"

Gideon giggled.

Vihaal *almost* smiled, but then managed to retain his stern demeanor.

"And you do everything I ask of you. Even if it's fucking depraved and disgusting. Because it will be."

"Yes, Sir," I panted, overcome with desire and love for these incredible men.

"Oh, yes, Sir," Gideon agreed.

"Good. Then we understand each other," Vihaal said, moving forward and pinning Gideon against the elevator wall. "You've got a smart mouth on you, don't you? I can't wait to fill it with...something."

He glanced at me.

"And you, standing there all quiet and innocent. Something tells me you can be *absolutely filthy*."

And I knew in that instant that I was home.

"Yes, Sir, I can be. I like to be. I want to be," I said. "For you. And for him."

Epilogue

One year later

"Do you smell that?" Gideon asked, lifting his chin. His hair had gotten longer and he pushed a few strands behind his ear as he sniffed the air.

"Oh fuck, I forgot about the cakes," I muttered, leaping to my feet and rushing into the kitchen, almost tripping on Rummy as I did. "Whoops, sorry!"

She gave a startled meow and tore off into the adjacent living room, where she leapt onto V's lap, as V gave me a stern look.

"You almost stepped on her. For Heaven's sake, be careful," he admonished, as I tore open the oven door and grabbed a mitt. I could hear his soothing words as I rescued my burning bake from the oven.

"You're all right, Rummy Tum Tum. You're safe with me now," Vihaal murmured and I couldn't help smiling, even as I gazed down on the overbrowned tops of the cake layers I'd made. The cats had been a bit of an issue when I'd moved in, and Vihaal hadn't been thrilled at the time. I was happy to say that they seemed to have won him over.

"The question is," Vihaal continued in a louder voice, "can the cakes be saved?"

"Yeah, I think so. I'll have to scrape the burnt bits off, that's all."

"Yes, and once the icing's on, nobody will ever know," Gideon said, coming over to have a look. "They aren't too bad. Leave the fan on to get this smell out. Maybe we can crack a window."

"Yeah, good idea."

I went to the window and opened it a sliver, looking out at the peaceful street. I'd never expected to be living in one of the most beautiful and swanky neighborhoods in Ottawa, but I did. With two of the most incredible men in the city. Possibly in the whole world.

"When are they coming?" Gideon asked. "That cake has to cool before I can ice it."

"Not until seven, so you've got lots of time. They've arranged for someone to manage things at the club, so they can have a Saturday evening away," I said.

We'd invited Jacob and Sebastian for supper, which we did every few months. Since they were our mutual friends and had been a major factor in the three of us getting together, it was appropriate to show them some hospitality. Plus, running Maverick Molly's took their time and attention seven days a week, and it was nice to have it focused on us for a few hours.

I'd moved into the house on Bellwood Avenue a couple of weeks before Christmas, and things were going well. Every once in a while, like right now, I'd pause to appreciate the strange turn my life had taken, once I'd allowed for the possibility that I might not be a hundred percent straight, and that I might just be hugely attracted to two men who were in an unconventional marriage with each other.

I was living my best bisexual life, committed to two gorgeous and caring men, with a past full of casual flings with women. It was tempting at times to call myself gay, since that was the lifestyle I was living, and planned to live as long as Gideon and Vihaal were with me. But I didn't want to deny a part of myself simply because of the circumstance I found myself in.

* * * *

The cake was a masterpiece. Gideon used some fancy icing techniques to spruce it up, and wrote J + S on the top, which looked adorable.

More importantly, the chicken casserole I'd made turned out just like Mom's, and the biscuits on top had baked to a golden brown.

"That looks amazing, Angel," Jacob said as I spooned a biscuit and some stew into his bowl.

"Sebastian?" I asked, passing the bowl to Jacob and holding my hand out for Sebastian's. "My mom's recipe. One of my favorite things that she used to make."

Sebastian gave me his bowl and I spooned some of the casserole into it.

"So, how is your store doing, Vihaal, now that you've switched over the management?" Jacob inquired.

Vihaal smiled placidly. "Profits are up. What a coincidence, hmm?" he glanced at Gideon, who shook his head. "Alice is doing a remarkable job. I should have put her in charge years ago. And Soresh is an absolute gem."

"That's fantastic. And how is Cory doing? He has nothing but good things to say about Tarnish," Jacob commented.

Vihaal had hired one of the molly boys on part-time, because Cory still wanted to work a few shifts at Maverick Molly's.

"He's wonderful. No complaints, and Alice says he knows more about furniture and design than she'd expected."

"That's fantastic. I'm so glad everything's going well."

"Yes, so am I. We saw Bridget last week," Vihaal said to Jacob, passing me his bowl once I'd handed Sebastian's back to him. "God, she's hilarious. Such a potty mouth."

Gideon laughed. "And she's always asking the most interesting questions!"

"Oh my God. I know," I said, blushing in embarrassment. "She loves you guys. You know her name isn't Bridget, right?"

"Yes, you keep telling us." Gideon rolled his eyes.

"She loves *you*, Angel. And she's happy that you're happy," Vihaal murmured.

"Yes, but she's also lusting after the two of you, the way only a seventy-nine-year-old woman can."

"Don't be ridiculous," Vihaal scoffed. "Wait. Bridget's seventy-nine?"

"Her name isn't Bridget!" I said.

Sebastian frowned. "For God's sake, Angel. Let her have the name she wants."

I held up my hands. "Fine. Fine."

"Geez," Gideon said. "I hope I'm still lusting after hot men when I'm that age."

Vihaal eyed him with suspicion. "Well, if Angel and I are still around, it had better be us."

Gideon sat back with a smug look on his face. "We'll see."

Vihaal's eyes widened and I laughed.

"Gideon *is* quite a bit younger than you, Vihaal," Sebastian said.

The smug look vanished from Gideon's face, and a concerned look replaced it. "Oh shit. What if I end up in one of those places all by myself? You're *both* older than me!"

"Oh, for Heaven's sake," Vihaal muttered. "I plan to be around to torment you for quite a bit longer, so don't worry. And Angel can do it once *I'm* gone. See? The beauty of a poly relationship."

"Jesus, that's true," Sebastian said, casting a contemplative look at Jacob. "Maybe we should expand."

"Not happening," Jacob stated, placing a spoonful of stew in his mouth.

Sebastian laughed. "Just like that. He ruins all my fun."

Jacob gazed at Sebastian sedately as he finished. "Well, it might be entertaining for a bit, but then your jealous nature will get the better of you. I don't think you have the temperament for it."

Sebastian frowned. "What do you mean?"

"Do you remember when you thought I was cheating with that bartender? After we first opened the club?"

"But that's different. That's cheating, not a negotiated and committed poly relationship."

Jacob held up his hand. "Correction—it *wasn't* cheating, because I'm completely loyal to you and you know it. And also, I can't see you agreeing to share me, nor I you. We're simply much too selfish. I admire you three," he said, addressing me and Vihaal and Gideon. "The way you seem to have an abundance of love between you, and no petty jealousies."

"Hmph," Gideon muttered. "Well, I do get jealous sometimes. But Vihaal spanks it out of me."

Everyone laughed.

"Do you ever get jealous, Vihaal?" Sebastian asked.

"No. Because these two lovely men are my solace and my joy, and I'm grateful for every minute I get to spend with each of them."

Gideon put a hand to his chest. "Oh my God," he said. "V, that's so sweet."

I cleared my throat. "And I'm about to tear up in front of our company, so thanks for that."

"Well, you should know. I love you both very much. Let's not think about getting older. We've all got many, many years left for shenanigans and profanity."

"Hell, I'll drink to that," Jacob said, lifting his glass.

Gideon's eyes shone as he raised his.

"Fuck," I said, lifting mine with one hand and swiping at my cheek with the other. "Fine. Happy now?"

"As a matter of fact, I am," Vihaal said.

Want to see more from this author?
Here's a taster for you to enjoy!

We Three Kings:
A Spoonful of Sugar
AE Lister

Excerpt

Christmas was coming, and even though I didn't have a partner and children to spoil, I had to think about my parents and siblings. We didn't go overboard with gift-giving over the holidays, but the adults in the extended family were expected to provide a few thoughtful presents to the nieces and nephews.

The men I'd met at a Halloween party and subsequently gone home with in October, Jericho Griffin and Pascal Olejatz, hadn't been available to meet up in person much this month, although we'd kept in touch via Facetime and text. I was busy, too, with marking and assessments.

I mentioned to Pascal on one of our phone calls that I had gift shopping to do, and he said he did as well and that maybe we could meet up on a weekday when the stores weren't crowded and go together. He said Jericho did most of his shopping online, but he liked to see what he was buying then bring it home to wrap.

So, Pascal booked off the following Thursday, and we went Christmas shopping at St. Laurent Center. I swung by their place, and Pascal was waiting on the front step, wearing jeans that showed off his muscular legs and bubble butt, black leather boots, and a short wool jacket, with a gray scarf wrapped casually around his neck.

"Hello!" he said cheerily as he got into the passenger side. He leaned in and kissed my cheek. "How are you, Scott?"

"Good! You ready to face the masses at St. Laurent Center in December?"

"It shouldn't be too bad, since it's a weekday."

I reversed out of the driveway and headed east. "Oh, it'll be bad—but hopefully tolerable."

I was right. Even on a weekday, Ottawa's favorite mall was full of shoppers looking for exactly the right gift or loading up with several. I had to search for a parking spot but found one fairly close to the entrance. The crowds would be worse on the weekend, so I was grateful we had a window of opportunity.

"Where do you want to start?" I asked Pascal as we entered the large, modern shopping center in Ottawa's east end. The giant Toys R Us sign shone blue and yellow above us.

"I have some things I need to get there. At least most kids will be in school, so there should only be parents with babies shopping."

"Sounds like a plan," I said, and followed him into the cavernous and fully stocked store.

There were a number of moms and dads carting their little ones around and trying to score gifts, but it wasn't too bad. The occasional toddler went into tantrum mode, but Pascal and I efficiently managed to get what we were looking for and book it out of there.

"Next?" I asked, after we'd dropped our packages back at the car.

"Is there a gaming store here? I want to get Jericho a couple of the new releases," Pascal said.

We popped into The Source, and he found the games he needed.

"Right. Now, how about a clothes store?" I suggested.

"Sure."

We made our way along the concourse and were about to pass La Senza when Pascal shouted out, "Hey! Vincent!" and lifted his arm in a wave.

A charming young man with light brown hair and intense blue eyes, who was dressed in tight jeans and a soft T-shirt looked over and smiled. He was holding a folded jacket over his arm and a blush-pink La Senza bag by the corded handles.

"Pascal. Hi."

He waved, and nudged the arm of the arresting shorter guy who was accompanying him.

"Hi, Nic. What are you two shopping for? Oh wait, let me guess," Pascal said as we approached.

Vincent held up his pretty bag and blushed a lovely shade as Nic chuckled and raised his eyebrows.

"Oh, just a little something pretty for my favorite boy, that's all. Who's your friend?" he said, scanning me from head to foot.

Nic embodied the spirit of pure androgyny, although dressed toward the male side, but I'd have to be careful about what pronoun I used. I thought he was a guy, but I couldn't be entirely certain. Luckily, Pascal had the courtesy to assist me.

"This is Scott. Scott, this is Nic. He's a friend of mine, and Vincent's partner-slash-Dom."

Nic inclined his head, evidently pleased with this description. "Nice to meet you, Scott."

"Same." I shook his hand.

"And this cutie-pie is Vincent."

"Oh, come on," Vincent said, rolling his eyes at Pascal and shaking his head in embarrassment but still smiling. "Nice to meet you, Scott."

"You as well."

"Doing some Christmas shopping?" Nic asked. He wore clunky motorcycle boots, loose black jeans and a soft leather jacket over a black button-down shirt. A pair of mirrored sunglasses were pushed back on his short, untidy hair, the sides of which were shaved close. His hazel eyes pierced mine with intelligence and curiosity.

I liked the look of him, and Vincent was adorable.

"Yeah," I said. "I don't have much to get, but I don't want to be anywhere near the malls in a few weeks."

"I hear you," Nic said. "We got most of ours done last month. But Vincent decided he needed some more lacy underthings, and I couldn't say no."

"Ha-ha," Vincent said.

"Okay, that's not entirely true," Nic admitted. "The fact is, I enjoy buying him beautiful things to wear for me, and he enjoys indulging my eccentricities. And he looks so pretty in them." Nic gave Vincent a sweet look, and Vincent bloomed with obvious pride under his gaze.

I tried not to picture this beautiful man standing in front of me in pink and baby-blue lace. I failed.

"Where's Jericho?" Nic asked.

"Working hard, as usual. I booked the day off to do some shopping and brought our new *patient* with me."

"Oh-ho! How nice. And what exactly is ailing Scott here?" Nic asked. He seemed fully aware of Jericho's sideline as a *pretend* medical practitioner. "What prompted him to, ahem, seek treatment?"

Now Vincent was looking me over and awaiting my answer with obvious interest.

"Pure desperation and a chance meeting," I said. "I was literally on death's door. Luckily, I fell into very good hands."

"Yes," Pascal agreed. "I'm happy to say his treatment is going superbly well. But there will need to be follow-up visits for quite some time, I'm sure."

I laughed. "Yeah, I'm counting on it. Can never be too careful."

"We were going to get some lunch," Nic said. "Would you boys like to join us?"

I glanced at Pascal for cues.

"Sure," he said. "Scott?"

"Absolutely."

"All right," Nic smiled. "Why don't we get a table at Moxie's? It's just down the road. It's Vincent's favorite." He shot Vincent a loaded gaze, which made the young man's cheeks darken even more.

Vincent whispered "Sir..." and ducked his head.

Hmm. I'm missing some kinky subtext here.

"Okay with you, Scott?" Pascal checked.

"Sure. Anything but the food court, honestly."

Pascal laughed. "I hear you."

We drove the short distance to Moxie's and found Vincent waiting for us inside the door.

"Nic has a table. Come on."

He led us to a booth, where Nic was sprawled on the bench, checking his phone. He put it away and stood, motioning for Vincent to slide in beside him.

Pascal slid in across from Vincent, and I sat beside him, facing Nic.

Nic leaned back and folded his arms. He'd removed his leather jacket and rolled up the sleeves of the black shirt, revealing slim forearms dusted with light hair and delicate wrists, one of which sported the latest in Apple watch technology on a brown leather strap.

"So, Scott, have you always been interested in medical kink or only since hooking up with Mutt and Jeff?"

"Nic, Jesus. Cut right to the chase, don't you?" Pascal snorted.

"Why not? I don't see any point in prevaricating. Vincent and I are as kinky as you and Dr. Jekyll."

My eyebrows flew up. "Oh no. Does that mean there's a Mr. Hyde that's going to appear sometime soon?" I glanced at Pascal, who was shaking his head with good humor.

Pascal said, "Don't listen to Nic, Scott. He's only trying to get a rise out of you."

Nic gave me a slow, sexy smile, and I knew exactly what kind of rise he was after. My dick began to swell in obedience to that dominant sneer.

I cleared my throat. "I've always had an interest but Jericho is the first person to, uh, exploit it."

"I see. And how did you meet? Craigslist? ChristianMingle?"

I liked Nic. He was funny and forthright.

I laughed. "Sonny's, actually."

"The Leather bar? *Really*."

"I went for the Halloween party. I almost turned around and walked out because it was so awful. But then I went upstairs, and that's where I met Jericho." I glanced at Pascal. "I had no idea he was a dog owner."

"Hardy-har," Pascal commented. "I've been showing Scott the basics of pup play. He used to be a skeptic, but now —"

"I'm definitely a convert. Not that I want my own or anything. But I get to play with Digger on occasion, and

I must admit, I'm starting to appreciate that particular lifestyle."

"Ah. Vincent, why don't you tell Scott what we like to do when you're in the mood for some pet play?" Nic said, maintaining eye contact with me. The charismatic intensity of the slim Dom was entrancing.

Vincent opened the menu and scanned it for something to order. He glanced at me and smiled sweetly. "*Meow*," he said, with a wink.

"Huh?" I asked.

"Vincent's been experimenting with some kitten play. And I must say, it's going extremely well. Isn't it, darling?"

"Mm-hmm."

Nic leaned toward me.

"When he climbs into my lap and wraps his fluffy white tail around my neck, grinding his cock against my belly and whispering naughty things into my ear, with those cute kitty ears on a headband and a pretty little bell collar around his neck..." Nic bit his bottom lip. "Well, there's nothing else quite like it, Scott."

I pictured the lovely Vincent dressed as a sweet white kitten and couldn't deny it made an intriguing image.

"I imagine that's true," I said, licking my lips.

Nic sat back. "What do you do for a living, Scott?"

"I teach anthropology courses at the college level."

Nic inclined his head. "Nice. I teach music theory and composition."

"Oh? Really?"

"Yes."

"Nic's teaching me piano," Vincent commented.

Nic winked at Vincent and bumped his shoulder. "It started as a kinky game, but Vincent's quite talented —

so now he has regular lessons, rather than only opportunities for kinky foreplay."

I imagined Nic having Vincent sit for a lesson and teasing him with the possibility of punishments for a lack of finesse or energy and swallowed thickly.

"I bet Vincent is an excellent student."

"Oh, he is…in so many ways."

We eventually stopped talking about sex and enjoyed a lovely lunch. Nic and Vincent were intelligent and pleasant company. Nic was charismatic and alluring, and Vincent sweet and attentive. I imagined the young, blue-eyed man made an excellent service-slash-sexual submissive. I had no doubt Nic was a stern but caring and creative Dom, and I got the feeling they were well-matched.

After lunch, Pascal and I drove back to the mall and finished our shopping before heading back toward his and Jericho's place.

"I haven't seen you much over the last couple of weeks because of school, and I'm having a really good time hanging out. Do you want to come in for a cup of coffee or some hot chocolate?"

"Sure, I'll come in for a bit, as long as I'm not disturbing you."

"Nope. I finished my big essay. Now I only have to study for the last test before the final exam in January. It's next week, so once that's done, I'll be free to enjoy the holidays."

"That's great," I said as Pascal keyed us inside. "I have some final marking to do this weekend, then my workload will ease up too." I followed Pascal in and toed off my boots, then hung up my jacket. "Hopefully Dr. Griffin will have some appointments available in the near future."

"Don't worry, he will. Things are always a little intense right before the holidays. Christmas is in two weeks, right? Another week, and he should be able to fit you in."

"I can't wait."

As we sat in Pascal and Jericho's snug living room and sipped our coffee, I asked Pascal how long the two of them had been a unit and how they'd met.

He told me they'd been together for four years, living with each other for three of those, and that they'd met at a pup night event when Pascal had been starting to get into the lifestyle.

"I was so nervous, and I didn't have any gear except a cheap dog collar with a tag with my pup name on it. I found myself in a pup mosh with all these experienced guys who had the full hoods and butt plug tails. And while it was awesome and I pretty much knew I was where I needed to be, it was also intimidating and intense. I was completely overwhelmed and kind of freaking out. Then this super-hot guy leaned over the gate and talked softy to me, got me to come over, gave me pets and scratches and made me feel like I was the cutest and most adorable puppy in the pit. And that was that. I've been his ever since."

"Wow."

"I'm so lucky to have met him, and the medical kink setup was an added bonus. I hadn't really explored it before and I don't think I'm as into it as you are, but I'll submit to anything to see Jericho's doctor persona in play. And being his assistant with others is a natural fit for me. It's pretty fucking hot when the patient is totally into it, like you are, Scott."

I laughed. "Ah, thanks."

We fell into a companionable silence, then both started speaking at once.

Pascal said, "Want to watch a movie?"

"Well, I guess I should be— What?"

Pascal laughed, blushing. "I just— But if you really have to leave, I get it."

"Did you ask me to watch a movie with you?"

"Yeah. But I understand if you're too busy."

"I'm not too busy. I simply didn't want to overstay my welcome."

"Well, you're not."

"Okay. Sure. I'd love to watch a movie with you."

"And cuddle on the couch? It helps me relax."

I smiled. "I'd love to."

We snuggled up on the sofa together, the way I'd seen Pascal do with Jericho many times—me underneath with Pascal between my legs and his head on my shoulder. Even though he was bigger than I was, it felt right, and I found my own seasonal stress dissipating as we laughed through the first half of *The Devil Wears Prada*. He smelled of clean cotton and fruity shampoo.

We must have fallen asleep, because the next thing I knew, the front door shut loudly, and Jericho's voice announced, "Hey, sweetie, I'm home!"

I blinked and tried to focus, swiveling my head to see Jericho step into the living room and take in the scene.

"Oh. Hey, Scott."

He peered around the room. "I thought you were going shopping."

I cleared my throat and jiggled Pascal, who lay snoring softly against my shoulder. "The stuff's still in the car. We came in to have a cup of coffee and ended up watching *The Devil Wear's Prada*. Well, part of it."

I nudged Pascal again.

Jericho laughed. "You won't wake him up like that. He's a deep sleeper." He walked over to us and gaze fondly on his boyfriend. "He's really in dreamland right now."

"Hmm, I don't think so. Wouldn't he be twitching and jerking?"

"True. Pups tend to do that when they dream." Jericho leaned down and kissed me on the lips, then pulled back. "Nice to see you."

"You, too. How was work?"

Jericho shrugged. "Busy. It always is at this time of year. I have a few things to do tonight, but at least I don't have to go in."

"I should get going."

"You could stay for supper?" Jericho suggested.

I smiled. "Thank you. But I should get back, sort out the gifts I bought and figure out if there's anyone left to buy for." I looked Jericho over. "Theoretically, if someone were to buy you a Christmas gift, what should they get?"

He rolled his eyes. "You don't have to get me a gift."

"I know. But I want to."

"Why don't you get me something to use in the 'office'?" he said, gesturing toward the spare room.

"I could," I said, blushing. "I thought of that. But then it would be a gift for me, honestly."

"True."

"Come on. What do you want for Christmas, Jericho?"

"Honestly? I want you to come spend Christmas week with us."

I blinked. The invitation surprised me. "The whole week?"

"Yeah. But you've probably got familial responsibilities…"

"No. Well, yeah, but I can do those visits in one afternoon, probably. I can spend most of the week with you two."

"Oh yeah?"

Jericho knelt down beside the couch and kissed me again, taking his time. When he pulled back, he said, "Maybe we can make up for lost time. I hate not seeing you. And I think Pascal has missed you, too."

It was settled. We'd have another week apart, but then I'd pack a bag and stay with the two of them over the holiday.

Although Jericho had said my company was the only thing he needed for Christmas, I wanted to get both him and Pascal something small to put under their tree. I simply had to figure out what.

I didn't want to get him anything for his medical 'practice', even though it was tempting. For one thing, I hadn't yet seen his entire inventory of instruments and supplies, so I was likely to duplicate something he already had. And for another thing, as I'd mentioned, that would be more of a gift for me, since I would be getting it for him to use during our medical play scenes.

I needed to think of something meaningful but nothing overly romantic or expensive. There was a delicate balance at the beginning of any relationship, in order to let a partner know you cared and thought of the relationship as potentially serious and long-term but that you weren't trying to jump ahead of them in the game. It could be tricky. And in *my* situation, where we'd already stepped outside the bounds of conventionality, it could be even more difficult to navigate those early weeks.

I settled on a gift card to the Sweet Basil Thai restaurant in South Ottawa, addressed to both of them. It seemed a good way to reinforce that I valued and respected the relationship they had with each other, even as I wanted to be a part of it. I liked them both equally, and their commitment to each other was part of the attraction.

I taped it to the bottom of an empty box and wrapped it up with some brown craft paper and a pretty green ribbon. I even went to the pet store and paid for a blue dog tag in the shape of a bone, engraved with 'To Jericho and Pascal' to attach. It looked beautiful, and I couldn't wait to present the gift to them.

About the Author

Alison Lister is a Canadian non-binary author.

They write graphic erotic romance (contemporary/historical/paranormal) as AE Lister, and sweet Young Adult LGBTQ+ romance as Alison Lister.

She/he/they

AE Lister loves to hear from readers. You can find their contact information, website details and author profile page at https://www.firstforromance.com/

PUBLISHING

Sign up for our newsletter and find out about all our romance book releases, eBook sales and promotions, sneak peeks and FREE romance books!